The CURSE of JOSEPHINE BAGLEY

CASSANDRA JOELLE

...the LORD turns my darkness into light.
2 Samuel 22:29

TABLE OF CONTENTS

CHAPTER ONE

KILLIAN

It was such a beautiful day, yet the man appeared to be the only one out. The businesses were boarded up, signs reading "Closed for the Season." Posters advertising tourist attractions were crumpled and faded on the streetlight poles. It was still warm in late September; the only sign of life was the phantom smell of cotton candy that lingered from the guests who had long returned home.

The man leaned his head back on the rickety bench, feeling the sun on his face. If there was ever a reason to come to town, this was it, he thought, as his home was shrouded in shade trees and always much cooler. The old homestead was designed to be hidden from Indian territory, and that included the sun. A dark cloud passed over the bright orb and a sharp chill followed. But it wasn't just a physical darkening; an ominous feeling washed over him as he opened his eyes.

Someone is here with me, he thought.

Then he saw him. A well-dressed, incomprehensibly eye-catching man was quickly shuffling down the cobblestone streets. His small eyes were in a scowl, and his brow furled as the stranger looked at him. Marking his destination, the stranger slowed his steps and leaned against a telephone booth labeled "Out of Service." He reached into his breast pocket, pulled out a cigarette tin, and exposed a chain pocket watch. His spiced scent was overwhelming even from a short distance. The man couldn't decide which was more peculiar, the stranger's clothing or the fact that he was here in the first place?

"Excuse me," the stranger directed towards the man, as though talking to himself. "Do you have a light?" The presence of the Zippo lighter in the man's pocket now heavy, he nodded while reaching for it. He held out the flame to the stranger, waiting for him to lean in with his cigarette, but he didn't. Instead, the stranger sat down next to him on the bench.

"There's something I need you to do for me." The stillness of the air around them froze time. How was the man to respond to that? "But first, would you like to hear a story?" The stranger's words again, directed at all the world and no one at all.

It wasn't often that the man was in town, let alone feeling particularly intrigued by a subject matter that wasn't his hobby. The camera around his neck was heavy after walking for hours, looking for any loose interpretation of inspiration, and turning up short. It felt nice to relax, and the stranger's voice was soothing. The man's breathing deepened and came to a snail's pace. He was in the trance of the stranger's presence, the one he felt just moments before, and now his body was begging for more. The stranger pulled out his pocket watch, and the man's eyes bore deep into it as the stranger held it out to him. The glass on the face had a large crack; such a shame, the man thought, for such an old piece. But the rest of it looked nearly brand new.

"Well then," he said, snapping the watch back shut. "What will it be, chap?"

Had he not answered yet? The man's body felt like it was lying in a tub of wet sand, and he tried to regain his focus. This was certainly unexpected. In fact, this was the most interesting thing to have happened to him in years. He rubbed his eyes and took the camera off from around his neck, setting it carefully on the bench between them, not looking this stranger in the eye. Taking a deep breath, he softly let the word flow off his lips.

"Yes."

"I've never shared this with anyone, but it's time I did." The stranger sat at the other end of the bench, taking a long drag of his cigarette. His slight accent was unrecognizable. "What do you think?" The stranger asked while turning to look the man in the eye.

The man had never seen someone such as this stranger before— so ambiguous, so strangely unique. His eyes sent a chill down the man's spine.

Feeling increasingly uncomfortable under the stranger's gaze, the man dropped his eyes as the sunlight caught the rings on the stranger's hand. He gasped under his breath. Never had he seen a stone such as the one this stranger wore. It looked like gazing into a crystal ball to determine your fate, but every outcome was very dark and twisted.

The stranger next to him cleared his throat and started telling his story. "My name is Killian. It is my middle name, and I always felt it fit me best." He took a puff off his clove, sending an O of smoke through the air. "Killian. It rolls off the tongue." He winked. "I was born in the late 1800s to Thomas and Ida Sparr. My mother died in childbirth, and my father wished I had gone with her. He could never look at me except to say that I wasn't wanted. He swiftly remarried, and they had as many children as years passed, most of which died in childbirth. Though that wasn't unusual back in those days, I always thought that was odd. I couldn't wait to escape his drunken neglect. I left home when I was fourteen to travel to the big city to follow my dreams of being a painter. In the early 20th century, I met Frank Bagley when he hired me at his weathervane company. I told him I could draw anything he could dream up. At that time, with no computers, you can imagine my skill being useful. I never let him down— on the job, at least. But it was the years before I left that really changed my future. You see, when you're young, you never think about these things."

The man nodded in agreement, feeling the lightheartedness of the conversation; since Killian couldn't be over 100 years old, the man imagined this story to be fiction.

"We lived in a time where Indians roamed their lands freely, and we, homesteaders," Killian pointed to himself, "were not welcome in any sense. There were no laws back then for things like this, and if there were, the Indians didn't have any reason to oblige. They could, and would, do as they wish, for their way of life wasn't going to change just because the white man invaded."

***

SARAFINA

The compact mirror on my desk reminded me to check my reflection before I saw Dean, as I did every day before he returned from his lunch hour. I applied plum lipstick, the only makeup I wore at work. It brightened my features and made my frizzy hair and puffy eyes look more professional somehow. Professional was the image I was aiming for as an antique dealer.

I slowly stood and walked out of my office as I heard footsteps coming down the hallway, and in an attempt to look natural, I grabbed a clipboard and camera as if I was in the middle of a cataloging project. My back was turned at the front desk for the utmost 'busy' appearance as the footsteps drew closer, expecting Dean to call out to me as he usually did, to say some snarky comment about his experience while gone. But the footsteps stopped at the desk, and I peeked through my bushy curls to discover it was not Dean, but instead, a messenger service.

"Hello miss, I am looking for a Sera-fine-a Rayon? Wait, that isn't it. I'm sorry, but the label got drenched in the rain, but I assure you the contents are fine as it is in plastic."

"Sarafina Rayne?" I cocked an eyebrow, unable to hide my curiosity at what someone sent to me via messenger to my work of all places. I couldn't think of a soul that knew I worked here that didn't have my apartment address.

"Whew! Thank you. Please sign here." Grinning wide, he held out a yellow order sheet. I quickly examined to see if a sender was listed, but it only said "L." I started to ask him who that was when his phone began ringing and buzzing with non-stop messages. Once I lifted my pen from the paper, he snatched it up and was gone in an instant, his voice carrying all through the building until he stepped on the elevator. He was arguing with someone in Mandarin, and from the limited exposure I've had to the language, it sounded as if he was fighting for custody of a poodle named Dodo. Once the elevator door shut, the screaming silenced, and the trance brought on by his argument was broken. I returned my attention to the package.

The thick plastic sheath wasn't transparent, and the suspense was dire to open it. I quietly stepped into my office and shut the door. Leaving the front of the office unattended while our secretary was away at lunch was generally taboo, but the other staff would have to manage on their own. There appeared to be no way to open the plastic without a pair of scissors as if it was sealed with heat, which I found peculiar. I half expected alarm bells to go off when I cut into it. Inside was a gold manilla envelope, a mundane sight compared to the intricate outward packaging. But it had weight to it, which intrigued me even further.

The front of the manilla envelope read, "Send to her when I am gone."

My face flushed, and my hands were shaking when I slid my letter opener into the back of it. I poured the documents out of their sleeve, and several bound wills, contracts, and legal jargon jumped out at me. But in front of it was a small handwritten note on journal paper, folded up with my name written on the top.

Just as I was opening it up, Dean knocked on my door, scaring the life out of me as he let himself in.

"Hey there, working hard, I see. Whatcha got there?" I realized that the entire time, I had forgotten to breathe, and now I appeared suspiciously winded. The part of me that was secretly in love with him felt like including him on whatever this was. The other part, mostly my brain, squashed that idea immediately. However much I wanted his attention, Dean was my boss, and I needed to act professionally.

"You know, I am not sure yet. But I promise I will tell you all about this very soon."

He was left looking stunned. I had never once shown an ounce of any mystery towards him whatsoever, but the office had a 'finders keepers' working policy, and we were allowed to investigate things on our own before bringing them to light, as long as we gave full disclosure after the fact to whether it was something important or not.

"Okay then." He stood waiting for me to spill the beans a little longer, completely blindsided by this unusual secrecy. He stood there shuffling his steps, expecting an invitation to my desk for a closer look. It didn't come, and we were left in a stare-off. "I'll leave you to it, I guess?" He slowly walked out of my office, closing the door behind him. The glass walls revealed that Jenny, our secretary, was back from her lunch hour and I could hole up in my office the rest of the day uninterrupted if needed.

I didn't care that he stood outside. I continued to open the note. A beautifully unusual gemstone necklace was wrapped inside.

"Sarafina,

I am deeply sorry for only just reaching out to you now. But if you are reading this, it means I am gone. I wish things had been different, but I couldn't bring you into my troubles. There is so much you should know, but I just wanted you to be happy. Know that I watched you from afar, heard of your successes as an antique appraiser, and I am so proud of you, dear.

Now, the legal side of things: You and I were the last living relatives of the Bagley Estate. I have been residing here since I was a young child. My grandmother Josephine, who was your great-grandmother, left it to me. And now I am leaving it to you. See the enclosed documents of my will, deeds, and any other paperwork you may need. Once you arrive at the estate, a complete set of keys will be given to you.

I find this inheritance fitting since you appear to love the old and mysterious, what better person to take this place over than you?

I hope you like this necklace. It is my gift to you. Wear it for good luck.

Leroy will be waiting for you.

Your aunt,
Victoria

P.S. Please, my dear— be very careful. Some things are not as they seem.

I could barely finish the letter before tears rolled down my face. The hairs on my body sent shockwaves down my spine, and though I was wobbly, I managed to grab my parka from the coat rack in the corner of my office and drape it around myself. 'The Bagley Estate.' I whispered to myself. 'Wait. The Bagley Estate? That sounds important.' My jaw dropped as the realization stung me. I don't know what I was more shocked by— relatives I didn't think I had— or inheriting a house? I wasn't familiar with it, so while I didn't imagine more than a modest homestead, I had no clue what to expect. Looking at the delicate necklace, I admired the beautifully cut stone cross. Without a thought, I put it around my neck. Then, I gathered all the files she sent me, or rather someone had sent me, put them back into the plastic sleeve, and grabbed my purse.

Thankfully, the secretary Jenny had returned from her lunch hour amid my surprise inheritance. "Jenny, would you please tell Dean I am going to the library? I am working on something, but I need to travel for research today. Actually, make that the rest of the week." I was digging in my purse for my library key, the one our staff has personal access to at the University. I pulled it out finally and looked up at a very concerned face.

"Is everything all right, Sara?" Jenny was eloquent in her words and a genuine person, but I still found her questions momentarily annoying.

"Yes, but I must leave. Thanks!" I started powerwalking towards the elevator when I heard Dean at Jenny's desk, and the words "travel" and "concerned" floated around. I didn't care to look up as the elevator doors closed.

Thankfully my parka had a hood on it as the rain was coming down in golf balls. I hesitated to grab an umbrella from the lobby. My apartment was already full of the ones I've borrowed. The doorman grimaced as I reached for one. He let out a snort, and I changed my mind. I'd rather get drenched than be judged by this guy. I ran outside when I saw a cab pull up and waved my arms while securing the contents of my crossbody bag.

"10th and Maple, please."

"Roger that." The driver drank coffee that smelled stale. I focused on minor details to keep myself from losing control of the situation, a trick I learned when my parents died when I was a teenager.

The flashback of that day came over my mind, uninvited.

"I am so sorry, Sara. Your parents didn't– " the doctor dropped her head, speaking firmly, "– They didn't survive the accident."

'Accident.' 'Accident.' 'Accident.' I kept saying to myself over and over before the word became a foreign object in my head, without meaning. Before this, the term used to bring imagery of carrying a tray of coffees that were spilling over, then tripping on a curb and dumping the tray onto your car hood. Or wear your shirt inside out after getting dressed in the dark so you don't wake up your family. Or running into a sliding glass door that had just been cleaned a little too well.

In no translation did it ever mean a driver high on methamphetamine would rail into them at a stoplight.

***

WILLIAM

"Hey, freak– over here!" A boy no older than ten shouted out to William. William was out pulling weeds in Mrs. May's Garden in the back of the orphanage. He'd much rather work outside away from the other children than be with them and live in a constant state of torment because of his facial deformity.

William peered over his shoulder at the boy, who, every time William was outside, harassed him. But he seemed friendly despite his language. It didn't faze William being called a freak anymore, he knew it to be true.

"Whaddya want?" He kept pulling weeds, detailing this small bed of dahlias. They were Mrs. May's favorite flower, and William took pride in treating her with respect. She was the only soul in the world who was ever kind to him.

"Let's go to the pier. My brother is there working, and he will give us tobacco!"

William scoffed at the child who was now swinging from a tree branch in the orphanage yard. "Come on now. I need backup in case we find some in-gens. We will be back with plenty of time for whatever it is you're doing." He was a young lad that wanted to use William for bait to save himself if anything were to go down.

Pondering the question, in truth, William had been planning his departure for years. It seemed like no one was watching today, and he could very well slip into the abyss. The home would likely even feel relieved.

William laughed at the proposition that this child had just presented him with. "Where did you even come from?" It was an unanswered question as the child was now climbing up the pecan tree, hollering curse words as he scaled the slippery branches. There were no houses in the area. It was very rural Indian land. William had often seen the Indians go by on their horses and thought they were beautiful, but Mrs. May had warned the children that they could be very dangerous. "Truthfully, they were here first. This is their land. We may have settled it, but they have the brawn and speed to take our lives from us. Never forget that, children. Treat them with the utmost respect."

Once, William was out working in the berry bushes on a day much like this. It was late summer, an exceptionally humid time of year. He had nearly filled a bucket of blackberries for the home when an Indian rode by. His pony shared the likes of him, William thought; both had long black hair and painted faces. William smiled in awe, feeling for the first time his spirit was wild and free, wanting to leave and live with them and in their ways. But then he saw what the Indian held in his hand; the feathers and beads hanging from the club made it no less ominous. The man dismounted from the horse, his hide-clothed feet taking small steps toward William, who was still holding berries in his hand. He clenched his fists together, the thorns of the berries causing him to flinch.

The Indian was inches from William when he stopped in his tracks, staring hard at the boy's facial deformity. The man, who was not much taller than William, put his hands up as if to say, 'do not come any closer.' What was that look, that William saw in the eye of this man, who not only furnished a weapon that could instantly bring death to a child such as himself? The man who was painted in colorful symbols, something that William wouldn't understand for years, but would later learn it was the colors of war. Was it fear?

He got back on his horse, circling the boy in the berry bushes, and was never seen again.

William returned from his memory, his new friend now down from the tree, holding a large knife and whacking down weeds with it.

"I live way over there." He pointed to the trees.

But William knew he was lying. "No one but the Indians lives out there."

The boy shrugged, caught in his words. "In-gens and us. They don't bother us— we don't bother them. My father has traded with them before. I'd much rather take my chances out there than live in that hell hole." Pointing to the home behind William.

William understood that. An orphanage was a terrible place to be. "What's your name?"

"Lowell."

"Ok, let's go. But we must wait for a few minutes. Mrs. May will be leaving for an appointment in the city, and her mother will be watching. So that means napping in the chair. We can just walk out, no one will stop me."

The child looked at William in amazement. "If it's so easy, why are you still here?"

It was an honest question with a complicated answer. Yes, he was physically and verbally abused in the orphanage. He tried to fight back now that he was older, but the children would all gang up on him at once. But William had someone he was close with, Mrs. May, the owner of the home. While she physically could not stop the abuse of the boys as she was a small, frail woman, she would listen to William. Which gave him something else that none of them had: a friend. Yes, he felt rage for his anguish, which he had bottled up for years, and part of him knew that simply leaving would not do the trick to relieve it.

But there was something he couldn't share with her or Lowell. William wanted to see his fellow orphans get what they deserved for his years of torment. He wanted to see them dead.

Occasionally, men from the transient ships would come to the orphanage and take a few young men for free labor on their voyages. William was always looked over, but it was a mixed emotion every time that one less bully lived under the same roof. He was relieved to the hilt that they were gone, but he always took mental notes of who they went to work for.

Mrs. May would always have a discussion with the boys before they would depart. "Be a strong, good man. Our country needs hard-working men. And remember, anything is possible. You are not where you come from, you are who you decide to be right now." It was always a beautiful speech full of hope.

Mrs. May told William that many years ago, one particularly troubled boy had been picked up by homesteaders that needed some strong men to work in their colony. Carl, the orphan, was no older than thirteen, but he was a man in stature. He had come to the home when he was six or seven. His parents died from some sort of violent crime, Mrs. May explained, waiting for William to react in any way to that revelation, but he didn't, so she went on. At times, the orphan's behavior had been frightening to Mrs. May. He would make weapons to use on other kids, but she treated him with as much kindness as possible through the fear. When the homesteaders wanted to take Carl, her eyes widened in surprise. But they seemed like very good people, and she said it was as good of a chance as he'd ever get. "Carl, listen to me, boy. This family is a hardworking bunch; that much is obvious. I've tried to always do right by you, but I can't help whatever happened to you before you came here. So, I just wanted to make sure you knew; you can't help it either. Nothing was ever your fault, nothing. Let this family take care of you, and you be certain to take care of them too, do you understand?" He nodded, the permanent look of defiance on his face waning.

Eight years later, a beat-up carriage pulled up to the home. Mrs. May shouted out, "Now, who could that be?" And all the boys, including William, straightened up as they did whenever a visitor came for a potential job opportunity.

"Well, if it isn't him!" Mrs. May ran out the doors to greet Carl, who had returned with his wife. They shared an embrace and talked for a long time before coming inside.

"Boys, do any of you remember Carl? He's returned with his new bride to take one of you home!" Jaws dropped all around the room. There hadn't been a legitimate adoption here in any of their lifetimes. Ultimately, the couple took a two-year-old home and named him Tommy. Mrs. May kept fawning over how happy she was for Carl and his wife, Sally. She would later tell William that it was the first success story that she ever knew of. William silently hoped to be another success story for her, though he didn't know how.

And she told William that while she always prayed for them, a part of her was still worried. They weren't rotten kids, but they felt slighted from the womb. "The feeling of abandonment runs deep, William. I want you to know that your parents didn't give you up because of any particular… reason," she was hinting at the elephant in the room, "But in actuality, they died." A ripple went through William's body when she spoke those words. "I have wanted to tell you that your entire life, my boy. But it wasn't until today that I felt I should."

"Why today, Mrs. May?" William asked her with wonderment. He had always assumed that when he was born, his parents took one look at him and gave him up because no one had told him otherwise. She was the only parental figure he'd ever known, and what she'd just shared with him changed his life.

Mrs. May took William's hand and held it. "William, you are an old soul. You see beyond yourself, beyond your ailments and problems, and you put up with disgusting, mean behavior from your fellow orphans. They beat you down, call you hideous names, and you do not react. But you haven't lost your spirit. There is an awareness of the world in you. One that I wouldn't wish on others, to be frank. But I know when you leave here one day, William, I will never worry about you. Because you have a will to survive that I haven't seen before."

Lowell threw a rock at Williams's feet, bursting him out of his daydreams.

"Actually, never mind." Lowell sneered in discontent. "This whole waiting around just doesn't work for me. I'm sorry. I promise I'll come back tomorrow with a pipe for you." Lowell took off in a skipping run before William could even protest his early departure.

This young boy, fearlessly living among the wilds and all its threats— and yet, William put himself through punishments and anguish for what, revenge? Revenge against his abusers? Wouldn't turning his back on them and starting his life be revenge enough?

William settled on leaving that night before Mrs. May returned; after the house went to bed. The weight of the matches in his pocket made him toy with the idea of lighting something ablaze on his way out. Like the bushes outside— he could create a ruckus that everyone would be focused on and slip away into the night.

But why did he think his fellow orphans would care? After all these torment-filled years? Not only did they tease him incessantly, but they offended him. He was disgusted with the cruelty a person could display, especially those with a sense of superiority but in an equally depressing reality. It all came down to his physical deformation. Of course, Mrs. May always reinforced to him that children were cruel because they were afraid of what they didn't understand.

A humid afternoon turned into a warm dusk when William quietly entered the orphanage for the last time. His eyes were squinted, his posture straight. A few children started heckling him the moment he stepped inside; but instead of listening to the words or trying to dodge the objects being thrown at him, he just kept walking, small wooden blocks and toys ricocheting off him all the way to the main bedroom.

"Not so fast, freak face." William didn't need to turn around to know who was next up to bat. Denny was a year older than William but taller by nearly a foot, thanks to his recent growth spurt. William had hoped more homesteaders would've taken him by now, but one look at this kid and you'd know why he was still here. If anyone had to narrow it down, it was the look in his eyes. He was capable of anything— in all senses of the word. He wasn't just fearless. He had nothing to lose, and it showed.

"I said, stop." William hadn't turned around yet to face Denny, and now he was getting angry. All the other children were frozen in place, waiting to see what would happen to William, and not wanting to tick him off in the process.

William gave in, turning to face his bully for the last time, he reminded himself. Denny tossed a wooden ball with one hand up in the air and caught it. "Where do you think you're going? Did I say you could go in there?" Denny was referring to the main room, where the children left what little belongings they had. Feeling the bulk of the matches in his pocket, William ran his hand over the box to remember his plan and calm his nerves.

"Whatcha got there, loser? Give it to me. Now."

William didn't have to imagine what situation he could find himself in if Denny obtained the matches. The entire house would burn with William inside. William felt a breeze of the warm outside air. There must have been an open window or Mrs. May had returned. He closed his eyes, savoring the scent of the floral sweetness that grew nearby, hoping Mrs. May would come and put Denny in his place.

"That's it." Denny charged William, pushing him up against the wall. Denny pulled his arm back as far as he could, wanting William to feel the fear of his impending punch— when an arrow went through Denny's neck. His eyes flared wide as he stumbled, gripping the arrows shaft before he fell to his knees and then onto his back, dead.

The shock of the twist that had just taken place was short-lived, as someone screamed out, "INDIANS!" Everyone scrambled as the painted men raided through, wreaking havoc in front of William who was still standing up against the wall, waiting for what was coming to him.

After a few minutes, he had been passed over by the men while he anxiously awaited his fate. William decided he would try and leave the house, slipping into the main room where several of the Indians were. Crawling up on his top bunk, he looked back. Still, no one cared to go after him. It wasn't clear who they were after, as Denny had been the only one killed thus far, but William felt thankful. Opening the window above, he pushed his lower body out at full speed, holding back a loud holler when he landed on his back. He lay still, frozen in a state that couldn't be considered fear because something deep inside William knew he wouldn't die that night. Instead, he had a deep understanding that his life had now changed, and he wasn't sure in which direction he was to go.

Up walked a barefooted man as broad and muscular as the horse he towed behind him. His face had been painted half blue, and his eyes were wild. The Indians all wore war paint that was individual to them, and though William understood they were here to fight the white man, he secretly thought they were beautiful. William sprang to his feet, wanting to meet the man eye-to-eye, and his pony who had colorful handprints painted on its side. He had a tomahawk in his extended arm that appeared to aim at William, and in his last moments he chose to admire the beading that dangled from the handle. But when the Indian saw his face, he stopped, just as Denny had a few minutes before. The man dropped his posture, pushed William down as hard as he could, knocking the wind out of him, and the Indian from the berry bush walked over. He looked down at William, in a look of disgust or pity, William wasn't sure. He had red lines painted over his eyes and eagle feathers in his hair. Saying a few words under his breath, he reached out to William, to help him stand. Without fear, he took the Indian's hand, standing up and looking him in the eye. Since William was a little bit older now, he was taller and felt more confident. The man wore animal teeth from his neck and fringe around his waist; giving William a nod, he turned and left.

William whispered, "Thank you." The Indian knew the phrase, stopping in his tracks, but must have wondered if it was for helping him up, sparing his life, or murdering his tormentor.

William let out a huge breath, analyzing the situation. He was spared. Mrs. May once told him that the world would be cruel to him because of his facial deformity. She said it may have come from syphilis, but he didn't have the disease in his body. The tribes clearly believed it to be contagious as well. She suggested if he ever had the means to correct it surgically, that he should. There were rumors of a surgeon performing miracles in New York. Instinctively, William reached to touch his upper lip. Other than some trouble annunciating plural words, he didn't feel any health struggles as though he was ill. He didn't even mind how it made him look. He admired himself for being born so drastically different that it caused people to fear him. And now that his bullies had been punished with an early grave, he finally felt at peace.

The Indian from the berry bush was standing outside the orphanage. He appeared to be the leader of the tribe of wild men, which all stood much further back now, burnishing torches and ready to light the only home William had ever known, ablaze. The leader spoke to William. It was a language he didn't know, but he understood when the man motioned to him to go with them. William looked at the fires the men carried, and back at the orphanage with regret. Now that his secret desire had come into fruition, he wasn't certain it was right. But whatever these men did, they chose it on their own accord, and William accepted that as he turned away from them and followed the Indian from the berry patch. The faint cries of his fellow orphans drowning out in the distance.

The Indian mounted his horse and muttered a few words to the tribe as they started their journey to their camps. William was trailing behind them, suddenly unsure of his steps and body, as he studied these men objectively. They had thick dark bodies yet were also lean, each with ornate symbols beaded into the scraps of clothing they wore. It was not much, but due to their stature, he assumed they simply couldn't find anything that may fit over their muscular bodies.

Only looking ahead for this journey, William saw a light out of the corner of his eye. There was a small farmhouse in the distance. An oil lamp glowed near a window, but suddenly the light was off. They must have heard the horses. William immediately thought of Lowell, who said his family lived out this way. He wondered why the Indians hadn't raided his house and instead chose the orphanage.

After hours of walking, William's bare feet were bloody; he was tired, hungry, and filthy but he knew better than to act like that. Mrs. May's voice rang in his head, "Never show your weakness. If you have a positive outlook, no matter the situation, the outcome will be positive too, William. Life can be anything you want it to be. The only limitations you have are those you put on yourself."

He smirked when his mind wandered, 'What would Mrs. May think about this situation? A group she taught us to fear, I am now willingly accompanying them.

The woods started to clear, and he smelled the distinct sweet scent of tobacco and a musky aroma of campfires. He looked up to the stars and saw smoke trails winding and curling. A few Indians let out some hollers to their awaiting camp, and after each step, the scene of beautiful tipis, women, and children came into view.
When they arrived at camp, William marveled at the culture.

The men who brought him in were very striking, but William had no idea it was only up from there. For one of the men wore eagle feathers fanned out on top of his head of long black hair, unlike the presumed leader who wore them on each side of his head. Some of the women wore fringe from their dress; others wore hides, in colors of golden yellows to dark tans.

William had never been one to notice fashion, but now he couldn't look away, for to never have seen this pleasing aesthetic, he may as well have been blind.

And then there was a girl about his age. Her hair was down her back in two long braids and a thin row of blue beads around her neck. She had a black rub of paint under her brow line with a red line going down the center of each eye that made them appear brighter. Her lips were naturally upturned; her dimples pronounced. She had a gap between her teeth.

The camp was a crescent moon shape with tipis lining the rim of the land before it dropped down into the water. The tipis were painted with scenes of hunter and prey; with a few handprints he knew to be from an animal's blood. Each tipi glowed from within, and the smoke billowing out the top let him know they were campfires inside. As he walked past one, he saw the ground was lined with luxurious pelts and furs.
William thought to himself, he'd never seen such a beautiful sight.

All eyes were on William, but no one openly acknowledged him, except a few children pointing to his face. He saw the children, who were younger than him, as playful and spirited youth that were no harm to him. He would return their wide-eyed stares with a smile, which seemed to scare them even more. He would laugh it off, but soon the question of his role overtook his mind.

The men all went into their tipis, greeting wives and children. He could hear animated voices, and even laughter and William imagined they were speaking of the raid that had happened just a few hours earlier.

He was alone now. The camp was just a few yards from a sandy beach, and only now that the tribes chatter had subsided, could he hear the water. He walked toward the smooth waves in a trance-like state, not feeling the sand mat around his bloody feet; instead, feeling the smoothness of the grains engulfing his wounds like pillowy socks. When he reached the water, he walked into it until it came to his neck, dunking his body into the abyss and washing away his life up until now. He was surprised to feel grief, thinking of Mrs. May discovering what had happened tomorrow. And what was it, that happened? Did the orphanage burn to the ground, or was its inhabitants, minus Denny, alive? William thought of Mrs. May being able to account for everyone except William and wondered how she would feel. He felt love for the woman who had tried to do right by him only weeks before disclosing that his parents may have as well, had they not tragically died.

His body rose to the top of the water. He had never learned to swim but felt it was instinctual to float. The saltwater stung his eyes and wounds, but he knew not to move his arms from their outstretched position. The waves slowly brought him back to shore, where he lay, arms still outstretched. After many minutes he opened his eyes, feeling the burn of his sadness for Mrs. May and the sting of the saltwater, only to see the leader, the Indian of the berry bush, standing above him.

He struggled to stand but tried not to show it, instead reaching out his hand to properly meet the man who he wasn't sure was about to kill him, enslave him, or maybe worst of all- leave him to die alone.

"Hello, I am William. I am told my parents are dead. I do not carry the syphilis disease though it appears I do from my facial deformity. I know how to garden and grow things. I think you are a beautiful people. And I respect you."

The Indian looked at William, who couldn't be much older than his own son. He was soaking wet and appeared to be in good health, besides being so pale and thin. William cocked his head and offered his hand, which the Indian decided to take. The child eagerly pumped it up and down, smiling. The Indian had seen other white men try to do this before they were killed.

"Hel-lo, Will-i-am." The Indian drew his hand back and patted his fist against his chest. "I- Wild Horse."

"You… speak English?" William's eyes were as wide as he'd ever seen. Wild Horse smiled at his revelation and recognized the spirit in this child as kindred to his own. He showed no fear, no pain though his feet were completely cut and bloody. He also showed obedience. Wild Horse decided to spare his life at least for some time, though he had planned on getting rid of him after bringing him back to camp to ward away evil spirits.

"Why did you come, Wild Horse? Why did you come to my orphanage?" William's voice was shrill, and Wild Horse felt the child was disrespecting him with so many questions. He took hold of William's jaw with his broad hand and pulled him closer until he was certain that William would not question him again, and he dropped the child and returned to his tipi.

William woke the following day to the sounds of women speaking. They were in the water, gathering buckets of it and returning them to camp. They slowed when they saw him slumped on a sandy knoll, speaking amongst themselves about him, but when he stirred, they nodded and continued their work as if to say, 'See? He's alive.'

He was given tasks later that day to help the women, as he couldn't assist the men with their skilled work. He was pulling corn husks and scraping hides with small carved tools. The women would scold him every few minutes, showing him again and again how to execute the task until he caught on properly. He took pride in his work, and Wild Horse noticed the sweat on his brow. But when William thought no one was looking, Wild Horse caught him picking up some of the Atlatls that had come out of the hordes of meat the women had been smoking. He watched as William quietly put them in his pocket and continued to work.

William rarely tried to speak to Wild Horse or any of them after his first night on the beach. Indians didn't want the white man, so he never wanted to use that language again. Instead, they conversed by pointing, motioning, and sometimes drawing things in the sand. He learned the words for things, but they would laugh when he tried to use them. But he was never laughed at here like he was at the orphanage. At night he would practice his pronunciation of the words until, eventually, they didn't laugh, instead only nodding. He serviced the tools that needed sharpening throughout the settlement, and at night, as he camped on the beach, would bring them back up to speed until they were pointed enough to kill a fly.

Time passed, and William found he was particularly gifted at sharpening tools. They all made pleasing remarks at witnessing his skillful cuts, Wild Horse only looking at him from a distance. One of the women said that could be his duty now, instead of her, as she was more gifted at mending than anyone else. Though he wondered if some of the praise may have been inflated in his mind, as he so desperately sought approval from anyone he could, William found delight in being useful to the Indians, and he hoped they would be his people one day.

Winter came, and William realized he'd been with the Indians for nearly a year. He must have been fifteen now, and he looked down at his body which had grown tan and muscular. He had replaced his clothes with leather hides that only covered his groin. The wife of Big Tree, the man who nearly killed him that night at the orphanage, had given him the greatest gift, a beautiful pair of moccasins for his feet. Although his feet were toughening by the day, the moccasins offered instant relief to his wounded feet and helped when he was walking through the brush and spikey vegetation.

One day William had been at the camp with the women and children while the men were away on a hunt. They were all working. Lihana had repaired one of Tatanka's bows that a horse had accidentally stepped on. William watched her restore it while he was working on flint, knapping some new tools, a trade he was just learning. The children were pulling corn husks, a job so mundane, and yet it was the only thing William was capable of when he first joined them.

When a branch broke a few yards away, towards the trees, everyone instinctively became silent as a mouse. The women kneeled, and the children tiptoed into the sand banks below, out of sight of any potential crossfire. Only William stood when a filthy man, a presumed robber who had nothing to show for his life except the knife he was wielding, came into the camp.

"Well, look what we have here." The man smiled the ugliest grin William had ever seen, and though it had been quite some time since he witnessed his own smile, he'd bet his life that this man's was uglier.

William, swiftly and discreetly grabbing the tools that lay next to him, walked towards the man, not breaking eye contact. As he crept closer, he picked up speed and broke out into a run that could outpace a gazelle. Hollering an Indian call at the top of his lungs, he flung himself onto the man who had not expected the move and proceeded to stab him repeatedly until he lay lifeless at the foot of the camp.

When the men had returned the next night, no one spoke of the robber, but Wild Horse knew something had transpired by the signs in the sand. He motioned to Tatanka to look, saying to him in the quietest voice he could that someone had been dragged away. Wild Horse looked back to his camp where his tribe awaited and saw William had been conversing with another tribesman who was proudly approving of some tools William had crafted while they were away. Wild Horse wasted no time and followed the tracks, so light-footed that he made none of his own, even in the sand. When he reached the corpse of the unknown man, who'd been buried in a grave only William could have made as it was far too shallow, he didn't know what to think.

After returning to camp and silently accounting for everyone, Wild Horse waited for William to come to him and tell him about the man. He even sat longer at the fire, while the rest of his men spoke of an impending war party, a topic Wild Horse would have to be the deciding factor on- he instead sat silent, an open invitation for William to come to him. But he didn't, and Wild Horse felt displeased.

Weeks had passed, when Wild Horse had announced that he would go and trade with the white men in a week's time. William had understood most of what he was saying and decided to present to Wild Horse a small, tanned hide that he had been working on in his evenings by the fire. He had beaded a fine border around it, a craft that Lazy Eye's daughter, Kateri, had taught him. Wild Horse was pleased with the item and said it would make a good trade. He then asked William if he wanted to attend the trade with him, to which William felt pride in his throat and nodded yes.

Wild Horse looked at this strange child. Although he had brought him back many moons ago to prolong his inevitable death and enslaved him to do work around the camp, this stranger never once protested any of it. Wild Horse felt he had been fair to William, almost taking pity on him that night they tore apart the orphanage. Wild Horse's people had never beaten him or starved him. He remembered that night as if it were yesterday. They had encountered a young boy in the woods who ran to them instead of running from them. He started rambling off that there was a house full of evil nearby. This child, who had been smoking, told them the area needed to be rid of all living there. He compelled Wild Horse with stories of how anyone who leaves becomes 'robbers and bandits and rapists who murder in-gens', which he'd seen, and his father had seen, and everyone begged for the in-gens to help. 'We would do it ourselves, but we can't have the law on us.' This wild child, who came off as a feral being, feared nothing of the men he spoke to— just the ones that he spoke of. Wild Horse felt the blood in his veins speed while his brothers nodded to each other in solidarity.

Wild Horse had been skeptical of the boy's claims but was also extremely superstitious. Though Wild Horse saw the look in the eye of the one killed with an arrow, and he had agreed there was evil in him, he hadn't seen it in the others and told his men to trash the place to discourage their livelihoods but spare their lives. And, in his superstition, that kept William alive and with them since. For if Wild Horse was to kill William himself, the evil spirits may join them forever. But since they let William stay with them, there have been many bad omens. The rest of that first summer they experienced a severe drought. The fishing had also been poor. And the forest the tribe had hunted for many years was lacking in gifts as well.

When hunting became poor, it wasn't unusual for the tribe to burn down the forest so it could regenerate itself. But doing so would require a moving of their camp, and he didn't think his tribe, which had a large amount of papoose and elders at the moment, was particularly up for that trek.

That night William joined Wild Horse, his wife Kaleena, Spirit Shadow, and his daughter Ehawee around the fire. Spirit Shadow was speaking of the men that murdered his wife, Lakeena. Twenty-three moons ago, she had been at the river one day near the old camp when a group of young male settlers came by. They offered her some shiny silver tokens in exchange for rations. They were weak and starving, having lost most of their supplies to a fire the week before. Lakeena took pity on these men who represented no threat and were so emaciated she could blow them over with a whistle.

They returned the next day with beautiful pony beads to trade for meat, which she gave them a white-tailed deer quarter and a few fish in trade. The Indians had treasured the beads, and she was pleased with the trade. It wasn't long until they returned, holding dozens of colorful beads in all shapes and sizes in their hands. Her son, Enahee was with her and said while she was pleased with the variety, she felt she had traded enough with these men, who suddenly had wild eyes. They then held out a silver pistol, which she took interest in. She agreed to give them one more leg of meat for the gun, saying to Enahee that his father, Spirit Shadow, could make use of the weapon.

She sent Enahee to get the leg of meat, but the moment he turned away, they grabbed Lakeena and held the gun to her head. She started crying and screaming to Enahee to get his father. Enahee began to pick up rocks to fight the men with, but Lakeena rebuked him and begged again to get his father. The men bound her and threw her over one of their horses, to which she screamed again to Enahee, promising that they would find each other again one day.

Wild Horse had a look of disgust in his eyes and shuddered at the memory. William guessed Enahee to be about a year younger than him, so the boy must have been around twelve when it happened.

"What makes you think she's dead?" William immediately regretted the words when Spirit Shadow stood up, pounding his staff into the ground. Everyone turned immediately to William, who had not spoken in English since the night he arrived.

"My wife is in the stars, her spir-it lay with-in me." He spoke as slowly and eloquently in English as he did in his native tongue.

Sitting across the fire from William, Ehawee gasped, showing her gapped teeth. But William wouldn't back down. To his knowledge, no one had any proof of Lakeena's demise. William felt Ehawee's intense gaze, as she suddenly sparked a feeling of manhood in him that he was experiencing for the first time. Wild Horse saw this exchange and immediately stood up, barking at Ehawee that story time was over. Spirit Shadow, confused at why his daughter was being sent away, looked at Wild Horse, who was staring at William. The wheels in his mind began turning and he muttered to Wild Horse, fast and in a rough dialect so William wouldn't understand, "I will not be disrespected. It's time to get rid of the white man."

William was none the wiser. He stoked the fire with thoughts of Ehawee's beauty and wondered if she saw something in him, too. After a while of sitting alone, he felt eyes on him once again. Looking over his shoulder, he saw Ehawee peering out from the side of a tipi, motioning to him.

As swift and silent as a cheetah, he walked over to her. They were out of view of the tipis and now standing behind a tree. They just stared at one another until he felt bold enough to kiss her, and she turned her head, him kissing her cheek. His cheeks burned and the elk ivories beaded onto her clothing glistened in the moonlight. She spoke softly to him in words he didn't understand because he'd never heard them before. Had he known he would've dwelled upon this moment well beyond his grave, he would've asked her what it meant. Or maybe he wouldn't.

The following day, he woke with a sense of peace, as if Ehawee had accepted him as one of them now. Though she turned her head, she didn't shy away from his kiss. He heard the men up and about, so he followed suit as Wild Horse, Tatanka, and Nanuka gathered the items for trade. After wrapping everything into a leather sack, they each got on a horse, except for William, who had still never learned to ride, or given the chance to.

As they waited on the edge of camp for Nanuka to gather the last of the supplies, William played out the conversation in his head, where he would ask Wild Horse if, when he was old enough, could he and Ehawee be together? In his mind, Wild Horse would laugh and smile wholeheartedly, and they would have a talk man to man and shake hands on it. William would rush back to camp, telling Ehawee of the Chief's blessing on their impending union.

They would spend the time getting to know one another deeper— her thoughts and dreams, his history and upbringing until they would allow him to marry.

But Wild Horse was in quite a sour mood towards William that morning.

Ehawee suddenly stood behind them, covered in bruises and had a split lip. She had tear stains as she held the blanket around her body firmly, and at once, all of the men turned to her as Wild Horse was demanding to know what had happened. She spoke of a young white man entering her teepee at night and abusing her. Wild Horse, Tatanka, and Nanunka immediately spun their heels to William. Tatanka took a swing at him as Ehawee quietly protested. Nanunka broke up the fight, saying it wasn't William, but another boy. William was as baffled and upset as the rest of the men. But wait. Another boy? She described a smaller, lanky young white man who smelled of tobacco and looked wild. Everyone instantly knew who this boy was.

Wild Horse swore to Ehawee he would find him and kill him.

Only a mile out of the brush from their camp did they travel, and William could see the men to which they would trade on the horizon. They all stopped at the precipice of trade and waited until the men came forward, then the Indians and William joined them. When they met in the middle, the white men started rambling in a language that William had only been removed from for a short while; but it felt like a lifetime ago. He now spoke only the dialect of the people he lived with— the wild people of the land.

All the white men stared at William, but William was no stranger to stares, and for the first time, he was pleased to live in a tribe that no longer gawked at him. He felt accepted by them.

The white men all stepped away after excusing themselves, to which Wild Horse glanced back at Tatanka with curiosity. Looking at William as they spoke, the white men seemed to come up with some sort of agreement, nodding and pointing to their saddle bags and guns.

Wild Horse was smarter than this, and he instinctively felt the trade was going sour as he reached for his tomahawk. The men saw this and shook their heads in protest, repeating that they come in peace over and over.

Wild Horse glared at them, and only for the second time did William hear him speak in English.

"What, then?" he barked.

Again, William saw the dangerous man that Wild Horse could be. But he also understood that while living with him, everyone was just a strong breeze and personal conviction away from violence. They were all capable of unspeakable things.

"We want the boy." Though they pointed to William, he looked around because he knew, surely, they couldn't be speaking about him. No one had ever chosen William— not even the Indians. He'd been merely allowed to exist in others presence.

Wild Horse looked at William, the child who had nearly become a man under his eye. He had grown taller and more robust, and his skin darkened up, and he was caring towards his people and had never posed a threat. But Wild Horse couldn't forget that he also saw darkness in William. A subtle sense of violence in his eye; not the kind that was deserved, it wasn't a rebuttal to something that had happened to him. Many nights Wild Horse had lain awake at night wondering when he opened his eyes, would William be standing over him with an ax?

There was also the signs of his evil; the crippling drought, the dead robber in the shallow grave and now Ehawee's attack. These things that come upon his people without his asking, the moment William was brought back. Wild Horse wondered if the evil that child spoke of, all those moons ago, was staring back at him now from the eyes of William.

Wild Horse turned back to the white men as they held out a bag of pony beads, tiny irregular shapes in ugly colors. Wild Horse had felt insulted by the trade but then decided these useless beads were good for getting rid of the threat that William posed. But why couldn't Wild Horse just kill the boy? He was still unsure what evil spirits may live inside William. What if he killed him and then got plagued? It wasn't a risk he was willing to take.

Wild Horse looked back at his brother, Nanuka, a simple man, nodding and showing his gap-toothed smile. Nanuka had been happy with the revolver he had traded for, and had no need for the beads, as no one back in camp would either.

William couldn't believe the words that came next.

"It is good." Wild Horse didn't look at William again, refusing to acknowledge the last year he'd spent with this person who was nothing more than a white man, refusing to believe that he had thought of keeping him with his people. His people, they were— this person was not.

Wild Horse dropped the bag of beads and William tried to search his eyes for answers, but he didn't look back at him. None of the Indians did, and William watched the men ride away, feeling that he'd been punched in the gut.

"C'mon, boy. You're with us now. Git up on this horse." An older man who smelled of honey and tobacco instructed William.

"I do not know how to ride, sir."

The man, physically taken aback at hearing this, shook his head. "It's time you learn, boy. You'll ride with me. But first, for heaven's sake, put these drawers on." He rummaged through a bag on another packhorse. The other two men were dead silent, and William wondered what would come of this.

"Where are we going?" Speaking, after not communicating in his native tongue for so long, he felt his voice sounded weak and singsong.

"I'm taking you to my sister's house, not too far from here. You can get ready for the war. We need soldiers. After you fight for us, you'll be free."

"I was already free." William, suddenly feeling defiant, spoke to these strange men who had just shaken his life up. He wished to return to the Indians, but he would never say that aloud, for fear of being called a traitor.

The men rode to the woman's house a few hours away. The further they traveled from his life with the Indians, the wearier William felt. During the trip, the men spoke of the impending war and mostly what they would expect of William now that he owed them a favor. He would stay for at least a month with the woman, who was married to one of the men traveling with them, while they continued to gather soldiers. She was a stern woman, they told him— an excellent cook, but if he disobeyed in any way, she would be at liberty to punish him by whatever means necessary. He was to always respect her and the Lord.

This was the first time William had ever heard of a Lord, and the men, though not surprised, were taken aback. They explained a few short things to him— that everything around him, from the dirt on the ground to the skies above, had a creator. He designed every one of us in our entirety. They said the woman would help him get right with this creator because he may "die by the hand of an in'gen during war."

That phrase caught William up. He heard only one other person call the Indians that, an abbreviated term for the lazy or inarticulate. He wondered if this man knew Lowell because William needed to find him and kill him for what he did to Ehawee. It was the same promise his tribe made- or the people he still considered his- and maybe, just maybe, if he followed through, he would be accepted back in.

William became angry in more ways than one with Lowell. Because of Lowell's actions, William was sold to these men. He wondered how the trade with Wild Horse ever came to be, considering that they were stationed so many hours away and surely several camps of Indians were close by, hiding in the trees. It was an ominous question, and his mind was racing. So, he let himself speak, and his words flowed on and on, reciting the horrors he'd been through. How he discovered that he could escape a mass scalping, living with the very people who killed those around him. How he murdered a white man to protect the Indians, and just how capable anyone was of violence given the right circumstances.

The men looked at each other with cocked eyes and didn't say anything back to William, only one mumbling to the others, "He will make a fine soldier."

But William knew that while he was capable of terrible things, so were these men. If not, more so, considering they each had two guns in their belts and one each on their backs. They had given the Indians some weapons for the tobacco which they incessantly puffed since getting on their horses— and, of course, the pony beads for his very life.

His mind went back to the trade. The beads were so small, and few, so distorted and discolored, yet Lowell had reduced William's life to a lesser value than ugly beads, and then Wild Horse didn't even take them.

The men finally rode up to the property. A creek ran through the wooded homestead, and a small porch lamp illuminated the entry. William was in awe of the landscape and instantly felt a connection to the cabin. Had he seen this place before? Maybe in his dreams?

It had a wraparound porch that he imagined the owners enjoyed despite this still being Indian country. There were neighbors, though, a little way to the east, which did give a false sense of comfort, considering the settlers were still vastly outnumbered by the native people on the land.

It dawned on him that this was the cabin he saw the night he left with the Indians. He instantly thought of Lowell, swinging from the branches at the orphanage. Suddenly he was filled with anger and rage again for what he did to Ehawee, the girl William longed for and, if it came down to it, would protect with his own life.

William's horse had been on a lead rope since he could not ride, and when they told him to dismount, his body wouldn't allow it. The men laughed, helping him down, where William wondered if he might be bow-legged for the rest of his life.

CHAPTER TWO

SARAFINA

The warmth of the cab with the rain hitting the windshield lulled me to a very calm state, and it surprised me when the driver slammed the brakes and shouted out, "Here ya go!"

I looked out. Yes, sure enough, this was it. The meter read $6, but I didn't have time to wait for change as I handed over a ten-dollar bill. I swiftly slid out of the cab, my feet barely feeling the one-foot puddle I stepped directly into.

When I reached the special entrance door, I already had the key in my hand, robotically turning the handle. The intoxicating aroma of books and a fresh brewing of a familiar spiced tea awakened my senses. I knew precisely what section, row, and book I was looking for as I broke into a slight jog to get to it. I recently researched an old manor in the countryside, and I found a captivating book with not only history but color photographs. I heard a few people speaking amongst themselves, and I didn't care that I must look insane, dripping wet and running through the library.

"Aha!" I pulled the book off the shelf, being extra careful to set my bag down as if the contents might break. I slowly slid down to the floor, silent as a church mouse, to get a better look at what I needed to find. I opened the index, and sure enough: Bagley Estate, pg. 167 jumped out at me.

My hands still shook from when the messenger dropped this off to me just minutes ago, but they were nearly paralyzed as I tried to open to page 167 of this book. '163…' Turning the pages one by one, '165/166…169.' What? Was the page missing?

I opened the book as wide as it would go and sure enough, it had been torn out. How peculiar, but why? Quickly scanning the shelf for anything else that might cover it, I found nothing. I grabbed my bag and ran the book down to the librarian as if she might be able to help.

"The page I need is missing from this book." My voice sounded urgent, but I was trying my best to whisper. I must have severely missed that mark because when I gazed around the room, I met a host of dirty looks.

"Oh, dear. That's not good. This is our only copy of this one. Hmm."

Me, always assuming this is some sort of conspiracy, "Well, who checked it out last?"

Her face reddened, and she shook her head. "Sara, you know this is a research library. We don't do check-outs here." Yes, I did know that, but in my moment of panic, I wanted answers.

Out of the corner of my eye, I saw a distinctly dark-haired, tan-looking man walking along the same aisles I had just been. "Well, can you tell me anything at all? Have many people been using this book lately?"

She turned it on its spine and was tapping her chin. "You know, it is odd since it is such a large library and all, but come to think of it, I can recall someone asking for it recently. He came in through the general entrance. That's all I can remember. Oh, and he was the most attractive man I have ever seen." She gave me a little sheepish grin and winked- as if we were old gal pals. I had no time for this kind of banter, but that was an interesting fact.

"See you next time," I mumbled, leaving empty-handed.

"Wait, you forgot something." I walked back to her desk as she held out a yellowed piece of notepaper. "This was in the book. Is it yours?"

It wasn't, but I picked it up anyway and read it. In nearly ineligible penmanship from a hasty hand, it said,

'I saw skies in your eyes,
Who is this perfect stranger?
Mouth full of lies,
Heart full of danger
j'

She handed me the book back after triple confirming the page was indeed missing. I flipped it open again to see if there had been any mention of the manor on the surrounding pages. Page 166 read: Bagley Manor, completed in 1905: Pictured, left to right, Frank Bagley and his associate, – " Darn. The page stopped right before saying who else was pictured.

"Thanks, Peggy."

The librarian offered her obligatory reply, but I was too preoccupied with my thoughts to hear her.

I felt like I was floating through water as I left the library, reading the poem over and over. I wondered about it, but not too long as I had things to do and houses to find. I waved down a cab while standing under the awning and made it to my apartment about fifteen minutes later. My mind was spinning. I needed to go to the estate as soon as possible– tomorrow at the very latest. I pulled out the paperwork again and got the address. It was at least four hours away and living in the city, I didn't have a vehicle. Or a driver's license. But I knew someone who did.

"Yello!" The way she answered the phone always made me smile. She was twenty-eight, going on a sixty-year-old man from Brooklyn who played coffee shop chess games and listened to baseball on the radio.

"Hi Megan, it's Sara."

"I know, silly. I have a caller ID. What's up, girl?"

"Well, I was wondering what you were up to this week. I may have inherited a house, and it's four hours away. And I can't think of anyone I'd rather go on a road trip with."

She gasped and started peppering me with questions I swore I would answer on the drive there, but how could I? I didn't know much yet. Megan would have to call out of work, but she didn't mind an ounce, and she excitedly agreed. Then she teased me that I was the only friend she had with a vehicle, but she was honored, nonetheless.

I let loose a huge sigh of relief as I hung up the phone. We were to embark tomorrow at 6am. I took a moment to reflect on how thankful I was for this friendship. Megan knew a thing or two about inheritances, as she was a trust fund baby, as we used to call her, so it eliminated the jealousy factor. She chose to work for fun but turned around and donated her entire income to animal rescues. Shuffling around my apartment and gathering my traveling necessities, a small photo frame of Megan and I sat next to my computer. It was from the first week we met— when my parents died. She was in the hospital visiting her grandpa, who was not long for this world.

"Hi there. Can I sit here with you? All these adults are making me more upset."

I nodded, only glancing at her long enough to notice she was very trendy. She had a blindingly bright diamond tennis bracelet on with her Juicy tracksuit.

"What are you in for?" she whispered. "I'm here because my grandpa isn't doing well. They don't think he will make it through the night." Just then, she started crying.

"I-I am so sorry." But I wasn't. I was feeling a grief hangover. I had just been given the news about my parents, and I was waiting for the staff to find someone to get me.

She continued to cry off and on for several minutes when she asked me again what it was that I was doing there.

"My parents are dead." Saying it out loud was a punch in the gut, and I buried my head in my hands. I was in a deep state of shock and hadn't started crying until that very second.

The new friend I had just made started hammering out questions. Where would I go, what would happen to me, etc.? I shook my head as I stammered, "Not sure, no family." I was now choking on my tears and gathering attention from the rest of the room.

"That doesn't work for me." She spoke confidently, in a manner that I had never interacted with, even with adults. She stomped off in her platform flip-flops, and I could hear her whisper-yelling to her parents.

I looked up just in time for them to make eye contact with me, nodding as they listened to her, simultaneously waving me over.

***

WILLIAM

Now under the woman's watchful eye, William waited for the moment the men would return for him to make him into a soldier. The woman would bring it up daily— not in conversation, but more scolding. She would make sure he knew what his purpose was, to thank the men for saving him from the Indians and protect the ground he walked on from being taken away.

But William's mind would wander off, though he felt himself nodding to the woman, to thoughts of the boy he met all those months ago. He felt the words gurgling up inside as he waited for the woman to stop talking, but she bore on and on. He remembered the warning from the white men who said she would punish him any way she wanted at her whim, but there was nothing that she could do to him that hadn't been done before.

"Do you know Lowell?" William blurted out, boldly interrupting her, and then he looked to see her face. She was piping mad and looked like she'd been slapped across the face. And that's just what she did to him, but she never answered the question. So, he repeated himself, but realizing she couldn't subdue him with a slap made her even angrier. "Boy, what did those Indians do to you? I'll do worse if I must."

William slid out of the chair he'd been sitting in, forced to listen to her speak all day. He stood, looking her in the eye, getting closer to her. There was a slight twinkle of curiosity in her eyes, though some might call it fear. William was as tall as the feeble woman but broader and more muscular. The woman took a step back, and he took one forward. William paused and spoke as clearly as he could, "It's what I did to them that they sent me away." Her eyes were wide as moons and she started screaming out, "Who do you think you are?" She was afraid and appalled and just now realized that she'd been housing someone that was possibly dangerous.

William told her, "I'll be leaving now."

She stopped screaming. He half expected her to forbid it, but instead, she was silent as he gathered the few pieces of clothing, they'd given him and walked out the door. He turned one last time to her before leaving the porch. "Do you know Lowell?" A sweat had broken out on her forehead during their argument, and her hands were trembling. "Y-yeah. He's at the boat docks."

***

KILLIAN

"There was this woman, Josephine Bagley. She was certainly the most beautiful thing you'd ever seen, soft reddish hair, olive skin, and light green eyes. But that's not what made her so interesting to me."

The man was intrigued, turning to Killian, his storyteller, who had his leg crossed over his knee and his arms up behind his head. "And what was that?" he whispered as if the sound of his voice might scare Killian away.

"She was cursed." The words slid off Killian's lips with no emotion. The man began to wonder if any of this was real.

"I'll get to how. But first, there is more that you should know." Killian pulled a matchbook from his pocket. As he slid the box from its sheath, the small sticks were perfectly intact.

The man wondered why he asked him for a light in the first place, but the embers from the flame put him in a trance. After a slow drag, Killian started speaking again.

"You see, Josephine's mother, Sophie, was a clairvoyant, except she was devoutly religious and refused to play into any of it. Her sister, Cora, had her own gifts and abilities too. She wasn't just clairvoyant. She could step into the vision and experience it firsthand. Like time travel."

The man let out a small, exasperated laugh, instantly regretting it.

"Did I say something amusing, chap?" Killian looked at him; his glare traveled to the man's core, sending chills down his spine.

"N-no, not funny at all. It's just that time travel is not possible."

"Well, let me make one thing clear: this family was very deeply woven into darkness. Well, to put it in terms you would understand," Killian's tone was very aggressive, and he took a drag of his cigarette, "Darkness has very few limitations, chap. And it's the very reason that I am sitting next to you right now."

The man looked over at Killian, who was meticulous in thought with his sharp words, and he started to feel as though he was in the company of the very darkness Killian spoke of. The man slowly looked around, waiting for another person that may be able to save him from this impending sense of doom.

"Shall I proceed?" Killian didn't wait for an answer. "One day, Sophie saw her own death coming and sent Josephine away to live with Cora, who had just been widowed."

"Josephine had no idea her mother was dying. Of course, Sophie kept it from her for reasons she never understood. Shortly after arriving at her aunt's house, Cora told her everything about her family, including her mother's visions and her own gift of time travel. She swore Josephine to secrecy, as now she and Sophie were the only ones who ever knew her secret."

"This frightened Josephine. She was raised to believe these things were of the occult and not to be dabbled with. But as the days went by, and Cora showered her in kindness, she began to come around.

"Sophie had always prayed feverishly that Josephine would keep away from these evil abilities. She was a Christian woman who chose to live as such; she believed her clairvoyance was not a gift from God but rather evil.

"But there was a time when it chased her dreams and screamed aloud in her mind- when her late husband died. She begged him not to go to the mines that day. He laughed it off at first, but then refused; for he had not known of her sight. He had to go. He had to support his family. After all, they were expecting a child. After the explosion, she decided it was because she was toying with the evil that he perished."

"She vowed to never listen to the visions again. But one day, she was getting a bucket of water out of the well when everything went dark. She lost all control of her body but could feel it spasming, then limp. She woke up from this episode covered in her own vomit. There was a flashing light around her. She was suddenly gripping her head as if it were in pain. Josephine witnessed the event and rocked with fear. The pain subsided, but these episodes started to happen again and again."

"Sophie took this as a sign of her own demise. She thought and prayed about it long and hard and accepted that she was sick— that death was near. The moment she did, she sent a letter to Cora, explaining how she would send Josephine there immediately."

***

SOPHIE

My dearest Cora,

I am saddened by the loss you are experiencing. No one will ever replace the love you had for Benjamin.

When my Robert died, I thought I would die, too. But Josephine is such a light in my world that I recovered. Now I am sending her so that you may, too.

She thinks it will only be a few days, as she worries about me. There's just one problem, I'm going to get sick, and I won't recover.

Please take care of my beautiful daughter for me, my sweet sister that I love so deeply. She's smart, hardworking and her eyes are remarkable. If it weren't for me, she would have found a husband by now.

Do whatever you have to. Just keep her.

Love always,

Sophie Sears Flint

P.S. I don't know how I've managed, but she doesn't know about us, or our family. Please don't tell her.

***

KILLIAN

"Cora, receiving the letter, felt sudden sadness but remembered Josephine having been exceptionally beautiful and thought she might use her for her own gain. You see, she wasn't the sweetheart that Sophie thought she was. Cora used people as pawns in her own greed. So, she decided she would travel to Sophie and poison her, to speed up the process and let her go out in dignity. So, she folded up the letter and imagined herself seeing her ailing sister, on the day the letter was dated— seven days prior."

"Stepping into the rickety cottage, it couldn't go unnoticed how clean and cheery it was, although nearly empty. There was a table with three chairs, a wooden stove, and a bookshelf. Cora didn't make a sound as she crept through the house, but she did peek into a bedroom. It had a patchwork quilt over the small bed, a nightstand with an oil lamp, and a cross hanging above. Figuring that it was Josephine's room, she continued to the second bedroom.

"Hello, Cora. I've been expecting you." Sophie spoke. Her back was to the door, as she sat in a small blue chair next to a window that had a view of a hillside brimming with sheep. The back of the chair had faded flowers stitched into it, with carved wooden feet. She was sitting at a desk, the pen she wrote her letter with still resting in the inkwell.

"You've already entered, why don't you make yourself more comfortable?"

Cora couldn't decide if Sophie was angry or relieved. "Hello, sister. I guess there are no surprise visits for the know-it-all of the family, is there?"

"Oh, you know I don't play into that gift from the devil himself." She turned to face her sister. "I did see you arriving today to kill me, though."

"I only wanted to help. Give you more options." Cora held out a small silver vial with roses carved into it. Sophie looked at the vial and sat it beside her on the desk. Staring into it, but not ingesting it.

"Will it be painful?" she whispered into the void, no longer speaking to Cora, but instead, God.

"Less so than whatever you're suffering from."

"Goodbye, Cora." Sophie went back to staring out the window, turning her back to her sister.

Cora pivoted and started walking out but didn't want to leave it like this with her sister. When she returned to the room, however, the vial still lay on the table.

"Goodbye, Sophie. I loved having you as my sister," Cora murmured as she slipped out of the room, suddenly very aware of the presence of death. She was transporting back when she heard Sophie whisper, "I love you, too."

"Cora was not a good person by any stretch of the imagination. She took full advantage of this ability and would use it to gain wealth. She married a man that she could leverage— a hard worker who would believe her when she had an idea, that of course, she learned from her peddling with darkness. She never loved her husband, on purpose. Cora thought love made people weak. She married a man she could use so that she would never lose herself. But they had been together for fifteen years, and it was obvious. There was plenty of love there."

"Benjamin was the kindest of men. They were superbly rich, though marriage was the most important thing to him."

"Then, one day, Benjamin left for work in the morning. Cora had 'teleported' as I call it, to the near future and discovered his weathervane invention was doing well, and since she had never been wrong before, Benjamin was acquiring the patent on it that day. He leaned in to kiss her on the forehead, and Cora caught herself closing her eyes, relishing the feeling of his mouth. She tilted her head and kissed him deeply. The gesture caught him off guard, but he was so happy that he started whistling out the door. She decided to look into the future later that day, because she was excited to see how things went. But when she got there, Benjamin was not at the business meeting; instead, it was a man they had dealt with before in business. One that she wasn't too familiar with. So, she went back a little earlier and started nosing around. Benjamin was in a heated argument in the alleyway with that man, Frank. Steam had been coming out of the nearby buildings, clouding her vision, so she moved in a little closer. It sounded like Frank had gone for the same patent that Benjamin was after, and Benjamin, not wanting to disappoint Cora, was threatening Frank to give it up, or he would make Frank disappear. Cora was shocked by this. She'd never seen this side of her husband. It excited her. More steam came from the laundry building next door, and once again, they men hidden from her view, when a gun went off. Footsteps hastened toward her, and a man emerged from the fog. But it was the wrong man. She abruptly returned home, back to her morning tea, still wearing her dressing robe. Cora leaned into her teacup as a tear fell in. When the evening came, she turned off the house lights and made her way to bed, not needing confirmation as she knew he wouldn't ever be coming home again."

"When the police arrived, Cora was ready to turn in the killer, but she had no proof, considering she technically hadn't left her house that day. She put on her best face for the police, thanking them for their work and detective skills, and would pray they would find the person responsible."

"But she knew they wouldn't because there was no justice at that time. If she wanted to make things right, it was up to her. Day and night, she would use her gifts to learn more about this man, who she now discovered was Frank Bagley. He was a widow, having lost his first wife and baby to Cholera, and had a large family. He had old money, generations before him in fur trading, but he also had his own fortune. His wealth came from his and Benjamin's collaboration on the weathervane patent, and he was building a large estate for himself and his family in the countryside. On land that he purchased from Benjamin."

"The moment Cora learned about Josephine coming to stay, her plan came together. Cora, mourning Benjamin, could now put all her attention and focus on Josephine, while also turning her attention to his killer. At the dinner benefit in Benjamin's honor, Josephine caught the eye of Frank, and he made his way over to introduce himself properly. Cora, at first, was shocked, considering he murdered her husband, but Frank laid it on thick. He explained to her that he had always been very interested in Cora's ideas, and he wanted to honor his late business associate, who had contributed to his massive wealth, by keeping an eye on his widow. When he turned his attention to Josephine, Cora knew then that she would ruin his life, piece by piece.

***

JOSEPHINE

Josephine was transported to the moment again after writing to her mother to the best of her abilities. She was articulate, but nothing could describe the feeling she had when Frank kissed her hand.

The room was brighter, and the people were different. The seasons had changed; there was sweet honeysuckle in the air. She was in a powder blue dress and an unforgettably tight corset. Frank looked much the same, which pleased her. He mumbled, 'As my eyes have seen, I wept.' It went as fast as it came, and she was in the moment again.

He kept her hand in his all the way to the ballroom dance floor. They danced to a sweet jazzy number, which she would hum for days. Frank never took his eyes off her, and she held his gaze.

His dark hair was swept perfectly to the side, and his mustache curled ever so subtly. He had a strong nose and soft-looking lips that she dearly wanted to kiss. The feeling of them on her hand would have to hold her over until she was graced with such an honor.

When the song ended, it had been over for a few minutes before Josephine and Frank broke their eyes from each other. Josephine glanced at her Aunt Cora, who she found nodding in approval.

Frank leaned into Josephine, softly speaking in her ear, "I have found the one whom my soul loves." He took her face in his hands and kissed her lips. His lips grazed her cheek on his way back.

Suddenly, Josephine's whole body felt chills like the pinpricks she felt when Aunt Cora was sizing her for a dress.

Josephine saw it so clearly: Waves crashing, pacing along the coast, searching the waters for him. A small boat outlined on the horizon. A presence with her while waiting for her betrothed. When the ship finally reached shore, it was empty of him, only containing a single black dahlia.

Josephine shook her head and her mind had returned to the room and heard no laughter, no talking around them. The party had cleared, and it was just them. Frank was staring at her in a peculiar way. "Where did you go?" he whispered. She shook her head; she really didn't know.

Frank took Josephine's hand and escorted her to his coach. Her Aunt Cora had left word with the doorman, seeing that Frank took her home, and to be careful of the killer lurking in the streets.

Later, Aunt Cora would tell Josephine that he was a very successful weathervane tycoon, and she was thrilled he took such a liking to her, as he had never courted a woman so publicly before. He reminded her of her sweet Benjamin, his success, and finding her as he was later in life. Cora was used to a very high standard of living, and Benjamin certainly didn't disappoint her financially. Josephine's mother once told her that they had a million dollars.

"Mother,

I had the grandest time at the ball tonight! Aunt Cora dressed me as royalty, I felt like Queen Anne.

Once we arrived, gentlemen kept coming over and talking to Aunt Cora, and she would tell me who they were, and after they left, she'd conclude with a humorous anecdote. One fellow has notably bad hygiene caused by a very strange diet of cheese and liver.

But that's not why I am writing to you this late into the night. Don't worry, it's not too late, but it is two hours past twelve.

His name is Frank Bagley. He was with colleagues tonight at the ball and was so handsome in a tuxedo. Much older than I, he has wise eyes that are so enchanting. He had a cocktail in his hand when he saw me, about to take a sip. But he never took a sip!

He came right over to me, mother. Aunt Cora stood straight up and said, "Josephine, meet Frank Bagley." But all I heard was 'Josephine Bagley'.

He kissed my hand, and this may sound peculiar, but I saw us marry right at that moment. In a grand room, much like the one we were in. I do hope it comes true!

Mother, I am worried about you. I haven't heard from you in the days I've been here. You promised you would write to me. Please write soon, Mother.

Love,

Your dear daughter, Josephine Flint 'Bagley'

***

KILLIAN

"Cora all but pushed them together after this, but it doesn't take much convincing since there was a natural attraction between the two of them. Frank and Josephine spent most of the evening talking and dancing, and afterward, Cora invited him over to her home for dinner the next night so that he may learn a little more about the price of the object of his affection."

"He arrived right on time, with a beautiful bouquet of wildflowers, which made Cora feel a little jealous. Out of spite, she played a little cat and mouse with Frank, making him first promise to listen to her ideas and agendas before he could see Josephine. He obliged, but the night turned sour when Cora made him swear to always give her fifty percent of his income. He objected as he too had family members who relied on him- but after a constant nagging and manipulation on her part- bringing up Benjamin, who Frank truly cared for so much and owed all his success to, he agreed to thirty-five percent. Cora is slighted but relieved to have the income as she has a costly lifestyle that cannot just come to a halt because her husband died. And she now had someone to do her bidding until she was ready to dispose of him."

"By the time Frank got to see Josephine, the visit was short, dinner service had passed, and they just shared a brief conversation in the drawing-room, and to his chagrin, Cora was present, looking over their shoulder. Josephine, however, had a lovely time, not being any wiser to the fact that Cora held Frank hostage for money in trade for time with her."

"Frank left, but not without asking Josephine to walk him out. Alone. Cora hesitantly obliged, worried that Frank may tell her the arrangement, but shuffled off. He asked Josephine if she would attend church with him tomorrow, to which she happily agreed. When she came inside, she excitedly told Cora that he was clearly a 'man of God' if he wanted to take her to his church. When she danced off to bed, Cora rolled her eyes. He was certainly a man, but not of God."

"The next morning, Cora woke her early. She decided it was now or never. She must let Josephine know that they all had unique gifts, hers being time travel and her mother's clairvoyance, and they would soon discover what Josephine's gift was."

"After a moment of shock, Josephine began to ask questions about her dear mother, Sophie. She immediately got up and started writing her mother letter after letter. Josephine would send one and start another— she had so many questions. Growing up, there were many odd circumstances, but most importantly, when Josephine touched objects or people, sometimes she would see things. But she immediately started to backpedal. Her mother had instilled such a deep faith in her that she felt this was inherently evil. She wanted no part of it."

"Cora, however, begged her to hold her hand and see if she, too, could time travel. Josephine was adamant and refused. Cora got angry. Her fuse was always short, and she ended up grabbing Josephine's hand. Josephine began seeing things— open water, death, drowning— and then she fainted. Cora decided that Josephine was much more sensitive in other ways and dropped the time travel idea."

"Frank arrived to take Josephine to church, and she hadn't even changed out of her nightgown yet. She was livid at Cora for delaying her worship hour with things of the devil and stormed back upstairs. Cora meanwhile invited Frank in, but he declined and insisted on waiting on the porch, smoking a cigar. He had a grand stagecoach with shiny silver wheels waiting for Josephine. Cora stepped outside, shutting the door behind her. When she asked him where his driver was, he replied just by pointing to the corner down the street, where the newspaper stand was. She nodded, pulling out a gun and holding it up to his back."

"She explained to him that she knew everything. He had murdered Benjamin for his own gain, and now he would do what she said or meet the same fate. Frank reached for his hat, removing it and turning around, the hat resting on his chest. 'Madam Cora, I think we can work something out, as we already started negotiations last night. I agree to your terms, but let's just keep this between us, shall we?' Cora nodded. 'Very well then. Let's start with you marrying Josephine, hmm?' Frank smiled, 'I guarantee it.'"

"With Cora's guidance, Frank quickly proposed much to Josephine's delight. They were to marry at his new estate, the one Frank had been constructing in the countryside, and he would return for them in two days to take them to see it."

"Frank sent for them, and they loaded up into his stagecoach and made the weekend trip to see the wedding venue. During the long drive, Josephine dozed off for a few minutes, so Cora took the opportunity to put her arm around her and try time travel again. It was a success, and they traveled back to the moment when Josephine sat with her mother, Sophie, at home. Josephine's spirit stumbled when her mother greeted her. "Hi, Josephine." A tear rolled down her cheek. Past Josephine smiled innocently and said 'Hello' back. Spirit Josephine said, "Mother, I don't want this. What do I do? Why didn't you tell me?" but her voice is so faint. Sophie closed her eyes, nodding. "I loved you too much to do that." She gave a soft smile. Present Josephine was confused but didn't say anything. Instead, she got up and went to her room, assuming her mother was having a daydream."

"Cora pulls them out of the time travel and back into the stagecoach. Josephine felt like she'd been dropped from the sky. 'What have you done?' She demanded of Cora. Cora pretended not to know what she was talking about. 'My dear, you fell asleep. We are on our way to your new home, where you will marry Frank and live for the rest of your life!' This brought Josephine back down to earth, but she was still very wary. Josephine was sure they had time traveled, as it was much too realistic for a dream. She clutched her chest, heaving tears and longing for her mother."

"Josephine swiftly realized she was without her necklace— the Brinley stone cross from her mother. She had worn it every day since she was eight. Her mother had seen it at a traveling gypsy market and purchased it. The gypsies said the price they required for the item, which Josephine remembered her eyes widening at, but Sophie obliged. She said she had been searching for a stone cross that could withstand the tests of time since her daughter was a baby. The gypsies gave Josephine a look over, whispering amongst themselves. They knew the necklace had some meaning, but they had all worn it and didn't experience anything. Back then, you see, people were very superstitious. They didn't know that it wasn't the stone, but the symbol, that had meaning. It was a multi-colored charm that sparkled in all different shades when the sun hit it. Josephine wore it all of her life, and this was the first time it wasn't around her neck, since her mother bought it from the gypsies."

"She had a sick feeling, and her stomach was instantly in knots. Where was it? When was the last time she wore it? Then it hit her: Cora had removed it to put on the pale Amethyst amulet for the banquet when she met Frank. How had she gone this long without it and just now noticed?"

CHAPTER THREE

SARAFINA

The drive up to the manor was peaceful and lovely. Although I enjoyed the silence, Megan loved to talk. By cranking up the radio, I thought that she would eventually get the hint, but it only made her talk louder. This, combined with the old hum of my car, was starting to make me feel nauseous. I decided to give in. "It seems a little dark and lonely out here." When I voiced my thoughts to my friend, Megan convinced me otherwise.

"Oh, Sara, I don't think so at all!" Megan exclaimed, her face inches from the passenger window, peering out to the vast hills and wooded land. "It's so beautiful!"

I couldn't disagree. The landscape was stunning in the mid-morning sun. The trees, in fiery colors, were vibrant and robust on either side of the road. We hadn't seen a house or store for miles, and the seclusion of the place made my stomach turn with anticipation. What treasures awaited me? Will this be the jumpstart to the career I've been dreaming of?

I cautioned myself not to be so excited. I had inherited the manor from a woman I had never known, but that didn't make the fact any less tragic. Besides, that woman, Victoria Call, had been my aunt. I don't even remember my parents mentioning her, but how could I? My mother and father had been laid to rest many years before Victoria, leaving me with many question marks on my family tree. Perhaps now, though, I would have a chance to replace some of them with actual names. I couldn't help but wonder: if she knew about me, why didn't she make herself known years ago? I've been alone in the world for years. It would have been nice to have some sort of family. The thought was putting a distaste in my body for the house.

"Oh, look!" Megan exclaimed as we came around a wide bend in the road, and the top of the mansion came into view. We both gasped in wonder, and I slowed the vehicle to a crawl as I took it all in.

It was more of a castle than a house as it stretched into the sky at a great height above the towering trees. The two side roofs were peaked, with large, metal crescent moons at the tips. Above the grand entry, the tallest center roof had two perched angels facing opposite directions. They held out a hand to me as if beckoning me to them, but even at this distance, the expressions on their carved faces looked mournful and desperate. The green speckles of moss covering each of them made the angels feel slightly less ominous, a sign of life. Between them, spiking upward, was an elaborate iron weathervane, a complex star shape sitting above the arrows lettered with directions.

As I drove further, more of the house came into view. I saw many chimneys scattered evenly, but no smoke curled from them. Of course not, for the place was now empty, but I wondered about the woman who had resided here. Was the home as cold as I imagine it will be? We turned into the main drive of the house, and Megan gasped at the vision.

The sides of the home were octagon, black pane windows covering the front sides almost wholly. The front came out like a half circle, with the grand porch below. The railings and steps were concrete, with shapes of stars and moons cut out inside. Moisture stained the façade, which made it even more beautiful.

Ivy and moss were invasive on other homes I had cataloged in the past, but in this house, it was magical. The moss was delicate and deep green, its leaf tips turning yellow and orange. I had never seen such intense colors before, and it reminded me of fire, making the house feel alive. Perhaps it would be warm and toasty after all?

I pulled the vehicle up in front of the sprawling home and shifted into park. I took a breath, and Megan grabbed my hand. "This is amazing, Sara." She was right. It really was. My head was leaning on the wheel. I was in shock. I lifted my eyes to get another view and suddenly felt like I'd been here before. Maybe I came as a child?

Megan and I unclicked our seatbelts and robotically climbed out of the vehicle as if we both felt out of place. The sweet scent of flowers immediately bombarded us. In late September, that seemed unusual. I scanned my surroundings but could only find dormant lilac bushes lining the mansion's porch. They were, however, pruned and well-maintained, which surprised me since my aunt had died more than a month ago. I breathed in deeply, savoring the aroma, wherever its source was. It reminded me of my late mother's scent— lilacs were her favorite. Megan didn't mention it, and I was about to ask, but when I turned to her, I was startled.

Suddenly a man stood before us. I didn't see where he had come from.

"Hello," he said cheerfully. "I'm Leroy. Welcome to the Bagley estate."

"Hey! It's lovely to meet you!" Megan jumped forward to answer him right away. "Megan Burnette." She didn't miss a beat, holding out a freshly manicured hand, which the older man took in both of his. "This is Sarafina Rayne," she said, stretching her neck toward me. "And she goes by Sara," Megan added quickly with a wink, knowing I didn't go by my full name. She swept her gaze over the front porch, murmuring at the beauty.

"A pleasure to meet you both," Leroy said. He shook my hand, not seeming to mind that it wasn't as dainty as my friend's.

"Likewise," I rasped. Then, after clearing my throat, "I didn't know anyone would be here."

"Oh, pardon me for surprising you, then. I am the groundskeeper. I currently live in the garden cottage around the side of the house." He spoke proudly, and I remembered the lawyer's paperwork mentioning something about a gardener living nearby. I didn't recall his meaning on-site.

"I'm so glad you're here. You can show us around the place, then?" Megan beamed joy when she spoke.

"Oh, yes." Leroy bobbed his head up and down, but there were somber undertones to his voice. "First, you probably want to see the guest house, which I had cleaned and made up for the both of you. The main house, well, I didn't think you'd want to stay there."

He didn't? I was about to ask why when Megan interjected.

"Thank you, that was very kind," Megan gushed. "I wouldn't mind dropping our stuff off and freshening up after our long drive. Shall we, Sara?"

I nodded mutely, half shocked, as I assumed she, too, was dying to get inside the main house and begin exploring.

Leroy took us to where a narrow, cobblestone path led up to a beautiful guest house. The entirety of the grounds was like something from a fairytale, and I was immediately enchanted. It was going to be difficult for me to sell, I already knew that, but I couldn't afford such a place and needed to be in the city anyway, for my career. I couldn't stop twisting my neck around in all directions when I suddenly saw something— someone— standing outside the corner of my eye. I stopped in my tracks and turned. The figure came from behind an iron gate and what looked like headstones in the distance. But when I searched, it was gone.

"What is it, Ms. Rayne?" Leroy asked, softly, almost a whisper. He too was looking in that direction before turning to me. I locked eyes with him. "Is there…someone else here?" My voice was inquisitive, almost accusatory. "No, madame. But sometimes we get deer in the area." His matter-of-fact response didn't leave much room for platitudes. His eyes never left mine, though. I reverted my attention in the direction of the movement. "Very well then, here we are," he said, motioning to the cottage.

I was still immobile. "Is that a graveyard?" I demanded, breathless. Let's just say a graveyard wasn't really in the brochure, not that I had a problem with it, but it proposed questions of its own. Who was in it?

"Yes." He spoke and swiftly turned back on his heels before opening the guesthouse door with a skeleton key.

After helping us take our luggage inside, Leroy left us to fix some lunch.

Megan immediately turned to me when the door shut behind him.

"What in the name of Mona Lisa was that!?" She crossed her arms and looked at me like I was crazy. This is the one person who knew me better than I knew myself. "Nothing, I just thought I saw something."

Megan smirked. "He's a very nice man, butler, or whatever his role is. It felt like the Spanish inquisition! You need a nap." She joyfully laughed, and I nodded. I was exhausted. I hadn't been sleeping well for weeks, and last night was no different. Leroy was a very nice person, I could tell. I had never had anyone looking after me before, and I didn't know how to feel about it, though I was grateful that he had readied the guest house for Megan and me and was so welcoming to us. I would make a point to be as polite as I could to him from now on.

It was a large house for just two people and had far more square footage than some of the ritziest apartments in the city. Still, it was only a fraction of the size of the main manor, even with its generous living room, moderately-sized kitchen, and three cozy bedrooms upstairs. Megan let me choose my bedroom first, and I set my things in the one that overlooked the main house. It had moody, dark blue colored walls and a tasteful mixture of wooden and plush furniture. It felt newly decorated, with its modern touches. I wondered if my aunt had done this herself. The guest house alone held a few rare antiques, so I couldn't even imagine what was in store for me inside the big place.

After a bit of settling in, I was feeling joyful and energetic again. "This is such a dream," I murmured. Megan agreed and began helping me put away the few groceries we had brought with us, thinking we'd find the kitchen unstocked. "I still can't believe it."

"Wondering when you're going to wake up?" she asked.

"Yes."

"It's such an amazing place, Sara, so hidden away from everything else."

"I know, I know. Wouldn't Dean love it?"

Megan groaned and knocked me on the shoulder. "Don't you dare," she scolded. "Don't you start thinking about Dean. This is the start of a new chapter, a new adventure. Dean-free."

"You're right," I said, sighing. Yet my mind couldn't help drifting to the handsome antique dealer whom I worked for. Dean Goetz. He would feel as if he were in paradise here. Who was I kidding? I felt in paradise here.

Dean was the man that I had always imagined I would be with when I was a girl: hard-working, funny, and an appreciator of fine pieces of art and craft. And, of course, wickedly handsome— molded straight out of my dreams. The only problem was that he didn't reciprocate my feelings. This house, or estate, was the perfect chance to impress him. Every item was an opportunity to be noticed and appreciated. When I brought him some of the rare finds the attorney had told me were nestled throughout the mansion, I wouldn't be invisible to him then.

"Come on," Megan urged as she shut the refrigerator door. "Let's go look at the main house!" I shook my head to clear my thoughts of Dean and followed her out of the guesthouse.

The sounds of my shoes on the concrete steps gave me a feeling of déjà vu as, once again, the floral scent intoxicated me. I turned to see if Megan noticed it. "Do you smell the flowers?" I whispered to her, not wanting to appear crazy since they were dormant behind me.

"You know I can't smell a thing with my allergies,." she replied without really contemplating the question. I dropped the subject and moved onward. The main front doors stood wide open. Leroy must have left them that way in invitation for us to explore. Megan gestured for me to go first and I didn't hesitate stepping over the threshold.

It felt as if I were entering another world— another time. The entryway was as large as a ballroom. The tile floor was a polished bone color, with hints of abalone. The stunning staircase curled up the right side and met a large landing at the top; the light poured over the second story begging me to race up the stairs. The wood banisters were dark and ornately carved, offsetting the light colors of the curtains. Furniture was beautifully placed around the entry, adding gorgeous colors for the eye to feast on. Fabrics on chaise lounges were soft and vibrant; the artwork surrounding them was dark and moody. I felt like a thousand eyes were on me, and yet, I'd never been so alone.

I took a few deep breaths, expecting the air to be musty. It had only been less than a month since Victoria passed, and the air tasted sweet and a little bitter. It felt different from the outside air and city air. It left me feeling somewhat lightheaded. I realized Leroy must still be keeping it clean.

Suddenly my eyes locked on the white owls carved into the banister. I raced over to touch them, and upon tracing my fingertips over the ornate feathers, it felt like I had done this before. I was so lost in the mesmerizing surroundings and didn't hear the footsteps that announced Leroy's presence.

"Hello, madame," he said. I jumped at the sound of his voice and twisted my neck around. Leroy was standing to the right, holding a tray of small sandwiches. The front hall had so taken me that I hadn't even noticed that Megan wasn't beside me any longer. She must have disappeared into another room. "Please, help yourself." Leroy nodded towards them.

"Thank you so much," I said, taking a sandwich from the tray. "You really didn't have to feed us, but we appreciate it a lot."

"Was it a long drive?" Leroy asked.

"Almost five hours."

"Long enough," he said, chuckling.

I smiled back at him as I took a bite of the sandwich. It was delicious, carved turkey, goat cheese spread with fresh chive and a hint of cranberry, all on unique artisan bread, thick-cut and still warm from the oven.

"Meg!" I shouted. "Where'd you go? Come get a sandwich!"

"I'm in the library!" Megan called from some distance. Of course, that's where she was. When it came to books, Megan was like a bloodhound, sniffing them out from a mile away. I laughed and asked Leroy if he would please show me to the library.

"Wait— Leroy?" I whispered, not wanting Megan to hear.

He turned to me, inquisitively, "Yes?"

"Have I— have you seen me before? I mean, have I been to the estate before? Forgive me but I am trying to put the pieces together; you see my parents— "

"No need to explain, Ms. Rayne." He cut me off. "I have been here longer than you've been alive and can confirm that you have never been anywhere on the estate. Now follow me."

I felt a bit slighted by his firm answer but appreciated it.

We passed through an exquisite sitting room with teal furniture and gold metal accents. The soft gray carpet felt plush to walk on, so much so that I kicked off my loafers and went barefoot. I was walking on clouds as I touched the pillowy furniture, felt its tufted buttons, and gave each metal table a tap. I was already cataloging it in my mind and it was thrilling. There was a large mirror on the wall facing the chairs. It was peculiar to have mirrors in a living area, and I was about to ask Leroy about it when he motioned for me to enter the next room. I let out a gasp as I entered. The vast library was shaped like a dome with its vaulted ceilings. Most of it was full of shelves, maybe twelve feet up the walls. Ladders sporadically hooked the shelves, and the room was broken up only by an oversized jade stone fireplace. A pattern of windows scaled the ceiling, different shapes that at first made no sense, but as if on cue, the clouds moved, and the light shone in with force. The windows illuminated, showcasing the detailed ironwork creating a beautiful star pattern that reflected onto the tiled floor. This tile had flecks of abalone as well; I could clearly see that now. Megan was in the middle of the room, standing near an antique globe, her jaw hanging wide open as she took it all in. I knew exactly how she felt.

"Sara— " She grinned. "Look at all of these books! There must be several thousand or more."

"Probably," I agreed. The spines of the books came in all different colors, burgundy, green, brown, deep purple, and black. Somehow, they reminded me of autumn leaves. The books and fireplace made this room feel somewhat cozy despite its vastness. Regardless of the September climate, the house was not all that chilly. I remarked as much to Leroy.

"It's a big house," he agreed, "but it's quite well-sealed. In the summer, it stays relatively cool, and in the winter, it is always quite warm."

"It must have been built well," Megan murmured, finally able to move her legs. She strode to the heavy desk and peered down at the titles of the books scattered on top.

"When was this built?" I wondered.

"It was completed in 1904," Leroy told us. "Sarafina's great-grandfather, Frank Bagley, had it built as a wedding present for his wife, Josephine." He turned to me, beaming. "Your great-grandmother."

Megan let out a low whistle. "This is some wedding present."

"Indeed," Leroy affirmed. "Josephine lived here for the rest of her years, most of her life. But unfortunately, Frank didn't get to enjoy it long himself. Victoria came to live with Josephine when she was a child, so it was pretty much the two of them for a while."

"When did you come to live here?" I asked.

"I came to work here," Leroy explained. "I've been here for many, many years. Josephine brought me on to help out, and Victoria needed me after Josephine died. She was all alone in this big house."

"You knew Josephine before she hired you, then?" I asked, curious about his relationship with my aunt.

"Oh, yes." He seemed to be working something out in his mind as he paused. "I've known the family for a very long time. There is much to be done here. In its heyday, there was a full staff, chef, a team of gardeners, and maids. Now it's a much humbler effort, and I have quite a passion for gardening. But when you see the trees and flowers bloom in the spring, you'll understand why I never left."

I looked down at my toes. I was sure I wouldn't be here to witness the blooming flowers in the spring. There was no way I could take care of this place, let alone afford the upkeep and bills that went along with it.

"And this is where I remind you to read the documents sent to you. While I haven't had the chance to review it myself, I am aware of a trust set up that pays the upkeep and the staff here, as long as the home stands." Leroy winked and waltzed off.

Well, that took care of that problem, didn't it?

"Look at this, Sara," Megan said from one corner of the library, saving me from my shame. "Isn't it spectacular?"

After we polished off the plate of sandwiches, Leroy took Megan on a tour of the kitchen and food cellars and I decided to start exploring on my own. According to the blueprints included in the documents I received, this house had two attics, seventeen bedrooms, eleven sunporches, six bathrooms, a library, a smoking room, a ballroom, and four dining areas. Although I stopped considering the rooms after I read the word "attics", because that's where I knew the really antique antiquities would be hiding.

***

WILD HORSE

The ride back to camp was quiet for Wild Horse, except for the occasional cry from his brother. He caught his mind wandering, wondering what would come of the boy, but he told himself he didn't care. And for a moment, here and there, he believed his own lie.

But his mind went to Ehawee and her tear-stained cheeks as he recalled his own wife when she was that age. A child. The faster they rode their horses home, with nothing to show from the trade except for the empty horse, the angrier Wild Horse became.

Spirit Shadow was again crying out, begging Wild Horse for justice for Ehawee. "A white man has stolen from my daughter." Wild Horse nodded in reply; there was no doubt in anyone's mind what happened. Now all they needed to do was find the boy who did it.

But the guilt of Wild Horse now lay in his mind as two roads diverged. He had begun to bond with William, the two were born enemies by geography but found common ground in respect, and Wild Horse saw what he could become. What he was becoming. He knew William's intentions to stay, to live with them forever. Nothing got past Wild Horse; except for the trouble that followed behind the White Man wherever he went.

That night the women were tending to Ehawee, and the men and children were around the fire. Spirit Shadow had his staff and was stomping it to the ground in a repetitive beat. The children began to dance with their feet, as Nanuka played his flute. A small chant broke out to the dancing as a few of the women joined the fire.

Wild Horse was relieved to see Ehawee sit next to him. He tried to respect her privacy and not give her too much eye contact, but he was her blood, and he put his arm around her.

Ehawee silently wept, her hands covering her face once again. Spirit Shadow saw his daughter weeping as he started booming his staff faster, speeding up the steps of the children in turn. Wild Horse looked back at Ehawee's tipi and wished he could've stopped the man from entering. The thought crossed his mind and spread like a snakebite in his mind: This is what you get when you pity the White Man.

He felt the emotions all around him, and with his heart full of revenge, he started chanting out to them in his fierce whip of a tongue.

"Watch me!
I will
take revenge
for the white man's
evil deeds.
I will!"

The entire tribe was now dancing and yelling as the fire crackled in a loud roar. Screams of joy ensued as their deepening anger subsided. But then an unusually large gust of wind came through their camp, brushing the fire among everyone sitting, lighting a blaze to Ehawee's blanket.

The dancing immediately stopped and Wild Horse ripped the blanket off of her, throwing it over the fire. Spirit Shadow was standing, shielding his daughter from the flames that no longer were a threat to her. But as he stood in that stance, ready to protect her, he wished he could stay there forever.

When Spirit Shadow turned back to the fire, the blanket was only ashes. He looked to Wild Horse, who held his gaze for a long time.

Many moons had passed and Ehawee was preparing to bring her own child to the tribe. Wild Horse felt unsure, considering her young age, but Spirit Shadow wasn't concerned about the birth. "Lakeena will protect her. She is with us, Wild Horse."

Wild Horse hoped he was right.

That night, the sky was full of stars but void of moon; Wild Horse silently tiptoed through the snowy tree line scanning the sky. Ehawee let out a low howl. It was unmistakable, the pain, the tremor in her voice. The women went to her, carrying their furs and hot water and Wild Horse found his brother Spirit Shadow at the fire.

"What does it mean?" Spirit Shadow asked his brother but didn't look him in the eye. Wild Horse knew exactly what he was asking. "It may be a good omen, Spirit Shadow. We don't know. Lakeena had Enahee on a very dark night if I recall." Wild Horse tried to calm his brother, but there was nothing either of them could do, but wait.

Spirit Shadow paused before speaking, looking up at Wild Horse. "And now, Lakeena is dead."

The cries grew longer, darker, and more helpless when at once, there only cries heard were from infancy.

***

WILLIAM

William took off on foot, venturing in the only direction he hadn't explored. He knew behind him was the orphanage, to the left was where he camped with the Indians and to the right was the forest.

He realized he was getting close to the boat docks as the air became moist. It was now well past sunset, and near the docks, no one was out or still working, so he waited until morning when he found a few sailors preparing their ships for the day's fishing expeditions.

He told them what had happened, and that he had been living in an orphanage when it was raided by Indians when he survived and lived with them for a few seasons. Then he was traded by white men to become a soldier, but he escaped that life and was now looking for Lowell. They didn't believe anything he said and laughed it off. So he asked them again about the orphanage fire, and they suddenly recalled hearing something about it.

"But no white boy ever livin' with ye Indi'ans." They wildly laughed.

He was defeated and decided that if he was ever going to get somewhere in his life, he could never mention his past. He had to be a new person. So he went down to the beach and found a spot where he could wash his clothes and dry them out of sight from the fisherman.

Returning the following day, he found another fisherman and offered his services of cleaning the galleys for a day's pay. That man took him up on the offer, but when they went out on the open waters, William had become horribly seasick and spent the entire day throwing up. The fisherman still gave him half of his pay and invited him to join his family for dinner. William accepted. It was the first time he had been in a warm family home. The moment the fisherman entered the door, his family had gathered around him, hugging him, and it seemed he couldn't wait to kiss his wife. He had a few children. One was a boy William's age. He spoke to William about his dreams of running a large ship after his studies were through. He had said he wanted nothing more than to be on the open water, but it was so important to his father that he learn how to read and write. He showed William a few of his books with elaborate ship drawings and told him a story of the great Sarafina's Revenge, a local ship filled with pirates and treasure.

"As the story went, Sarafina's Revenge came upon Fairn Island. The residents of Fairn Island watched its approach, assuming there were sailors aboard. However, as the boat drew closer, the people on Fairn Island realized not a soul was on that ship. But in the next several days, bodies began to wash ashore." William was fascinated with this boy's retelling of the story, which took hold of his soul when he heard it.

"But I know something that isn't written down anywhere." He smiled at William, who was instantly begging the boy to tell him. "A few days go by, and the settlers bury all of the bodies, right? Well, a small wooden boat washes ashore. Laying inside is the Captain of Sarafina's Revenge, Scarsbeard. And the best part? He was alive. He took the settlers captive and enslaved them to work aboard Sarafina's Revenge."

William was floored by this story and continued to pepper the boy with questions until his father said they must go to sleep. The fascinating mystery of what happened to the men on that ship was so compelling that William decided he would find a way on board.

William had continued to work on a few ships from different fishermen over several years. He became very good at his trade while growing into a solid body with brawny sea legs. William rented a small bedroom from a barkeeper and usually had just enough left over from paying his rent to eat. In his new love of sailing and fishing, he had let go of the dream of returning to the Indians. But he always maintained his love for Ehawee, though her image in his memory faded over time.

One day, he couldn't believe his eyes. Sarafina's Revenge was on the horizon. It kept its distance from the docks, much to the locals' relief. Almost everyone had a story about the ship. None of them were good. Local lore said it was filled with murderers and thieves, immoral men who would kill you for bread. William didn't leave the docks that night; he would wait for the ship to enter the harbor. He made his bed amongst the rocks on the beach that night, and sometime after the full moon rose, a low horn that can only be heard by those anticipating it blew.

William shot up in his light slumber, eyes immediately on the ship slowly chugging towards him. The ship was nearly invisible in the night and would have been if they hadn't had such an exceptionally full moon. He feared they would spot his light-colored clothing in the moonlight and quickly ducked behind a giant rock.

It took the ship an hour to reach the bay and another half or so until he started seeing movement disembark. They were being careful, trying to go undetected. Better that way for when you are sneaking up on someone. Not surprisingly, the first few men who dispersed into town went to the brothels and bars. Then a few more followed in their footsteps. But the last group of men who got off the ship stayed put, guarding Sarafina's Revenge for everything inside.

At daybreak, William decided to approach the ship, aware the action could get him killed. He would ask to speak to the captain, whom he'd heard from the fisherman's son, was named Scarsbeard.

The men all turned to William as soon as the creak of his foot touched the dock. They were heavily armed and as filthy as a person could be. He could smell them before he made out their faces.

They burst out in laughter as he made his way closer. They, too, were surprised by his bravery.

"Good-day, gentlemen" He spoke as confidently as he could, to which they replied with more laughter and mockery. But here's the thing about William, he had been through the worst. He'd faced death and came out of it. And he had nothing left to lose.

Suddenly their laughing ceased when they made out his facial features. The pirate in front appeared to hold back the few behind him, and William felt the tables turn in his favor. They were now in fear of him for his facial deformity.

"I am here to speak with Captain Scarsbeard," William squinted his eyes, focusing on the one in front, who appeared to be a leader.

"And who may I say is asking?" He attempted to sound like he was mocking William, speaking in a proper dialect, but it didn't work. You could hear the uncertainty in his voice.

"The one who isn't afraid of him."

William nearly couldn't believe the words as they slipped off his tongue, but he had to start somewhere.

The laughter ensued again; this time brief. It faded completely when everyone turned to the wooden banging above them on the ship.

A man with the stature of a beast appeared. He had a wooden peg from his left knee down, and his gait appeared lopsided due to the peg. His silvery hair was long and dreaded, but his clothes seemed much nicer than any of the men William had seen. His back was to the crew and he stopped in his tracks. The guards looked like they were sweating bullets, and William felt the adrenaline of the Indians sparing his life pulsing through his veins once again.

The man turned and locked eyes with William, whose jaw dropped at the site. This man had the same facial deformity that William had. They gave each other a visual inspection, and the man walked out on the ship's plank, towering above William, and spoke as stern as the horn.

"I am Scarsbeard."

The voice echoed throughout William's body, the docks, and the town. He heard shutters close in the distance, women calling out to their children as all chatter stopped. It was William's turn to speak, but his voice had no sound, having been taken by the boom.

"I wish to join your ship, Captain."

The guards looked at each other with wide eyes. William didn't know this then, but he was the first person to ask to be a part of this ship.

Scarsbeard squinted his eyes, to which William reciprocated the glare. Scarsbeard spit on William, and instead of wiping it off, William just stood there, glaring. He showed no fear because, truthfully, he had none. This man reeked of evil, but William had tasted death, and it wasn't so bad.

Scarsbeard nodded and stepped back from the plank, leaving for his chamber once again. William took a breath, walked past the men guarding the ship, and entered. But not before spitting on their feet.

The ship set sail a few hours later, after a horn blew, alerting the men in the town that their raping and pillaging had come to an end. They all climbed back aboard, and even with their sea legs, half of them couldn't stand up straight.

William felt he had been treated with cruelty his whole life but did not act like a victim. But that first night, he was shown what cruelty really was. The captain invited William to join him in his quarters for dinner. William obliged, and they were served by a man who, when William muttered thank you, Scarsbeard shook his head, saying, "I cut out his tongue." They were eating some kind of mushy bean course with crackers and cheese. Everything was room temperature. He devoured his meal, and William kept up the pace. Scarsbeard let out a burp and the odor was foul, William tried to hold back his disgust, but the look reached his eyes.

"What's the matter, fool? Ye never heard a man belch b'fore?"

William looked away, choosing his battles. If this man was truly as evil as he'd heard, he knew better than to partake in petty chatter.

"Where are ye parents?" He spoke with the same booming voice and came off like he actually cared. William told him he was an orphan. "I am an orphan as well." Scarsbeard, squinting, was suddenly uncomfortable at the similarities.

"Why are ye here?" He growled, to which William replied, "The same reason as you."

Scarsbeard planted his fist on the table. With a smirk across his face, he twisted the hairs in his beard, staring at William while he came up with a solution for this brazen attitude. "If ye know so much, I am now one man over my capacity. Ye can choose who walks the plank tonight."

William's heart sank hearing the news that he would kill a man tonight by drowning. His mind started to reason with him, it would be indirectly, but still, he would be the cause. The alternative was clear, he could choose his own life, but he'd made it this far. Besides, humanity had not been kind to him. He had taken more than one man's life, but many times he had felt it was just.

Scarsbeard sent him to the deck after finishing his meal, reminding him not to get used to eating with him. "Ye never know when I offer ye same deal to some'ne else, and ye walkin' the plank ye'self." William knew there were worse ways to die than by drowning. He had just hoped that day wouldn't come.

A loud horn blew, and the men started wailing out. They knew what was about to occur as they emerged from their berths and living quarters. They lined up, careful not to make eye contact with William, fearing being chosen. William wondered how many times they had been through this routine.

But someone was missing.

Scarsbeard got up in William's face, holding a rope in his outstretched hands, asking William, "What ye matter, boy? Can't make ye decision? Well, we can throw you instead!" The men cheered at that response, Scarsbeard clapping, egging them on.

"No, I have chosen, but he's not here." The men fell silent, looking all around. Scarsbeard, starting at the end of the line of men, took inventory in his head, deducing who was missing.

"It's Gregory, Captain. He's not here." A younger man, who couldn't have been older than eighteen, shouted out. He had a French accent, which was a beautiful reminder in despair such as this that there are places that aren't here.

Scarsbeard nodded, pointed at the Frenchman, and snapped his fingers. He immediately took off looking for him.

Less than ten minutes later, Gregory emerged, but it wasn't the man who mocked him. It was a disabled man covered in food. He must have been the chef. His eyes were going in two different directions, and it appeared he had little control of his limbs. William felt pity for him, and shouted, "That is not the man I chose." But Scarsbeard was already roping him up. Gregory looked very calm, and William was certain he couldn't grasp the situation.

"No, that is NOT who I chose," William screamed, and felt himself getting choked up, but knew he couldn't show any emotion.

Suddenly, the man who mocked him came out of the ship's stern. William forced himself between Gregory and Scarsbeard and got right in Scarsbeard face. His body was trembling, but his tone was unmistakable. "That man— that is who I choose." Everyone turned to look and gasped. He was the First Mate, but as it turned out, Scarsbeard didn't care much for titles and didn't like much of anyone.

"Very well then, but ye have to rope him up ye'self." The ship again roared in laughter, still not believing this boy could handle any of this and, in turn, would end up dying himself.

"That won't be a problem, but I will need your weapon, sir." The laughter stopped, and Scarsbeard instinctively grabbed his blunderbuss that was resting on his hip. It must have been the shock of the request, but Scarsbeard had a sudden smirk on his face and handed William the gun. Everyone looked stunned, but Scarsbeard didn't specify he had to be alive before going overboard.

Since never having held a gun before, William gave it a good look over. Scarsbeard snapped his fingers at two men and pointed to the man in question, and they ran and each grabbed one of his arms.

"Tell me somethin' boy," the man, who was the first to mock him this morning when he approached the ship, spat. He looked William dead ahead and asked, "Why me? There are several men here who laugh at you. In fact, everyone here does. I am just one of the many."

After inspecting the gun from the books he'd studied on the matter over the years, William decided it was loaded and ready to shoot. He took it in his right hand, feeling the weight of it, and raised it, only then returning the man's gaze.

"Because... I choose me." And with that, William shot the man in the neck. He had aimed for his head, but it wasn't far off for his first shot. All the men cringed as the man choked from the wound for a few seconds before falling. It was such an unpleasant sight to see. A few of these men, who had no doubt witnessed the lowest of humanity, looked away.

William spun around to Scarsbeard, who had a cock-eyed glare of surprise on his face, and handed him back his weapon. "I didn't know ye had it in ye, boy." He let out a cackle, but it wasn't a laugh. He recognized so much of himself in this child. And that made him feel fear for the first time in his life. Because he knew what the boy was capable of.

William tossed the rope at the men standing around and asked them which cabin he would bunk in. The Frenchman, whose voice was far too eloquent to match his mangy appearance, sang words as sweetly as a songbird when he spoke. "You will take his bed, which is in my cabin, over there." He pointed to the cabin with three beds, which had a circular lookout window.

William shuffled to the room, which wasn't much more than what he saw from a distance. A small painting hung on the wall, as out of place as anything high-class would be on this dump of an operation. It was of a countryside full of lavender that butted up to some similar-colored cliffs. It had a twisted sky for the landscape as if the artist didn't know which way he was painting, pleasant or dark. William was locked into the art and crawled up on the bed to get a closer look.

"Oui, isn't that interesting? I thieved it from an art dealer in New York. Worth big money." The Frenchman kissed his fingers and made a slick gesture.

"Yes, it is quite interesting." William scanned the portrait for an artist's name. 'KS' was all there was on the bottom of the painting. "Do you know who the artist is?" William asked, turning around, but no one was there. He heard his voice echoing from outside the cabin. William wasn't sure who this man was and why he was on a pirate ship, but he was curious to get to know him more.

He was finally alone, and he lay on the bed that sat below the window. There was a very thin blanket that smelled about as poorly as the men on this ship and a small ragged pillow. But it beat sleeping on the rocks of the beach last night. In fact, the lulling waters below made it better than his closet-sized apartment above the bar, though he would miss the perks of living there at all hours of the night. The bright crescent moon aligned perfectly in his window when his head rested on the pillow. His hand started spasming in the motion of pulling the trigger. He had killed a man, and immediately after went to admire the artwork. It was just like that, then? Did he have no remorse or value for human life? Or had he just had enough of the nameless monsters who treated him so? Like Denny in the orphanage had had it coming, just like the man tonight.

Yes.

They deserved it.

The more he quelled his own conscience, the faster he fell asleep. And it was the most profound slumber he'd ever experienced.

William opened his eyes just before dawn after a short but restful sleep. It was still dark when he wandered into the captain's cabin. The door was closed but slid right open when William gave it a push. The captain's bed was on the opposite wall of the small room, next to the door where his navigation was. William slipped inside and slid the door shut behind him.

Scarsbeard was lying on his left side; face pointed at the wall, which immediately struck William as odd. Who in their right mind would ever sleep with their back to the door? He was asking for something terrible to happen.

William crept up to him, searching his features. He was a mid-sized, average-height man with long scraggly silver hair that had dreaded ends. His facial deformity was the same as William's, with about the same severity, going into his nose.

Scarsbeard, lying in this state of unconsciousness, was just a man. There was no evil in his slumber, and William started looking around his room for information. Anything that he could learn about this man could be used against him. He searched through a wooden chest, but it only had clothing and linens. It started to rain outside, and the volume helped cover William's tracks. He decided to investigate the navigation deck, right through the door next to Scarsbeard.

That door, much to William's surprise, had been locked. So that must have been the deterrent in killing this man in his sleep. You wouldn't be able to take over the ship unless you could find the key.

The ship suddenly hit some choppy water, and William almost fell on Scarsbeard, barely catching himself within an inch of physical contact. Scarsbeard appeared to stir, about to break through that last bit of sleep, and William slipped out just as quickly as he had entered. Upon returning to his room, his roommate woke up, and for a brief moment, William had worried that someone may have seen him in the captain's quarters.

He would shrug it off as sleepwalking if so, and he crawled back in bed, closing his eyes for the last few minutes before the rest of the crew would awaken.

At dawn, Scarsbeard awoke to the nagging feeling that someone was in his room. He half expected William to be standing over him with a gun, but when he opened his eyes, no one was there. The feeling still lingered, so he stood, dressed and went to William's cabin to see if he was in fact there.

The door was open, and he could see from twenty feet away that William was dead asleep under the natty blanket with his bare feet sticking out. Yet he couldn't shake the nagging awareness that this boy brought with him. 'It is only a matter of time until he kills me,' he muttered. Everyone had always feared Scarsbeard, except for William. Gregory was standing behind Scarsbeard at that moment and offered him some breakfast. Scarsbeard lingered in his gaze, ultimately obliging, and wandered back to his quarters.

What was only supposed to be a pretend slumber, to his surprise, William slept another several hours. He woke only because he dreamt of being thrown into the water and drowning. When he opened his eyes, Gregory had a bucket of water that he was slowly submerging William's feet into.

Three men around him had burst out laughing as William realized he lay in his own urine. He swiftly covered himself up, but it was too late. "Don't worry matey, ye just a foolin' with ya. Don't go throwing ye overb'ard now ya hear?"

The men shuffled out of the room while William gathered himself. He pulled on his pants and stood in the room for a moment, looking out the window. While he expected to see islands, birds, or even other ships, it was just water, as far as the eye could see. The only way off this ship was death, and William would do everything in his power to avoid that.

The ship's captain had a soft spot for orphans, having been one, but was otherwise a cruel man. He would often toy with William, just waiting to catch him in a moment of weakness, any excuse to throw him off the boat. One night he had asked William to choose who, out of three men, was responsible for a slimy film that covered the galleys, and that man had to walk the plank. William immediately chose, much to the crew's disgust, as no one actually thought these men were guilty. He didn't know it, but the captain was testing him. It just proved how ruthless he was willing to be, and he became his first mate after that.

When he was a little older, William, the captain, and two mates were in Scarsbeard's quarters playing a game of poker. Since the two mates had no money to bet, William said the winner of the game could choose the next round, which he announced while holding the winning cards in his hand. They obliged, drinking and laughing amongst themselves, which was notable to William in part that he had such a grim reality for them waiting.

After revealing his hand, they nodded and clapped while waiting for him to announce the game. Scarsbeard never said a word when William pulled out his revolver. Opening the shaft, he removed a bullet from the chamber, leaving three bullets inside. The men knew what game this was as he shut the six-bullet chamber, spinning it. But instead of pointing the gun at himself, he aimed it at the two mates.

"What er ye doing, William!?" Peter, the one in the crosshairs shouted, jumping up from his stool and falling backward. William moved the gun a few inches to the right, aiming at Solomon. The captain stood up, reaching for his weapon, and William shot the two men dead.

"Those are some odds," he spat over their bodies.

A click of the gun and pressure to the back of his head let William know he had moments to speak before his own demise. He decided to let the captain know that it was actually him that was nearest to death.

"Cap'tain, it's been a real honor sailing with you. But now is not my time."

Scarsbeard scoffed, breaking his silence and wailing for him to stand. "You better believe it's yer time, boy! I've let this go on long e'nough." Scarsbeard let out a cough, followed by a choking noise.

William turned around, watched him fall to his knees.

"With all due respect, it's my time to lead. How did I know you would reach for ye gun tonight? You see, I've poisoned your weapon, sir. Have you any last words?"

Scarsbeard, fighting to the end, whimpered out a whisper, "Ye... are... Evil."

CHAPTER FOUR

MRS. MAY

When Mrs. May returned to the orphanage after that fateful night, she thought she would die of a broken heart. It wasn't just her calling to look after the children with no parents or homes or families of their own; it was what she loved to do. She thought that, if she treated the children with kindness and respect, she ought to make a difference in the world; a world that was full of dark deeds, violence, and crime. And yet now, as she stands in front of her home of ashes, she cried out to the heavens as she looked for its inhabitants.

It only took a few minutes of her calling out names for her to locate the souls under her care. They had fled to the forest and came out with a fascinating tale of fire, arrows and Indians. The children wildly described the gruesome scene. Mrs. May knew they would all be carrying this trauma for the rest of their lives, but oh, was she thankful for it, because it meant they still had breath in their lungs.

Everyone in her life had been in the building when it was raided. She found it nearly unbelievable at first how everyone had survived, except Denny. As she accounted for each one, it didn't go unnoticed that William wasn't among them. For that, she held out some hope that he had escaped and would start a new life somewhere. She hoped too that one day he would return to visit her, like Carl had. She pictured the meeting in her mind; William, grown older with a beard and suspenders on, as was the trend these days for young men. He would have a wife with him, and Mrs. May would comment on what a beautiful couple they made. She would recount stories of Wiliams childhood, remitting the bullying and torment from the other children of course. And she sat and cried and hoped that just maybe, William had gotten away.

A stretch of time passed and Mrs. May had a handful of her previous group were old enough to leave on their own accord, there were more that went to the war effort. Later, she had six more children back under her care, for which she wasn't surprised, as there was never a shortage of death to put a child on the streets. But this time, things would be different, as Mrs. May now had people traveling through on a regular basis who'd heard of the tragedies of that night, years before, that would check on her and the children. A few times a week they would stop by, telling her the rumblings of the city or the shores, and telling her the news about the inklings and rumors of rebellion.

Mrs. May had worried her whole life about the threat of the land her people had taken, settled as they said, but it didn't dawn on her she may face the threat of her own people fighting each other now too.

Months passed and the war was nothing more than some randomized shootouts, but many men perished, and she buckled down for an influx of orphans. But the only one that came was on one lonely, winter day. A homesteader knocked on the door holding a bundle in his arms. Mrs. May gasped when he came inside and revealed it was two small infants, twin boys, holding one another for body heat.

KILLIAN

"I was on the property living in the cottage when the Bagley's returned for the grand wedding event. By now, the wedding was a day away, and they brought a brigade with them to prepare for the event. Frank sent word to the cottage that the last stagecoach to arrive would take me back to the city. As I gathered my few belongings and headed to the coach, I spotted Josephine in the grass, writing a letter."

"She was twirling a twig of lavender in her fingers, closing her eyes while experiencing the intoxicating aroma, before letting go to write another sentence. I watched her for a few moments; after all, I was an artist looking for inspiration. She looked so innocent as she lay in the meadow, mumbling while carefully writing her script, but I thought I heard her sobbing. I took another few steps, this time determinedly louder, that she may look up at me if she wished as I passed by. She didn't. I didn't say anything to her. Instead, I just dragged my equipment to the stagecoach. But I did steal a look over my shoulder, and her head turned to me, catching my gaze."

"Frank wed Josephine in the most lavish affair. In the grand ballroom." Killian motioned with his hands a grand landscape. "There was a live band, all the cutlery was gold, and white doves spontaneously swarmed the skies above, but that wasn't even the good part. The good part was the unveiling of the manor to his friends and foes, the likes of which no one around here had ever experienced before."

"To see that place in its heyday— well, I suppose it was about what it's like now," he said, shaking his head. "But the house had a living breathing warmth. It sparkled with life and was meant to be filled with laughter. It was also the first home with electricity", he laughed. "That alone was magic. But the true enchantment was his love for his bride and how lovely she was." Killian reached out and lit another cigarette. "She was as beautiful as they come." He pulled back on his clove, turning to the old man as if he had something profound to say, but just stared at his face. It was the most intimate feeling to be examined that closely, and the old man felt Killian's hesitation before releasing his gaze.

"Josephine was twenty-one when they met but still just a girl really. She had never left her ailing mother's side before coming on the trip to stay with her aunt Cora. Cora's husband, Benjamin, had just passed away and he worked with Frank, you see. And died by his hand." Killian put his hands into fists and emphasized his words.

"Frank told me he recognized Josephine the moment he saw her, as his wife, I mean. They were attending some gala in Benjamin's honor, and he saw her from across the room. Frank said with every stride she took; she was further down their wedding aisle. He lit up a room after he met her, and his joy was contagious.

"Frank had purchased the land from Benjamin well before he ever died at his hand. The land was from Cora's father, but her mother had told her it was cursed with a burning cross, so she didn't want it. Instead, she sold it to someone they didn't like all that well." Killian rolled his eyes.

"Frank had already owned the land, and the house had been under construction for a few years by the time they met. He came out once a month to check on the status of the construction. I was invited out to paint the landscape; it was to be a gift to Josephine when the house was completed, which it nearly was. I set up my easel in the back corner as I wanted to paint from the perspective of Josephine as she was overlooking the estate from her garden. She loved flowers." He fell silent.

The way Killian spoke of her made the old man feel a little uncomfortable. It was clear Killian was infatuated with her. Before the old man could inquire, Killian continued on. His account was compelling.

"I was to stay the entire time he was gone, and part of my task was also to keep an eye on the comings and goings for him, because Frank was paranoid." Killian shrugged. "Sure, he had enemies, he was exorbitantly wealthy and, in that time, if you were wealthy, people assumed you had stolen from others. I made myself indispensable to him over the last few years and he appeared to be very trusting of me. Besides, I didn't mind. It was a beautiful late summer and I had slept under the stars, though there was a small cottage on the property, which was all mine." He put one arm on the bench, gesturing to the sky. "I used to love stargazing. It made me feel connected to something bigger than myself. It gave me hope for my life. I even saw a comet my first night there. But after a few weeks, the weather changed, and so did my mind."

"The days got so chilly I had been doing most of the work inside the cottage. While it may have been the fumes of the paint thinner or the isolation, I don't know. But time started to pass frantically, and days would go by when I wouldn't even recall painting. I would go to bed with paint on my hands and smelling of the lacquers, but that's all I remembered."

"As a lightning bolt broke across the sky, time stopped when Frank arrived. I heard the carriage come up the hill and the sound of horses. Had it been a month already? What day was this? Where am I? I had been standing in the entryway of the main home that I didn't remember walking into. The easel was behind me. Alarms went off in my head; my instincts said I needed to leave because Frank had given me strict instructions on my living quarters and where I was allowed to paint; he didn't want to risk anything prolonging the move-in. I grabbed the painting and drop cloth, and took off for the cottage."

"When the carriage stopped out front, I greeted him, immediately asking him for a return ride back to the city. He was happy to do it but wanted to see the home's progress, and the painting. Though it wasn't completed, I knew I would have to show it to him. So, we decided that before I packed up, he would come to the cottage to see it."

"I was surprised to see Josephine had accompanied him, as he'd been so secretive about the estate and was calling it a 'gift' for his bride. She wore an emerald green dress, matching gloves, and a mink coat. I remember thinking wealth looked good on her," Killian said with a smile. "It was the first time she had seen the estate after it being furnished. When she stepped out of the cab, she was shaky from the bumpy journey, so she grabbed onto my arm as I was standing closest to her. Frank immediately put his hand out for her to go with him, but her eyes were locked on the house.

"Why, it's the most beautiful thing I ever did see, my dear Frank. It's...so...I'm speechless." She squeezed my arm a little tighter, and for a moment, in her daze, she thought I was him. I reached out and touched her arm with my hand, though Frank could see, and I could feel her body stiffen."

"Josephine's laughter abruptly stopped. She turned to me, looking me up and down, snatching her arm back. Her eyes were twisted, glaring at me, and she was just about to say something when Frank took her other arm, walking her into the manor.

'Shall we go inside for a look, dear?' She gave me one last glance over her shoulder when they made it to the steps— and that's when I gave my heart and soul— whatever was left of it— to this woman, who belonged to another man. A very rich and powerful one at that.

"The thing is, when she touched me, I saw something. I had a disturbing vision. You see, I saw her future, heavy with child, watching someone as they buried her family members under the very ground I stood on."

The old man's face felt like it had been stung as Killian said that.

"Disoriented, I waited as they entered the manor. But they didn't come out until near dark. I had considered following them, but that would have been a major intrusion. And I was a hired hand. When they finally did emerge, it was joyful. Josephine was singing about not wanting to leave, so Frank whispered in her ear and left her in the doorway. Her posture looked relaxed as she gazed at me from her grand mansion."

"'Come on, chap! Let's see what you've created for my bride.' Frank was floating over to the cottage with me, but I had grown so anxious waiting for him that it felt like I had four legs. I could barely walk straight at all. He chatted about the chill in the air and how I needed warmer clothing, even offered me his second jacket back in the stagecoach. 'We will get you warm on the ride home.'"

"But as soon as the door opened to my work, prominently displayed on the easel, he fell silent.

"'What is that?' he asked me, repeating the question over and over again. In my confusion, I said, 'Well, sir, it's the landscape. What do you mean?' I even laughed because he was making me nervous. I was standing between him and the painting, and he became irate. Before I knew it, he stormed out, and they left without me. I was choked up with embarrassment. I turned around and looked at the painting, and I couldn't believe my eyes. I had painted Josephine standing on the edge of the cliffs, arms spread wide in a golden dress. The same dress he'd just made for her, but there was no way I could have known that. That day was the first time I ever saw it with my own eyes."

"They left me there, and I stayed in the cottage that night. Someone else arrived the next afternoon to take me 'anywhere but back to Frank', but the wedding was near, and I chose to stay. I needed to see Josephine again to see if she felt the same. The driver shuffled around before he shared some devastating news. Frank returned to his weathervane factory to find it had experienced a fire and collapsed with workers inside. He was distraught but found hope in his future with Josephine, swearing to retire after that. He was ready to start a family and had a new sense of interest in his own. They were to move into the manor, have the wedding, and then send for his family so he would have everyone he cared for in the world under one roof."

"And that's when the real tragedy happened."

***

JOSEPHINE

What a lovely gift my dearest has given me. The estate is captivating, with its broad landscapes, grand buildings, and foggy speculations. I feel that I am in Europe while I stand among the architecture, though I am in New York. Frank wanted our home to feel like the hotels in all the luxurious capitals of the world. We are to be married in the ballroom and then take residence here permanently.

I have written to my mother many times since leaving her, and am still waiting on her response. She must have fallen ill, and I have also been ill with worry over her. I have extended an invitation to her to take residence with Frank and I. He, too, has invited family to live in it, as the home is now complete.

What a dream my life has become. Frank is very wealthy, and I am his bride. He is wiser than me and enjoys showing me the many wonders of the world. I enjoy his presence, his beautiful green eyes, and dark mustache.

His family shall arrive any moment. They have been called on from the north and east, traveling by automobile.

As Josephine leaned into the grass, basking in the intoxication of lilac bushes, she slowly started drifting off.

Standing at the fountain in the middle of the estate, Frank stared at her longingly. He seemed to feel such pride that she was his bride. "Darling, don't overheat!" he hollered, laughing. She coyly smiled and blew him a kiss.

Josephine was the niece of a late colleague of Frank's. She fondly remembered the night they met, not long ago. She had only attended the gala as her uncle had passed away the weeks before, and she took to caring for her aunt, who was indebted to participate.

Benjamin and Cora Kennedy were very wealthy, and Cora didn't need her help. She had maids for that, but Josephine's mother wanted Cora to have family by her side, as they never had children.

Josephine's mother, Sophie, being a widow herself, knew the pain that Cora was in. "You should go up and stay with Cora for a few weeks. You've felt the grief she's experiencing. Help her through it." Josephine wanted to please her mother but worried about her being alone. "Don't worry about me. I will be fine! Worry about Aunt Cora." As expected, her mother left no argument for Josephine to make. A few days later she took a stagecoach to the city where Cora lived.

Cora had been happy to see her. She admired what a beautiful girl Josephine was, with her long red hair and delicate freckles on her cheeks. Natural rosebud lips and very light eyes with a dark rim around them. Striking wasn't a strong enough word for her appearance.

The days that followed were full of sadness, but Cora felt hope for Josephine. She had decided to show her a good time. "There is a very special party I've been invited to tonight. Benjamin would have wanted me to go, and I will take you as my guest." Cora winced at the mention of his name. Josephine was concerned it might be too much so soon but also panicked at having nothing to wear.

"I would love to attend, but I didn't bring any evening wear." Josephine was too embarrassed to say she didn't own any, either.

Cora laughed, "Of course you didn't, sweet girl. Do not worry yourself. We are around the same size, and I have the perfect gown for you to wear." She got up to leave the room, taking another look at Josephine. She was a woman now, in little girl's clothing. Since her father passed, Josephine had been strictly helping her mother with chores and the upkeep of their modest home. But had it not been for that mining accident, she would probably be married off by now. If she was sent home, she would live that life forever.

"Josephine," Cora whispered, getting her attention, "don't be surprised if you find a husband tonight." Cora smiled with guilt, as she knew what that would mean for her sister, Sophie. But that wasn't the life she would want for her niece.

As Josephine dressed for the ball, she felt excited at the prospect of meeting a handsome prince. Her uncle had been in oil, and this event tonight would host his colleagues and hopefully, handsome strangers.

Josephine was not to stray from her aunt outside of the party. If they were separated, she was to come straight back, no stops, as this part of the city had been plagued by violence recently. Stories of women being murdered and disfigured were splashed across the chronicle. Her aunt sternly reminded her of the chronicle over and over. "You mustn't keep me waiting, Josephine. Please don't leave me to worry. I've had enough on my plate." Her aunt had definitely had her share of woes with losing her husband, Benjamin Kennedy...whose recent death had been quite mysterious.

"Now, we need the finishing touch!" Cora exclaimed as she finished getting Josephine into her green noir evening gown. It had a sweetheart neckline, almost off the shoulder, but not quite, and three-quarter sleeves with a delicate black embroidered mesh overlay. It nearly looked like the stars in the sky.

Cora came up behind Josephine as she was admiring her dress in the mirror. Cora fastened a gemstone necklace around her neck. The gem was in the shape of a star.

"Oh my!" Josephine cried out. She had never felt so beautiful in her life!

"You are a sight for sore eyes, Josephine." Cora was proud of her niece for turning into such a beautiful woman. "And to think, yesterday you were a girl."

Hearing a noise, she awoke from her daydream to see that the first group had just arrived. Josephine hadn't been graced with most of Frank's relatives yet; she wanted to make an elegant impression.

After she gathered her inks and papers from where she was writing her mother, Josephine patted down her hair. Warm from the sun, she cherished the delight of its touch before putting her hat on. It perfectly matched her gray dress, with a lovely black flower atop. When her gloves were straight and the parasol open, she strolled over to meet her new family and housemates.

"Josephine, how beautiful you are! You have such unusual eyes." Frank's mother greeted her, reaching for her hand. "Oh, my heavens! Ahhh!" Frank's mother screamed as a starling fell on her like a rock, taking her hat down to the ground.

Puzzled and surprised, Josephine reached for her hat. The bird was under it, dead as a doornail. "It must have died mid-flight. How strange." She bore into the creature, hypnotized by its intricate feathers and fine thread of colors. It was reminiscent of sunlight hitting oil in shades of deep blue and purple, with hairs of white and orange on its chest. Its beak was sharp and defined.

Without warning, his bright red eyes snapped open. A rapid pulse returned to his lifeless body, and Josephine intuitively extended a finger, which he hopped onto. "How peculiar!" Her new mother-in-law gasped in amazement.

She stood up to see more people had come over when the bird fell, and they had come out of the stagecoach to see what the ruckus was about. The little bird had clamped onto Josephine's finger and his pulse had steadied. His heartbeat seemed to be in step with her own.

"Go on, now. Return to your family, little birdy." Speaking softly so that no one else would hear, she encouraged him to fly away. He took one last long breath and flew off.

Josephine's back was to her new family, and she stayed there for a moment, feeling shame. What had just gone down? Whatever it was, it wasn't supposed to happen. It wasn't usual. Nor was it good.

"Josephine, my darling?" Frank's voice broke the moment, and she returned to her new family. He had just joined the gathering, and by the look on his face, he was confused about what they were all doing. "Well, now that you've all met my lovely bride, you know she is as special as the daybreak." Josephine cherished his love for her. "Let's all go get settled inside. We will put tea on the kettle." Frank was warm, handsome, and kind. She was the luckiest girl in the world to have found him.

A black cloud started rolling in as everyone gathered inside. Josephine held back a moment, pretending to admire the grand fountain. Running her hands through the water, she disturbed the lilyponds and vines that grew inside the deep well. A feeling came over her all at once. She desperately choked back tears. "Something is very, very wrong with my mind."

Mother,

My wedding day is tomorrow, as I have told you. I was in my room with Aunt Cora, playing with my hair, trying to decide what tomorrow would be like, when she told me the strangest stories I've ever heard.

Is it true, mother? About your– OUR family?

Aunt Cora said we have gifts, but to me they are of the devil and I would like no part of it! Nothing about me is magical– and I thank the Lord for it.

Why didn't you tell me?

Anxiously awaiting a reply,

Josephine

"Mother,

Life with Frank has been grand! He is very attentive and doting, I know you would approve. I am beginning to plan a trip back to see you, as I've become so worried. I hope you show up any day now, or at least write me back.

Forget what I said before. I know you are a righteous woman, and I don't care what Cora said.

Frank's family has moved in with us. All's well, but for the little ones. They have been feverish often. Many people now reside here. But still plenty of room! Mother, this house is so exquisite. You could move in and have your own wing if you choose. You'd never have to see anyone if you felt like it.

I think of you when I look at the gardens, mother. They are wild yet kept, overgrown by design. The colors are shades I didn't know existed before now. How strange it was, but we had someone come and plant Lilacs, and the rest of it just came with the spring rain. There must have already been a garden here. At my request, Frank hired a specialist to come here and make sure things weren't poisonous— with the children around and all.

Most of it is.

Love,
Josephine Flint Bagley

***

KILLIAN

"After the wedding, Josephine became pregnant nearly immediately. Frank was over the moon and had a strong paternal instinct. He couldn't wait to be a father and even picked out names for the baby. Henry James if it was a boy, and Rose Lily if it was a girl." Killian's mind wandered off. "Frank wanted everything to be perfect, and his baby would grow up around its entire family. But Josephine had a wish too, which was for her mother to be there for the birth. So, one day, she went to her mother. Frank had wanted to accompany her, but she had so many feelings about that trip that she thought it would clear her head if she went alone. In the end, it was probably for the best.

***

JOSEPHINE

Mother,

Tomorrow I will travel to see you. Frank is sending me in a stagecoach now, as I will not be able to make the trip in a few months' time. I am with child

89

and would like you to return with me. There is plenty of room in our home for you. I even have a separate area for the baby.

By the time you get this, I will only be a few days away.

See you soon, Mother.

Josephine Bagley

My dearest Frank,

I made it to my mother's home, but not in time. I found her in her room. She hadn't received my letters since I arrived. The devastation has taken me. I will stay an extra day to make arrangements and clear out the home. You don't need to come.

All my love,

Josephine

Mother,

This is my last letter to you. I will send it into the grave. You seem to have died just days after I left, from your appearance and the odor. I feel I abandoned you when you needed me the most, and I will regret that until I meet you in eternity. The tears haven't stopped for you and they never will.

We bury you today and I chose a plot with wildflowers growing around it in the summer. Purple and yellow and white. It's beautiful, cast in the countryside near the mountains. I also chose a very comfortable arrangement for you to rest, and I hope you do.

When I first arrived on my quest to stay with your sister, she told me we all had gifts. At first, this scared me. But now that I've lost you, I am afraid that the darkness will try and take hold of me.

Cora had also said I wouldn't see you again.

But I will, Mother. I will stay righteous and you will see me in heaven.

Your loving daughter,

Josephine

***

KILLIAN

"I'm sure by now you gather that her mother had passed months prior, and yet, Josephine was the first to find her. She was devastated, but I heard that her mother had written her a letter and left it on her nightstand to find. She never spoke about it, but one wonders what it read."

"She returned home, shattered, but with some closure. The loss of her mother was nearly too much to bear, but there was much to look forward to. Frank was beaming to see her home and once again wished to be done with work altogether so he'd never have to be apart from his family again."

"Frank had Cora crossed when he decided to end their arrangement. He'd already given her a lot of wealth and offered her a share in his electricity patent, but Cora was livid. So much so that she tells him she is okay with it on one condition— that me must take one last trip to check out a new invention overseas and promises he will return right when his child is born."

"Josephine was devastated when she learned Frank was to leave for a long trip. He told her his hands were tied. His business partner, whom he's never disclosed, is Cora, is finally letting him off the hook when the trip is complete, and he will be home right in time for the baby. He will be returning home by ship right around when the baby is due. After all, he's taking the Triton ship, renowned as the worlds fastest. But we all know what happened to that ship." Killian turned to the man, who nodded, letting out a snort. 'It was only the most infamous shipwreck in history. Very few made it out alive, mostly women and children."

"His family was there, though, and she truly loved his family. They were helping her prepare for the birth, which was very enjoyable. Frank was hiring a few people to take care of the grounds, cook, and clean, and they would be arriving soon. Frank explained that one staffer was a notable pastry chef who sourced all of his ingredients from his garden. Josephine had quite the sweet tooth, so this pleased her very much. Time would pass quickly; he promised as he kissed her on the forehead and left forever."

"Less than a month later, the family started to come down with something.

It began with the children, a late-night fever, and an upset stomach. Out of eleven children, each one came down a few hours apart. Then the adults started a cough or a fever. This mysterious illness had reached a few staffers and the gardeners, who didn't even live in the house. A week later, the situation was grave. One of the maids insisted on Josephine going to town so she wouldn't catch it, and as she was begging Josephine to leave, the maid broke out into a sweat on her upper lip. She covered her mouth with a cleaning cloth and pushed Josephine out of the way."

"This shook Josephine, and as much as she didn't want to leave her home in case Frank returned, she decided to take the advice and rode into town, where she would stay with Cora until the illness passed. However, once she arrived, Cora was so guilt-stricken at what she had sent Frank to do, to die, that she couldn't even look pregnant Josephine in the eye. She ended up fleeing with the excuse that Josephine must quarantine in private since she had been exposed to the illness. But truthfully, Cora was embarrassed at the measures she took out of anger, and poor Josephine was blameless. But when Cora returned, Josephine was ready to bolt. She missed her family, though she was thankful to Cora for giving her a place to stay well. So, before Josephine left Cora's uptown apartment, Josephine, being the sweetheart she was, turned to Cora to hug her."

"For weeks, Cora had been giving her the cold shoulder. Josephine, being pregnant, had enough on her mind than to worry about what Cora thought, so she ignored it. But when they touched, awareness flooded through Josephine. The specifics, we will never know. 'Cora, what have you done?' Her words were like fire. Josephine didn't know, but I had been on the porch, having just finished a business meeting with Cora. She and I were discussing a proposal for my Art Gallery. She had a zest for the arts, you see." Killian nodded to the old man, as if they were old pals, sharing a secret about a mutual friend.

"Cora didn't have anything to say, pushing Josephine away and returning to her porch with a check for me, mumbling something about being the only one truly alone now. I left thereafter, but not before I saw Josephine get into the back of a stagecoach. Josephine didn't look back to see if Cora waved, but she didn't."

"When the stagecoach arrived back at her estate, a torrential downpour broke out. She ended up walking the rest of the distance, encountering a man standing outside. It was one of her new landscapers, and she excitedly waved to him, assuming everyone was well. But the landscaper warded her off when she got closer to him, saying she needed to stay away. He explained that everyone was doing poorly. He, too, was leaving but promised to send a doctor from a nearby town as soon as possible. Being on foot, she begged him to take the stagecoach she had just returned on, but he had no money, so she offered to pay his fare. The only problem was that all of her money was inside. He demanded she not go in the house, but she was desperate for the doctor if it was as bad as he was saying. She decided to go in anyway."

"Upon entering the household, the stench had her doubled over. It was nearly as bad as the death she experienced finding her mother but also had a completely different air to it."

"Frank was nowhere to be found. She surmised he hadn't returned yet after she tore apart the house looking for him. Almost everyone was dying. If they weren't deceased on her arrival, they would be within a few hours."

The man gasped at the horror of Killian's tale.

"Josephine found a handful of coins and raced out to the landscaper," Killian continued, "but he was long gone, along with the stagecoach. She considered making the journey to town but didn't want to risk losing shelter for the birth. Just at the bottom of the well of despair, she saw a stagecoach approaching down her driveway. It was the pastry chef; who was months late but right on time to save her."

CHAPTER FIVE

SARAFINA

I uncovered a few dressers, a set of chairs, and a small bookcase, but nothing older than what was already in the house. Beautiful nonetheless.

Then when sliding one of the dressers to the side for better lighting for photos, I noticed an ornate trunk. My heart raced with excitement, a leather trunk inside the attic of a Victorian gothic estate? It was my definition of treasure! I scrambled the dresser further out of the way, leaving my camera on top.

Upon closer inspection, the trunk was made of immaculate wood with brass inlays, which had small vines carved out in their entirety. The wood was dark brown, but the front was a lighter olive shade. It had two parallel latches running on each side, attached by leather straps. There were additional lateral straps with buckles, each shaped like a star. The center closure was a sizeable circular lock that felt more aftermarket, as it wasn't the same shade as the brass buckles everywhere else. My professional opinion would date this well back to the 1800s, and running my fingers up and down was an absolute no-no for antiques, but I couldn't help myself.

Suddenly feeling for the keys down deep in my pocket, I pulled them out and started trying them one-by-one. Not a single one fit, but I wasn't surprised— this was a well-maintained chest for such a dusty attic. I was anticipating the treasures inside would warrant a hidden key. I just hoped Leroy knew where it was.

Standing up and brushing the dust off, I realized this was an event that would give me my own firm. All of this was mine. Turning anything over to my current employer— albeit one of the world's top dealers would be foolish of me. I had a slight pang of guilt as I thought of my great aunt who had been so generous to leave this to me, though I was her only heir— did she have a choice? I just wished I had been able to meet her.

I remember only one occurrence of her name growing up. My mother had received a letter, and my father asked who it was from as it lay unopened on the counter. 'Victoria,' she said in a small voice. I jumped up and screamed, 'Victoria, the singer!?' They both laughed. I was maybe only nine years old and was going through a bit of a phase. All I did was listen to her music, try to dress, and talk like her. My father looked at me, made big goofy eyes, and kissed me on the forehead. My mother never answered me, so I continued to think there was a letter from my icon on the counter. I knew it stayed there the rest of the night because I kept checking. My parents weren't secretive, but they had an entire life together before they had me. This gave them boundaries in their love that I instinctively never crossed. For instance, I wouldn't have pressed it on the letter. The next day it was gone from the counter, and I never saw it or heard that name again.

My lifeline in all of this may very well be Leroy. I was happy to have him here, as weird as it initially may be. At least he could fill in the blanks.

***

JOSEPHINE

After a few weeks, Josephine had not yet fallen ill, and she felt the baby was getting closer. Her doctor had planned on visiting her at home next week anyway, so she decided to make the journey and return to her family. Cora was not family; only a blood relative. Her attitude towards Josephine was intolerable, and in her emotional state, Josephine had to leave. But as she was leaving Cora, she had a vision. Frank, her dear husband, was calling out to her in distress. She didn't know what it meant, but she did know that Cora was intertwined with evil, and ever since her mother died, Josephine let herself get pulled in as well. But to harm her husband? She realized that she must leave at once, and she did. These visions, this place, Cora… Josephine instinctively clutched at her chest, looking for the cross necklace she once wore, that was taken off some time ago and she let out a small prayer for protection from the evil that surrounded her.

She hired a stagecoach to deliver her home, but the weather had turned sour with massive rain, and one of the wheels on the coach had caught itself in a pothole. Josephine always enjoyed walking, so she gripped her umbrella and requested to walk the rest of the journey. Her legs had been restless as it was. At home, she had been used to walking long distances, but at Cora's, she'd nearly been bedridden in preparation for an illness that never came. The driver looked at her nervously and suggested she shouldn't in her condition. After all, she was nearly full term in her pregnancy, but since she was so petite, she looked farther along than she was. Josephine handed the driver a small velvet bag of money for the trip and, without a word, got out of the coach. The driver slowly rolled away. As his horses trotted off, the coach wheel was now riding a little smoother without the weight of a passenger in the back, and he looked at her one last time before giving the horses the nudge to leave.

As Josephine started her walk home, she was instantly breathless. From where she got out of the coach, she could see the outline of a man outside. Relief washed over her, and the chill in the air felt colder than usual as she tightened her coat. Her red velvet gloves were already dampening from the sideways rain, and her hands were freezing. Her feet had become wet only a few steps into the walk, and she regretted sending the coach away. But it felt good to walk and get fresh air; for that, she was exalted. She kept her trail on the firm part of the roadway, where a little foliage had grown so she wouldn't become stuck in the mud the road now was.

As she got closer to the house, she became so excited at the prospect of seeing the children run up to her and give her pregnant belly a hug and a kiss. She knew the maids would immediately draw her a hot bath, and the chef would make her some tea with extra cardamom, just how she liked it. She knew the fireplaces would be roaring and imagined kicking off her shoes and warming her frozen feet while laughing about walking home. But at first sight of the house, no curls of smoke were coming from the many fireplaces. As one of the first estates to have total electricity, there were no lights on, despite it getting very dark in the corners and east-facing rooms this time of day. She didn't hear any children laughing or see them playing in the puddles. Only the one man milling about— not the usual groups of workers inhaling the fragrance of the rain or enjoying the storms under a willow tree. There were no signs of life, besides this man, anywhere at all.

He remained motionless even when she walked up with her clothes slapping against each step. Perhaps he didn't hear her over the rain, so she called out to him. He ducked at her voice as if someone had thrown something at him, but she saw the fear on his face as he turned to her. As Josephine was excitedly waving at him, he was waving both arms and hollering not to come any closer.

After the man shared a disturbing revelation that the entire household was on death's door, if they weren't already gone, he forbade her from entering the home. He was leaving and would try to send a doctor, and she pleaded with him to take her coach. If she was swift inside to collect money, he could still catch up with the coach on the road. Josephine wouldn't take no for an answer and went inside the home, despite his pleadings not to.

As she reached the steps leading up to the front door, Josephine collided with a pungent odor. Her stomach had felt nauseated before this, as she hadn't eaten yet that day. Still, this essence that could only be described as death itself purged any contents left in her stomach over the railing. She vomited until she was nearly on her knees, begging the Lord for mercy from this sickness. She feared she, too, had just come down with it, but after a little while, the nausea passed. She still breathed in its sour fragrance but was able to stand and hobble over to the door.

The musk grew stronger the closer she got, and she removed a wet glove from her cold hand and held it over her nose and mouth as she entered.

The scene was horrific. Josephine trembled as she stepped inside. The floor lay covered in blood-stained sheets or rotten food remnants. Dirty hand prints and scattered papers tainted the walls. She peered into some rooms and discovered no one inside. She had made it through the downstairs chambers except for the ballroom when she started to climb the stairs. Her muddy shoes traced every step she took, the wet soggy noise of her feet pressing into the steps the only noise in the house— the only noise, for miles.

She stood at the top of the stairs to assess the situation. Turning to go down the hallway on the right, she gasped at the sight of her nephew's body lying lifeless on the floor. Jakob, the poet. He was only nine years old. She ran to him, bending down and choking on the scent from the room he was lying in front of. It appeared Jakob had not been gone for very long. His body was still warm. Josephine screamed and cried out. She had loved this child as her own. His mother was Frank's sister, whose husband had died in a coal mine, just like Josephine's father. She looked up at the door beside her. There was a note attached to the knob: Have mercy on— the note had been torn in half, and Josephine's instincts told her not to turn the knob, but she twisted it anyway, saying a prayer before she did. Pulling the door open revealed a scrap of paper on the floor. – the children, please sir, I beg of you.

All of the children had been inside the room, huddled around the fireplace. They had all expired, and from the vomit on the carpet, she knew the illness had taken them. She picked up her dear nephew Jakob and placed him in the room, on the bed to be with his family, until she figured out what else to do. She had buckled under his weight, though he was very slender for his age. As she looked down at him, she didn't see any signs of illness in him now. His skin had looked bright, not sallow and sweaty like the others. His lips were rose-colored, and she kissed him on the forehead before turning out of the room as she felt bile again climbing up her throat.

She began to sweat as she thought the illness might be coming for her, but it was the adrenaline catching up. She broke into a rage as she went from room to room, some rooms completely undisturbed as if the maids had just finished up, while others had been ransacked thoroughly.

It appeared someone was looking for something, or someone— but what? Or who?

There was only one more room to look at— the ballroom where she married the love of her life, Frank. She didn't even have to enter to know everyone was inside. Instead, she started going around the house and opening all the windows, still crying herself into a fit. A cool breeze had gusted through the home, making a mess of the scattered papers everywhere.

She had gone into the butler's pantry and retrieved some table linens, sorting through the piles until she found napkins. Using a piece of twine to tie it over her, she put a folded-up lavender oil-doused napkin over her mouth and nose and entered the ballroom, her eyes soaking wet from grief. The rest of them were indeed inside. Their bodies lay in twisted positions, some with arms reaching out, others doubled over. One thing they all had in common, it appeared they spent their final moments in enormous pain.

Meanwhile, a thin, young man of small but sturdy stature was dropped off outside by stagecoach. He asked the coach driver if Mr. Bagley had already paid his fare, at which the driver nodded yes.

"Good day, Leroy," the driver tapped his cap and turned away. Leroy slid out of the coach, parked off to the side of the estate, and immediately smelled something he detested: tobacco. But not just any tobacco, the clove-infused kind. How odd that he'd only ever encountered one person who smoked that specific blend, his estranged acquaintance, Killian. Killian had known Mr. Bagley, and in fact, that is why Leroy was standing here right now, per his recommendation, when Mr. Bagley was looking for staff. But that was months ago, and why on earth would Killian be here now? He decided it was best if he quickly saw where the smell was coming from, so he set down his suitcase on the wet grass and paced around the house.

The winds changed as the scent grew stronger and threw him off course. He was around the back of the house when his steps led him to the edge of an enormous cliff. "My heavens!" Leroy nearly fell backward out of fright, not quite ready to fall over the edge and die today. The winds changed again as he lay, leaning back on his elbows in the sludge grass, and a foul stench assaulted his nose. He knew the scent and immediately rose, his clothes now wet and his bones shivering. A slight flare off in the distance, accompanied by movement caught his eye. "Killian," he called out, and it wasn't a question.

Killian had a very distinct shape; he was of medium height, stockily built with larger-than-life thick hair that he could never quite wrangle. There was no doubt who the figure was that disappeared behind the side of the house.

Leroy sprinted after him, but his shoes got stuck in the thick mud on the back side of the house, where rocks replaced grass. He shouted again, waiting for Killian to show himself. As he continued around the house, there was no sign of anyone, not even a footprint. Surely his feet would have made indents in this atrocious washout.

Leroy shook his head. He must have imagined it; experiencing the scent of death and seeing a vision of Killian didn't surprise him. There was something very wrong with Killian. He had told his family and begged his mother to see it, but she cut him out of her life completely, which was hurtful. Still, Leroy mostly felt fear when it came to Killian. When Mr. Bagley contacted him for this job, he raved at the recommendation from Killian. Hearing that name, Leroy was going to turn it down immediately, but then Mr. Bagley mentioned his young pregnant wife, Josephine. Leroy accepted the job, feeling he would need to protect her from Killian.

But what exactly was Killian going to do? And why did he want Leroy involved in it? That was the matter in question, and it appeared Leroy was already too late. He broke into a run, fetching his suitcase and racing up the steps, the revolting sour air ruminating around him the closer he got, his hand unable to keep it away.

Inside, Josephine was distraught. She was all alone, afraid for her life and the baby. What was she going to do? She couldn't stay here tonight, and it was growing dark out. She opened up the windows of the ballroom, went to grab some clothes, and left for the gardener's cottage, where she would figure out her next steps. Once she opened her front door, she shrieked at the sight of a man standing on the porch, also covering his nose and mouth with his arm.

"M-Mrs. Bagley?" He squinted at the odor, and Josephine, frazzled being an understatement, nodded yes. The man had a youthful appearance but wise eyes. "I am Leroy, the pastry chef...?" Covering his nose and mouth with his free hand, the other holding a small suitcase, he peered inside. "Forgive me for being months late to the assignment; I had family matters to attend to. Yet, it appears I have made it just in time to be of your assistance."

She cried out in mixed emotions, relief being one of them. She had a small bundle of clothing tucked under her arm and pointed to the cottage on the side of the estate. Leroy nodded, taking the bundle and leaving his suitcase behind. He took her by the arm, leading her to the cottage. Josephine continued sobbing, and being in this man's presence made her realize she'd been doing so since she arrived over an hour ago.

Leroy went inside first and found signs of someone living there. He brought her in, immediately drew her a bath, and started a fire in the hearth, placing a pot of water for tea inside. It was a clean and tidy two-bedroom cottage, with one room as an upstairs loft. He found fresh linens and placed them near the porcelain tub, and at her request, helped her into it. Josephine's body was ice cold, her stomach marks from her pregnancy nearly navy blue on her translucent pale skin. Once she was in the tub, Leroy made the bed downstairs. The cottage kitchen area appeared to be well stocked, to his surprise. He cut into a loaf of seeded bread and spread some butter on top, finding a few jellies to add in and some water crackers and olives. Locating a small amount of cheese and raspberry wine in the storm cellar, Leroy was puzzled by the decadence. Was all of this for the help? Who was living here?

Josephine emerged around an hour later, wearing clean clothes, but none that belonged to her. It appeared she had taken clothes from the maid's bureau, as she donned a loose-fitting muslin dress with wool socks and a sweater underneath. She looked smaller in the clothing than she did in the nude. Leroy felt sad about her being in this state, but he still didn't know who had died.

"Madam, I have prepared you a meal with what was here. Please, eat." He motioned to the small wooden table covered in slices of bread, cheeses, figs, and olives. There was a small bit of wine and a large cup of hot tea, which Josephine could smell had a very distinct ingredient she was unfamiliar with. She sat in a chair with his assistance, her knees suddenly wobbly, taking a sip of the tea in question. It was an adventure on her lips, a trip to another world in her senses. She felt as though she was in a far-east teahouse, the kind she and Frank had visited on their honeymoon. She was immediately starving, devouring the food, which was also incredible.

"Can you tell me what happened?" Leroy whispered, looking through the window at the estate.

Josephine knew she had no choice but to tell. Someone— perhaps this man— had been hired to care for her by her dear husband. She felt a little stronger from the sustenance, chewing her food slowly, savoring every bite.

"My husband's family— they fell ill weeks ago, and sent me to my Aunt Cora's so I wouldn't catch it."

Leroy nodded, understanding the sentiment of wanting to spare her.

"They are all gone. I am so sorry." Just hearing the words caused bile to rise again in her throat.

Leroy rushed over and refreshed her tea, telling her to drink. "It will help with the nausea. Go ahead, drink up." He helped her hold the teacup while her hands shook violently. "And Mr. Bagley?" Leroy didn't want to ask, but he had to know, so he whispered it.

Josephine shook her head. "He is away, he will be returning any day. He doesn't know, I myself just found out a few hours ago." She started crying again, but this time, for Frank. His family was gone. All he had left was Josephine and their baby.

Leroy looked puzzled, inquiring whether she had an address or a way to contact Frank. It was crucial he returned, as Leroy had seen women give birth too soon after grief. Josephine nodded and explained she had an address for him in a drawer in her drawing room loft. It was where she penned all of her letters. She had sent Frank one already but wasn't sure if he replied since she had left immediately after.

"I will go and fetch it. And I will also take care of the house. Don't worry about a thing, Josephine."

She was crying still, but again from relief. The house was a disaster and too much for one person to handle.

He led her to the couch before the fireplace, getting her settled in with blankets. He lit the large oil lamp on the nearby table, which produced a dreamy rose glow. Leroy threw one more log on the fire and proclaimed he would be back. He just didn't know when, he thought to himself.

The chill in the air when Leroy stepped out of the cottage made his teeth chatter. The rain had turned to sleet, and he was trembling after only a few steps. He felt fear for Josephine. He prayed this mysterious illness wouldn't take her and the baby too— if it was, in fact, an illness. For Leroy felt things were rarely what they appeared.

As he traipsed closer to the house, a stagecoach appeared in the distance. He hoped it was Mr. Bagley returning early and he wouldn't have to enter the death house at all. The horses neighed, the mud in that stroll had been too thick for him to cross earlier, and he expected the carriage to stop, but instead, it kept moving forward slowly. The anticipation was building like a steam engine. The closer it came, the louder and more ominous. A deep rumble sounded as it pulled into clear view. Leroy's heartbeat matched the ticking of the wheels when it came to an abrupt stop. His hands were shaking, though he didn't know if it was from the cold, or from fear of the unknown.

"Good evening, chap." The driver's cheer pulled him out of the moment. "Where ye headed?" He looked at Leroy, waiting for an answer, but saw the confusion on his face. Instantaneously, one of his horses started behaving wildly, kicking and snaring. The driver tried to laugh it off, but the horse persisted. "Excuse me horse, sir, this is unlike him." With a fluid movement, the driver hopped from his seat atop the carriage onto the horse's back. "Get yourself together!" He pulled a carrot from his pocket, but the horse refused. Instead, it started snapping in Leroy's direction.

Leroy, having grown up in the countryside, was never considered a threat to animals, and this behavior was startling. But he had seen it before. He held his hand out to the rabid horse, and the driver screamed, "what do ye think yer doin' there?" His eyes widened. But the horse calmed down to the driver's surprise.

Leroy didn't skip a beat, "Where am I heading, sir?" He couldn't fathom why he'd ask such a question. Did this mean the carriage was empty? The driver looked side to side, not understanding the question. Leroy grabbed the door of the cab, pulling it open with such force that he felt it deep in his shoulder. Yes, that's exactly what it meant. No one was inside. Who would send a carriage so far out of the way?

"Sir, I believe there has been a misunderstanding. I did not order this coach. Could you tell me who did?"

"That I cannot, chap. I got ye no information, for I'm just doing what he told me to do."

"He? Who is he?" Leroy demanded, but the driver was still immersed in his horse's behavior.

"If ye are not coming with me, sir, I'm heading back. These roads are doing me no good in the dark."

The driver slid back into his seat, looking onward. He tipped his cap and grabbed the reins, making a clicking noise with his mouth and took off.

What a strange interaction, Leroy thought. His eyes followed the horseman's carriage well into the forest brush. The fading glow of his lamp made Leroy feel as if it were all a dream. He looked back to the house, remembering the foul stench and imagining the bodies inside, and thinking to himself, how much easier it would be to take that carriage and never look back. But when he looked again at the forest, there was no sign of it at all.

The sour air flooded his senses as his feet touched the steps. His stomach churned, but it wasn't as bad as before. The door was slightly ajar, and he pushed the remainder open. He went to the linen closet as Josephine had described, found the napkins with the lavender oil, and created a makeshift face covering. Then he moved on to the ballroom, twisting the door handle slowly, but a strong wind gust resisted. He pushed into the door harder and fell when the wind let up, just inches away from one of the bodies. He jumped to his feet and glanced to see that everyone was, in fact, deceased, and then he started dragging them one by one out of the ballroom. Out of the house. Out around the back, so Josephine couldn't see.

There were seven adults, and it took nearly all of his energy to wrap them up in linens. He had considered digging a mass grave but was tempted to push their bodies over the cliffside instead. Recalling the children, he quickly tossed that notion aside.

Back in the ballroom, Leroy took the handfuls of the sage he had found in the kitchen and placed them atop the wood in the fireplace. The chimney flue looked like a giant star as it swung by, releasing the air cleansing properties into the home. He left the windows open, despite the relentless downpour, as any mess it made wasn't as bad as the smell, he thought.

He grabbed the large white owl carving at the base of the banister to steady himself, taking in the home around him for the first time. What an improper introduction, he thought, but he was relieved to have saved Josephine from attempting this task.

She had told him where the children were, and he had quickly located the room with the note on the door. He analyzed the lettering before entering and found the sight heartbreaking. To put a prayer on the door of the sick was both a cry for help and a realization that things were not getting better.

It was one thing to see an adult perish, but quite another to see a child, let alone in multiples. Leroy went into the room, already feeling teary, but was so shocked when he entered that he let out a cry. One of the children, a little boy with fawn hair, was sitting up on the bed, looking at him.

Leroy ran to him, wanting to save him from the horrifying scene and get him into the cottage with Josephine. But when he grabbed the boy, his stiff body fell to the side. Leroy screamed again, the stillness of the room devastating.

He carried the children down the marble steps, the slap of his wet shoes on each step the only noise for miles. He had wrapped the children's bodies with precision and care as he had the adults, but also with love. The little boy on the bed was the last to go, as he must have been the last to die. "I'm sorry you had to go through this," Leroy whispered. He slid his hand over the child's eyes, closing them, and carried him down to be with the rest of his family.

Carrying the child, he caught a distinct musk. It wasn't the rotting stench of the others but rather a more profound fruit smell that had soured. He recognized the scent as many did with overpopulated sewer rats. Bromobenzyl cyanide.

***

ROSE

Rose Lily was born on a stormy night to Josephine under the care of a midwife Leroy sent for. This innocent child, born out of the tragic remnants of Josephine's life, would never know her father; or her mother, for that matter.

As soon as she was of age, Rose was sent to boarding schools and raised under the care of many different headmistresses. She enjoyed the companionship of other girls her age nearly immediately, but when she would return home on holiday and summer breaks, she would revert to a painfully lonely existence.

Her mother, Josephine, always had her guard up. As the years passed, Rose would understand the impact on her mother of the compounded losses she had faced in such a short time. When Rose tried to ask questions about the family she never knew, her mother would let on about a family curse but never would elaborate. Rose eventually stopped asking and settled on the fact that her mother would never be much of a mother at all.

When Rose was fifteen, she grudgingly came home for winter break after a friend's invitation to go with her to the slopes had fallen through. It was Christmas eve, and while all of her friends had been calling her telephone to speak of wrapping presents and the excitement over upcoming family festivities, Rose paled in comparison because, at the Bagley household, there was nothing of the sort. Her mother had always been a depressive type, and though they were extremely wealthy, she didn't care much about the facade of holidays.

Rose had grown to be tough as nails, however, and this fact about her mother no longer bothered her. The real treat was her new interest, Daniel, a boy she had been talking to from her boarding school. Rose was madly in love with him, and though they hadn't even touched hands due to the strict rules of the boarding school, there was a spark between them that couldn't be extinguished. He even promised her a Christmas present when she returned to school, to which she was elated.

She had spent the evening in the library. Snow fell gently outside, and she had a piping hot cup of cinnamon tea as she wrote poetry about her love.

A salty kiss on my lips waits for you.

All of her daydreams included a kiss from Daniel. She closed her journal and laid her head back on the chaise, staring up at the ceiling. It had a beautiful triangle motif of specialty cut glass, always letting the light in no matter the weather. Nighttime was her favorite time to admire the library ceiling. As the stars shone, they sparkled in reflection, and she wasn't sure how that was even possible. She lay gazing up as a shooting star passed by and gasped, suddenly longing to share that moment with someone. Anyone. She felt the sting of not being close with her mother as her friends were with their own, and she decided to see if the relationship was really as bad as she imagined.

She took the hallway off the library and cut across the foyer in search of her mother. Josephine could usually be found in the ballroom, listening to the music that played at her wedding on a phonograph. As she got closer to the room, she heard the music playing and slowly twisted the doorknob.

It was disturbing to find her mother dancing with herself with arms extended, near the ballroom stage. Her mother had shared little with her over the years, but she mentioned her father's desire to have a platform for bands to play on. Frank wanted to host galas, dances, and all kinds of parties. As Josephine silently danced to the music, she didn't notice Rose's presence, and her arm was out as if she'd been dancing with a partner.

"Mother?" Rose whispered. It appeared Josephine was in a trance. She laughed out as if hearing a joke. It was the first time Rose had ever seen her mother so happy. Suddenly Rose felt indecent watching this scene that was nothing short of madness. She tried to duck back out of the room, but then the music stopped. With her back to the ballroom, Rose felt a cold chill run through her body, and she froze in place, her heart racing.

She slowly turned her head to glance behind her at her mother, who still hadn't made a noise. But when she looked back, Rose screamed at the top of her lungs as she saw her mother not even an inch behind her, with wide eyes like she'd seen a ghost. Josephine's head dropped, and for a moment, she stood silent before letting out a wailing cry. Rose was frightened and tried to step back from the mad woman, but Josephine took hold of her arm.

"Mother, let go of me," she shrieked. Josephine's touch was freezing cold and shocked her senses. "Mother, please let me go!" Josephine's head rolled backward, and finally, her eyes closed, and she loosened her grip on her daughter's arm.

Rose fled down the hallway and raced up the stairs as if the devil himself had been chasing her. She reached the top of the landing and turned left, running to the end of the hallway, where her bedroom was. She ducked inside, not waiting to see if her mother had made it in behind her.

She slid into a small corner of the room that was trapped in shadows, away from the starry night sky, and put her head on her knees, trying to control her breathing. As she waited for the fear to subside, she covered her eyes with her arm. If she couldn't see evil, it wouldn't be there. A cold sweat took over her body. The only thing that stopped her panting was when she heard the footsteps right in front of her.

"Rose, I'm sorry to frighten you. I mean you no harm." Her mother's voice had been steady, but lacked its usual pride. One could say there was a hint of shame in it as she looked down on her distraught daughter.

Rose choked out a terrified wail, yet no words formed.

"Would you like me to explain? I will tell you everything and answer any questions you have."

Rose looked up with wide eyes at her mother, who in the dark hallway had been just a shadowy figure, but the light from the chandelier illuminated her, and it appeared she was glowing.

Rose took a gasp of air, still breathless from the adrenaline, but this time able to choke out a word, "Yes."

"Alright then, meet me in the library once you gather yourself." Josephine left the corridor.

Sweat dripped from Rose's forehead, and the salty taste hit her lip, as if her poetry had been a premonition. But she didn't want this scenario, where her mother was clearly ill, or worse. Troubled. Possessed. Evil. She stood, wobbly, and made her way through what now seemed like a foreign house. She stopped by the washroom and fumbled for the light. A hum of the fixture and initial flickering of the bulb startled her, though it always did that. The buzz was louder than the ringing in her ears. She went to the basin. Her hands were shaking so bad that she couldn't cup enough water to wash her face with, so she just let the water run over her palms, cold as ice and sobering. Once she regained calm, Rose opened her eyes and looked in the mirror. The reflection staring back at her was unrecognizable— filled with anguish. Her mother had never shared much of anything with her, and she had accepted that. But now, she had the chance to learn more about this mysterious unloving woman and ask questions about her father. About the estate. All she knew about him was his obituary, along with very cryptic hints here and there from her mother. Now she had the opportunity to learn everything. She just hoped her mother would honor what she said and respond to anything she asked.

Rose hobbled into the library like a feral cat, not trusting anything. But Josephine looked normal again, and the pride returned to her voice as she offered Rose a cup of cinnamon tea from the bar cart that she had brought with her. Rose obliged, desperate for the comfort and warmth the tea would provide. Josephine poured her a cup and approached the jade fireplace to throw on another log. Rose was freezing. She felt the temperature drop in the night, and the house went with it.

"Shall I start from the beginning?" Josephine asked, but it seemed much like a rhetorical question, directed at no one, so Rose didn't answer. It wasn't her turn to speak.

For Josephine, it was a story she had rehearsed at every turn but never wanted to share the burden of its weight with anyone. But it was just as well that Rose knew the truth. Josephine stoked the fire for a few minutes until the flames came roaring to life. Rose's eyes locked on the embers as they engulfed the log. With the aromas from the hot tea and the warmth of the hearth, she let go of everything that had happened before this evening, which was the most she'd ever felt of Christmas time.

"Tonight, I will share with you about my family." Looking at Rose she added, "our family. My grandfather was William Sears. It was not a name he was born with— he earned it. You see, he grew up in an orphanage after his parents tragically died. A fate that almost came upon himself."

Josephine would go on to tell Rose the entire history that she knew.

"Have you ever heard of the infamous ship, 'Sarafina's Revenge'?" Josephine asked, staring at the hearth.

Pondering for a moment, Rose was a brilliant student and also was constantly reading history in her spare time. Her mind wandered, and she took a stab at it.

"Is that the ship that washed ashore, empty of its crew, with no one on board?" She recalled the story from a history report by a classmate. The ship had made its way into the French trading harbors of New York without a soul on board. But the ship was owned by a man who later appeared half-dead in a lifeboat, from what she remembered.

"Yes, that's the one." Josephine paused, wishing her daughter had not heard of the tale, and that she could tell it herself. But alas, Rose went to the best boarding school money could buy. What did Josephine really expect?

"The ship was later captained by someone else." Josephine recited. "That captain was your great-grandfather, William."

Rose gasped, and the chill in the air returned. Without saying it, they both felt as if he had just been summoned to the room.

"He was born in a time that many children never lived to adulthood," Josephine started the tale, as she made her way to the library window, gazing out at the snow. "When he was still an infant, he was found next to his deceased parents, in a storm much like this." Rose shuddered at the thought of a baby in a snowstorm. "It too was Christmas eve, in fact." Josephine felt no emotion at the meaning of the holiday since it had none for her personally. "He was sent to an orphanage, where he stayed until he was eleven or twelve. People were not able to adopt children back then like they are more likely to now. And your great-grandfather was maimed. He had an abnormality around his nose and mouth, a cleft palate, that people back then thought was a symptom of syphilis."

Rose was entranced by the flames and the story when she absentmindedly took a sip of tea, realizing it had gone cold. She grabbed a fresh cup from the cart and poured herself another.

"Of course, we now know it wasn't syphilis, but your great-grandfather suffered greatly from others' misunderstanding."

Josephine, stoking the fire, turned to Rose who was propped on the chaise. "How do you know all of this?" she asked. Josephine stiffened. She had two options, tell the truth or continue the charade. She looked at her daughter, who was wide-eyed and frightened, and made a choice.

"There is a man that told me. He knew your grandfather when he was a boy, you see. And that man is still alive today."

CHAPTER SIX

SARAFINA

"Miss Rayne, are you up there?" Leroy's voice startled me once again. "I turned the power on for you. Can you hear me?" His voice was smooth for his age; it didn't quiver.

"Yes, I am here. Thank you for turning the lights on." My pitch was higher than I had intended. He quickly ran up the steps and I was surprised by his buoyancy. "I— I think I will come back tomorrow to look through all of this, as there is so much, and I'm still quite beat from the drive." There was enough furniture in the attic alone to keep me for a week anyway.

"Very well then, madam. Ring tomorrow for me, and I will make sure everything is on properly," he said, while extending his hand to me as I reached the bottom steps. My gaze lingered on his hand. Speaking of rings, a gemstone he wore caught my eye. It was in a ring on his middle finger, in the shape of a star. He coincidentally turned his hand, directing my course down the stairs.

"Oh my, what an interesting ring you have!" I had never seen such a peculiar color before. "May I see it closer?" I asked, but the air felt heavy between us. Leroy started to extend his hand but yanked it away before I could inspect it any closer.

I remembered the necklace that Victoria had sent me. Was it the same stone? I reached for it around my neck but realized it must have fallen off somewhere.

"Oh, silly me!" he gasped, reaching into his pocket. "Here is the master key. A few things don't work with that set I gave you. Let me know if you have any questions about the property at all— any of the art, or decor— or if you want to change any color schemes. And be sure to see the gardens. I, of course, have always had quite the green thumb." He smiled proudly.

From the brief look I had; it was true. The gardens and landscapes Leroy kept for my aunt were something out of a fairy tale. Roses as dark as the evening sky and as big as a dessert plate thrived next to centuries-old willow trees that spread a deliciously sweet smell through the air. The fire-like ivy covering the grand sides of the home even looked maintained. Everything was carefully tended and trimmed.

I looked him up and down. "How do you..." I couldn't find a way to say something without mentioning his age and instantly regretted opening my mouth.

"How do I stay fit?" He laughed and explained he walked the property daily, tending to the plants across all the vast acreage. "For the love of it," he affirmed. "Besides, I have a duty to the countess of this home to keep it in perfect order. Now my dear, that countess is you." He made a slight bow.

My eyes fled to the ground and heat rose to my cheeks, but this was as good of a moment as any to confess. 'Well, Leroy, as soon as my work is done here, the estate will be auctioned off by– my firm." I can't even speak those words without my mind going to him. "But, according to my aunt's will, your house will always be yours, and you will not have to work for anyone here. You will just be a very close neighbor." I tried to sound confident and assured, pointing to the lawyer's name on top of the documents I was still carrying around, as if someone was going to jump out of a closet somewhere and demand I show proof of my ownership.

'Why, Miss Rayne...I am very saddened by this news," Leroy said. 'It's just that, in her last days, Victoria hoped you could enjoy it here. Giving it to the highest bidder...just doesn't sit well with me. Perhaps you need more time here. Dare I say the last few hours you've spent here, thumbing through her things, haven't been enough to make a proper decision!" He slowly stepped away before spinning on his heels and storming off.

I felt a gust of wind and sudden remorse wash over me. I scanned up and down the halls as I held the beautiful, intricate skeleton keys in my hands. At the top of the stairs, my eyes were level with the chandelier. It was like a sky full of stars. Each jewel was beveled and twinkled with its incredible shine. I had to let this feeling go. I had to do what was best for me. Although at this very moment, I wasn't clear on what that was.

My mind torn, I returned to cataloging the house. I closed the door behind me to the attic stairs. This had been the first of two attics. The second, I would leave for tomorrow. But on my way out, I might as well check some of the bedrooms.

The hallways were shaped like the inside of an octagon. One side was covered in grand oil paintings, and the other had the carved wooden banister. Bending down to inspect the carvings, I thought they almost looked like curved V's, but no, they were small birds. How magnificent.

Starting on the first door up the stairs, I matched it with the correct key and stepped inside. It was a peach-toned bedroom seemingly decorated for a young girl. It had tangerine bedding on a light wood headboard, with carved angels on the four-poster bed. A chiffon net draped the bed like an antique veil.

There was a built-in nook on the room's west wall, the two chairs facing each other with a table center. A marble chess set lay on the table, perfectly untouched. Again, the plush carpet had me instinctively kicking off my shoes. Coming from the city, I have been deprived of soft surfaces for my feet. I shuffled around the room and found no trace of life. No toys, no clothes or photos. The window on the north wall had some light draperies covering it, so I pulled them aside to see what the view was. It was a stunning landscape of colorful trees in bloom. The light gave the room a soft glow and I discovered something new. The nook had two small bookcases on each side of the chairs, and first-edition copies of childhood favorites were sitting on the shelf. I will have to bring Megan here as soon as I find her!

Beyond the bathroom was another room just before the attic entry. I gasped at the sight. It wasn't any standard room. It was an atrium of sorts; no plants or birds, just a panoramic view of the beautiful forest of aspen trees. The room was glowing from the golden hour of daylight pouring through the oversized windows. The grove of aspen tree eyes bore into me. There must have been hundreds of trees just outside this window. After a few steps into the room, my gaze climbed upward. The ceilings were painted to depict the starry night sky. There was sunlight coming through them, but I couldn't see from where. A silk rope controlled the brocade drapes, so I gave it a tug to cover the windows. All of the stars shone sunlight through them, the most magnificent thing I'd ever seen.

I could lay in this room all day and look at this work, but I was tired and overwhelmed from all the magnificence I had witnessed. I would gather my wits here and then search for Megan.

I knew what my conversation with Megan would cover: the gilded, oversized glowing glory of everything in this estate. It was nearly overwhelming, as I'd only seen half of the rooms so far. There was still the other side of the manor to explore.

One room in the middle of the hallway remained locked, and I'd been meaning to have Leroy open it for me, but then I remembered he gave me the keys. Besides, after his scolding me a few minutes before, I doubt he wanted to help me right this second.

I held up the set of almost identical skeleton keys to pick one to start with. No. Not that one, either. The last key on the ring did the trick; the satisfying click of the locks made me excited to discover what was inside. Gripping the glass knob to turn it, halfway through it felt like someone was turning it from the other side. Just my exhaustion making me jumpy. Laughing at myself, I took a step back and tried again, this time successfully.

I peered in, half expecting someone to be standing at the door, but it was empty. Like the other rooms, this room was circular but had a unique winding staircase, made of beautiful, oxidized brass leading to a loft. In the corner, an ornate gold bird cage sat on a wire stand, below a painting of a songbird. The painting looked sun-damaged, which I immediately found unusual, considering the pristine condition of everything else in the manor.

I robotically decided to go up the stairs, my limbs on autopilot as I climbed up the windy steps, dizzying my way to the top. A portrait of a woman stared back at me as I stepped into the loft. She resembled my mother in some distant way.

The woman in the painting was dressed in a yellow gown, and appeared to be around twenty years old. I sometimes dreamed of a night wearing a dress such as this. I leaned in to touch the frame, loving to feel the materials to assess the quality, which everything in here was the best of the best.

A small inscription on the portrait's frame read, "Josephine Bagley." As beautiful as this was, I felt chills down my spine as I could sense someone's presence. Megan must be nearby.

A yawn overcame me, and suddenly I felt like I could collapse from exhaustion. There was a perfectly placed seat next to me, so I curled up in the chaise lounge next to the homage of Josephine. There was a small mirrored end table with the drawer propped open to my side. A small-scale key of the ones I'd been given for the doors lay on the table. I picked up the key, adding it to my larger ring. Inside the velvet drawer was a page torn from a book. It had the fine print of a novel, but someone had written a poem with a calligraphy pen over the text on the backside of the page.

A salty kiss on my lips

waits for you.

My body lifted by the waves,

promising to carry me away.

I never told you, but you knew

that deep inside me was a sadness

I could not subdue.

I leaned back and closed my eyes, wondering about the author. I connected with that person in shallow ways— feeling a loss but not wanting to die. To feel so hopeless that you commit suicide? That brought my troubles into perspective. I felt incomplete. Dazed. I honestly didn't care about anything, and if Dean were to call me now, I'd give this house up in an instant for him.

A loud scuffling noise downstairs averted my attention. Closing away the drawer and its haunting poetry, I traced my steps back to the hallway, and locked the solid mahogany door behind me.

Leroy was in the atrium when I made my way back downstairs. I politely said, goodnight, and he swiftly appeared to walk me out with a smile. He stepped ahead to open the door, escorting me to my quarters.

"Madam, what do you know about Victoria?" he asked with a raised brow. He nudged me as if we were old pals.

"Well, not much, actually. I hope to learn more about her as I spend time in her home."

Leroy stopped in his tracks. After a pause, he raised a handkerchief to his nose. "I'm sorry, madam," he said, choking up. "It's still…so fresh, the wound of losing her."

I nodded in condolences. I knew the weight of loss— its every shape and form— the gaping emptiness, the joyless years. Loss lives with you, rent-free, forever. It is impossible to ignore and likes to remind you of its presence when you least expect it, like finding an old photograph in a shoebox under a bed.

When we finally made it to the guest house, we both turned, looking back at the mansion. It was quite an impressive view from my guest quarters.

"What about the history of the home? Did you find it intriguing?" Leroy crossed his arms, not taking his eyes off the mansion.

I knew what he was up to. He wanted to spark that exciting mystery that he felt would entice me to keep the manor. While it was amazing, this is what I did for a career, which was the most important thing in my life. It was my identity.

"Well," I said, "after you told us about it being a wedding gift, I did a web search. Wiki says this house was the proposal, and it wooed Josephine enough to leave her cherished family behind and move upstate. Then, she married Frank

Bagley, here in the ballroom." I turned to him, feeling smug.

"Well, Madam, that is technically true. But, it's not the whole story. You see, Frank and Josephine were married, but not for long. His family all relied on him for their affluent lifestyles. So after the marriage, they moved into the estate, as there was plenty of room! Tragically, a year after they were wed, all members of the family had died of…Cholera."

His pause was noticeable. Sarafina thought he wanted to emphasize the sadness.

"Later on, a magistrate heard about this from a worker who'd made it to town before his death. The magistrate went to the home to verify the bodies and prepare the estate for auction when it was discovered that Josephine was alive and well. Josephine was never ill, as she had gone to visit her Aunt Cora during her pregnancy, only to return to the mass death. All living generations from one of the richest families in America had perished, and now his new bride owned it all." Thick silence spread between us momentarily. I'd been schooled.

"Josephine was plagued with grief. Soon after, she discovered Frank too had perished on the Triton Ship. I should know, as I was here, back then." With a flat-lined look, he bowed and retreated to his home with a flourish of the hand.

"Mic drop!" Megan hollered from the guest house. "Do you need me to pick up your jaw from the ground, Sara?" She winked and closed the window.

I must have looked like a deer in the headlights at that revelation. It took the wind out of my sails to imagine the things Leroy had seen here at the estate. Looking at him, you know he's in his upper years, but he looked great for being that old.

"I didn't know you were in here. I thought you'd still be in the library." I was too tired to chat, so I just waved to Megan as I shut the bedroom door behind me. I had planned on staying upstairs, but needed a bed now.

My thoughts raced as I delved under the cool sheets, after stripping down my jeans and top.

How unfortunate for Josephine to lose everyone and survive. It was impossible to imagine what that could have been like— having to bury her whole family while carrying the next generation. I felt grief-stricken, suddenly ill, with her thoughts mingling with mine. I felt the loss of Dean again. Though we were never betrothed, I would have married him in a heartbeat. A silent cry escaped my throat as tears bubbled behind my eyes.

I wallowed in pity when I fell into a deep unconscious state.

When I emerged from the room, it was nearly dark out, and Megan was nowhere to be found. I took the robe hanging from the bathroom door and stepped outside the guest house. A screaming flock of bats flew overhead; the squeaking was muted until they were right above me, and one bat even touched my hair. I stumbled over in fright, covering my head, screaming in return. After the shock passed, I turned to look at the illuminated manor. It glowed from the inside.

What a beautiful estate this was, especially under the soft shades of dusk. It was symmetrical from head-on, but the house was built at an angle on the property. This made all the rooms face the gardens. Even in the daylight, the brick was dark as if the stonework was always moist. I thought I heard Megan ask something about a water source to Leroy, if only I had been listening.

Suddenly a flock of bats flew from the house into the rising moonlit sky. An owl call echoed through the valley, then through my mind. They certainly added magic to the place.

My eyes devoured the land and I felt guilt. If it really was Victoria's desire to have me inherit and live here, couldn't she have expressed that sooner? Were her— our— other relatives already living in multi-million-dollar castles and had no desire for this enigmatic home that attracted fog and ravens?

And why did I want nothing to do with it? Was I so desperate to get ahead in my job that I could easily turn this once-in-a-million lifetime event over to them? Yes, but maybe not. I was starting to feel a twinge of regret and uncertainty. Maybe I would stay. But without Dean, what did it really matter?

I took a deep breath and realized how full of regret I was for doing this. I couldn't believe it myself, this was such a special place, and here I was going to piece it out and get rid of it. I told myself, 'This won't make him notice you if he hasn't already. Getting ahead will not make him reciprocate your feelings. A man is not worth this. There are plenty of fish in the sea.'

My daily self-chants rarely worked, but the truth was hard to swallow. I had been infatuated with my colleague for as long as I've known him— since he hired me on as his assistant dealer. The day we met, I had just interviewed with the hiring manager, who then told me to help myself to a coffee or tea while I waited for the owner. My back was to the door as I tore open a sugar packet. Suddenly, I felt him in the room and I spilled the sugar everywhere. His presence excited me before I even saw him.

Back to reality, I knelt to feel the softness of the grass. Running both hands through it, I couldn't remember the last time I felt happy.

Wait. What is that?

Suddenly I glimpsed a shadowed corner of the mansion I hadn't noticed before, to the north. I stepped inside the cottage and changed back into my jeans, grabbing a pair of rubber boots that had been sitting out by my luggage. They weren't mine. Maybe Megan's? Although I doubted that, I even laughed at the notion. Megan's shoe prerequisite required it to have a red sole.

I remembered when we arrived earlier that there was a flashlight sitting on the front entry table. I reached for it before leaving, but now it was gone? Maybe Megan had grabbed it. I opened up a few drawers in the kitchen, finding a small one that wouldn't do much, but it was better than nothing.

I walked back through the grounds to investigate, grateful for the rubber boots, now slick from the moist grass. My legs were sore by the time I reached the back of the property. The sounds from the river below were frightening since there didn't appear to be any sort of railing.

"Hey, come here. I want to show you something."

I couldn't tell where the voice came from, and while I assumed it was Megan— there was no way she would be out here alone, at night, where the 'creepy crawlies' are. And the voice was much deeper.

"Who's there?" I shined my flashlight and thought I saw someone concealed in the trees. I diverted my path, aiming the weak beam when it slowly went out. "Darn batteries!" I hit it a few times with my palm, to see if I could kick it back on. Shaking it didn't work either. I slid the defunct light into my pocket, calling out once more to the voice in the woods. "Hello? Who are you?"

"Madam, it's a little late to be out here alone." Leroy appeared out of nowhere, placing a cold hand on my shoulder. I let out a shrill scream at the touch. "I'm sorry to startle you," he apologized, "but I fear that area is off limits for now. It is a cliffside, and the rocks have proven to be unstable in this wretched weather."

I respectfully nodded, not wanting to cause a stir. "There is someone out there. He spoke to me."

Leroy stopped in his tracks. "He?" His face was now visible by the glow of the house as we got closer.

"I think so. Yes, it sounded like a male." Truthfully, now I was unsure. I turned my head to look back in that direction. In the darkness, the twisted trees poking out from behind the lush forest of aspens, pine and willows appeared darker than the night sky. The thought of someone out there gave me the creeps, and I suddenly felt eager to get back inside.

"Must be an owl," Leroy mumbled. "Now, let's go have dinner. I've prepared a lovely welcoming spread for you. Megan is waiting."

The following day, Megan used the vintage rotary telephone in our living quarters to call her fiancé, soon-to-be 'husband' as she always said. They had a plan on eloping soon, but it was so top secret that she wouldn't even tell me when. He was sharing some great news that the offer they put on a house was accepted. I had a feeling them buying a home together would speed up the engagement. She was overjoyed, but ruefully looking at me when she got off the phone.

"I have to leave today. Please don't be angry with me. I will come back and get you in a few days. Would that work?" Megan was compassionate; the thought of hurting someone's feelings or putting even the slightest strain on a relationship just killed her.

"Oh, of course! I am so ecstatic about your future home. Tell me about it while you pack up?"

Relieved to know that I wasn't upset, Megan went on for nearly an hour about the house with its modern fireplace and built-in sauna, butler's pantry, and walk-in closets that could double as a guest bedroom.

"Well, that sounds bigger than my new place!" We both laughed. It was good to laugh with a great friend and share our joys. Hearing her excitement made my stomach twist up about the manor as doubts about selling it started to flood my mind.

"And about coming back to get me— you know, I haven't even cataloged a single thing yet. And today Leroy was going to show me the wine cellars. How about I just give you a call in a few days? You don't have to come all the way back here. I can hire a car or something." I was hesitant on the last part because I wasn't sure if anyone would service such a remote location.

"Oh, Sara, you are just the best! Thank you. I am so happy for us!" She leaned in and hugged me, her hair smelling like roses. "I'll call you when I get home? And you can tell me what you found today!" Megan opened the door to the guest house, clutching her designer weekender bag, and left. Leroy was in mid-route to his quarters when he saw her depart, so he came over to me to check if everything was all right.

"She's off to sign for her own manor that she will share with her soulmate." I didn't mean to sound so jealous because I certainly had it pretty good myself. Glancing at Leroy, it appeared he thought nothing of it, waving her off.

Lifting my hand to wave her goodbye, a small bird landed on it and wobbled to perch on my finger. "Oh!" Surprised, I almost shook it off. It looked at me with its little beady eyes and puffed up its chest. "It's a sparrow, milady.

Birds loved Victoria as well." He issued a coy wink.

Sniffling from the sudden cold, I looked back at the tiny bird on my hand. My heart suddenly began racing, and it matched the breaths of the sparrow. It took off just as the rain picked up, and I heard thunder clapping in the distance. "Shall I be expecting you today for lunch?" I nodded yes, and Leroy happily trotted off.

Since Megan left, I gave the guest quarters another once-over. A pale velvet tapestry hung over a wall, with a cord begging to be pulled. I tugged it to unveil a large painting of a woman standing on a cliffside. Her back was turned, and the wind blew through her hair. A white comb held the tresses together, but her hair was like fire— out of control and long. Her yellow dress was bright against the bleak, ominous backdrop. Was this the same woman in the yellow dress, that I'd seen in the study?

The rest of the day was spent back in the manor, with fresh eyes now that I was alone. I had the chance to dwell on each item and started to get a feel for the eras they originated from.

As I lay in bed that night, I went through the inventory of today's discoveries. A few pieces were perfect for our clients, and maybe one or two that I'd claim for myself. One, in particular, was a table with clawed feet. It had a velvet-lined drawer with an ornate key on a ribbon to secure it. I wondered if Dean would like it. Or would he prefer the sterling silver jewelry box lined with turquoise silk, also with a key?

The countess sure liked her privacy. I realized almost everything I had looked at so far with drawers or compartments had a key to lock it. Very little had been inside these items, mostly just the keys themselves. The only drawer with contents of any sort was the one in the study where I found the poem ripped out of the book.

My mind returned to Dean one more time, before drifting off to the place that I could never truly hide from. I fought sleep by reaching under the bed and pulling out a mahogany box full of pictures of my mother that I brought with me. I don't know why, but I felt like I had to hide it from Megan. To hide my grief. The box was lined with dried flowers and mint leaves from her garden she kept when I was a child. The scent of lilac and honeysuckle intoxicated my senses.

My mother, Lilith Rayne, was breathtakingly beautiful, with long, thick dark hair and eyes that matched. Her long eyelashes used to tickle my cheeks when she kissed me. She would leave lipstick kiss prints on my forehead while I was sleeping. My father, Robert, always spoke about the shine in her eyes. They had me later in life, after spending twenty years together. When I was a child, my father told me that they decided their lives felt incomplete one day. They decided to have me right then, and eleven months later, I was born. They loved me completely and also each other more and more every moment. I had great respect for their marriage.

They died when I was fourteen. I will never forget that day. A teacher pulled me aside at school. A strange sense of calm washed over me. It was like a dream when she said, "There has been an accident, Sara. I am going to take you to Providence Hospital right now, ok?"

The following forty-eight hours whizzed by. I met Megan that day. She and her family's kindness overflowed like a river. They helped me plan the funeral and took me in. Her father, Marcus, handled the life insurance paperwork and helped set it up for me in an account. Her mother, Kady, was the stand-in motherly support figure that was there just in case. When I tried to thank them, they would shake it off and smile. Her mom would say, "It's what I would want for Megan if she were in this situation." I was eternally grateful.

My parents never spoke of social life, and yet, their funeral and reception were full. Hordes of people showed, claiming they were their friends. They offered me anything I could ever need; housing, money, support. Each was more mysterious than the last. One woman, as Megan let me know, had head-to-toe designer clothes and wore brooches on her shoes. Her husband was strikingly pale, so pale it frightened me. Another woman had olive skin and the most beautiful blue eyes. Her husband was dark with a mustache. Then there was the man in the green sweater, with eyes to match. His immaculate appearance didn't have a hair out of place. He never said a word or took his eyes off of me.

***

WILLIAM

The next morning, William sat in the captain's seat as the men emerged from their beds. Their wide-eyed looks revealed the fear they felt at such a sign of disrespect to Scarsbeard.

"He's killed his crew for less, mate." One man cautioned. "Come down from there, boy!" Another yelled.

But William sat in the chair, shaking his head. "I am the captain now. Scarsbeard is dead, at my hand." They froze, motionless bodies ogling him in disbelief, until one let out a cackle.

William ran Sarafina's Revenge for several more years before it dwindled to a skeleton crew. No one had wanted to work on the ship, and they either mysteriously disappeared or had died in the galleys. Anyone who opposed him would be thrown overboard. Their days were spent sailing, which he loved, but as with any ship, it eventually must dock. And the days that followed became all too predictable until William grew tired of the life of debauchery and thievery.

He caught his appearance in a stained mirror hanging in a brothel, shocked to see he looked similar to Scarsbeard, with his scraggly appearance and overgrown hair.

One day, after much contemplation, they docked and William sold the ship to some French merchants whose ship had sunk. They were in a desperate place to pay more than something was worth. He gave the Sarafina one last look over and decided the only thing he wanted was that small painting of the countryside. After that, he had been somewhat well off, but it wasn't enough. He had a hunger for wealth. Real wealth— the kind that opened doors— the kind that made people afraid of him.

Weeks later, while renting a beautiful hotel on the sea, he heard a woman calling his name out the open window. He was on the twelfth floor, yet it seemed she was directly outside. He looked out, but no one was there— yet she called again. He suddenly felt like he was in a trance, his feet floating to the door, down the hall and stairs. "Come here, William," she sang in a familiar song as he scuffled out to the beach. The moon was full, brightly illuminating the waves. No one was there but he started to see pieces of shiny metal sparkle under the moon, all along the beach. He went towards them. As he got closer, he realized they had significant size and shape and were, in fact, bodies. He ran and fell on his knees to check if they were alive, sprinting from body to body. They were all dead— maybe a dozen of them, but then he recognized someone, and then another. They were his remaining crew members still on board when he sold the ship, now dead on the beach. Then he heard the woman's voice again.

"What is the matter, William?" Her voice is twisted now, not so much a song but a chant, and it's swirling around him. It is neither in front of him nor behind, rather the voice is coming from inside his own head.

"Wh-who are you?" He demands, but his voice is frail, for a moment, he feels afraid.

"Don't you know? I am the one who got you here, in this wealthy existence, paid on the backs of these souls."
He nervously looked around and the bodies, they had died at sea, nothing more.

She suddenly appeared to him. Her face was almost translucent pale, her golden hair was impossibly long, almost brushing her ankles. She wore nothing more than a red cloth that covered a third of her body. He was immediately attracted to her, in an animalistic way, to the point he reached out and grabbed her. She allowed it to happen, laughing in the twisted chant. Then she became stronger than him, forcibly pushing him away, kicking him back several feet instantly.

"Now, I am here to see if you would like MORE." He was breathing heavily, laying on his back from impact, but trying to regain his balance. She got down on all fours, crawling towards him, her body twisting impossibly. It was as if she had 6 legs how she was moving, like a black widow.

She got up in his face seductively, licking her lip with each phrase. "More wealth, all of the wealth, so much wealth, no one can ever take it away." He boldly reached out and kissed her on the mouth, to which she obliged, and her tongue went so far down his throat he almost choked. Coughing, gagging, she laughed once more. "I need to hear you say it, William."

"Yes," breathing heavily, "I want it all. I want so much wealth that people fear me. But I don't want to be alone either." He looked at her curvaceous body, picturing immoral things he could do right then and there; things he had done with many women over the last few years.

Suddenly her body twisted around like a tree root. She grew as tall as a tower, the red cloth becoming her skin color, with horns growing out of her head. She no longer had a gender, but rather had feminine and masculine features. It spat out, "Very well then. You and your descendants will always have extreme wealth, you will marry and have children. But there will be a curse."

The creature vanished, and Ehawee stood before him, just as she did all those years ago, with tear-stained cheeks, holding a blanket over her body. She was looking around very confused and afraid, shouting out in her native language, one that William no longer remembered. "Ehawee! It's me, William." She squinted her eyes, then widened in the overwhelming realization it was him, given his facial features. She mumbled out, "Where am I?"

William looked around and looked back at her. "I can't explain it, Ehawee. But somehow, you are in the future." She was panicking, breathing heavily. William recalled the night she had somehow traveled from was the night she met Lowell under very tragic circumstances.

"Ehawee, what did that boy do to you?" The rage inside him had just been triggered once again.

Her eyes became angry, "Do you do this, Will-i-am? Do you want this to happen?"

William was shaking his head profusely when Ehawee started chanting words, louder and louder. "No, no, Ehawee, I loved you, I still do." William scrambling to explain himself, Ehawee, now drawing something in the sand with her fingertips as she called out for help in her native tongue. Just when Ehawee covered her ears to the chants that swirled around William, Lowell appeared unconscious, laying in the sand. The chanting became a scream.

William stared at Lowell, committing his grown features to memory. Lowell stirred, awakening slowly, and gaped up at them. His eyes were full of fear when he saw Ehawee and heard the chanting.

"What's happening? How did she get here?" Lowell tried to question William, but the chant turned to laughter and the noise once again grew louder and louder.

The woman's voice, once light and seductive, turned deep and masculine as it answered Lowell's question. "You have caused death among this woman. There is a price you must pay, so you will live as long as William and all of his blood."

William's body went limp, falling backward into unconsciousness. When he woke, it was morning, and he was the only one dead or alive on the beach.

CHAPTER SEVEN

SARAFINA

That night I dreamt of a wildfire. A roaring burn, taking miles in strides, devastating everything in its wake. People were screaming, crying out. I ran closer to them and I heard a strange rhythm. They weren't asking for help as they were burning. They were chanting my name.

I was holding the gas can.

Upon waking, I found the sky so bright. I hadn't seen the sun in several days so I stepped outside to find a pomegranate tree. I don't like pomegranates, but had an urge to touch everything of beauty. I reached for a fruit when Leroy spoke to me and scared me into letting out a shrill cry.

"I wouldn't do that if I were you!" Leroy ran over to me. I laughed, turning around, thinking surely, he couldn't be serious.

"Madam, these fruits are off limits." He was very stern.

"What— oh, I'm sorry, I didn't realize." Confused and waiting for an explanation, I was somehow relieved that I hadn't picked one yet.

The angst in Leroy's eyes faded. He gave me a friendly smile. "Miss Rayne, why don't I give you a tour of the gardens?"

"I would love that." His abrupt change in demeanor was now a memory. I wanted so much to feel the sun on my hair.

The landscape was even more enchanting than I initially thought. A grove of aspen trees surrounded the property from the sides up to the gate. Their white scarred trunks were covered in large eyes that stared right through your soul. Dahlia's, which Leroy said were Victoria's favorite, were the centerpiece of the gardens. They came in every shade of red. Crimson crabapple trees were at the end of their cycle, yet still full, while the weeping willows seemed older than the mansion itself. Leroy explained that the lilac bushes lining the porch were planted when the house was built, over a hundred years ago.

The fruit tree selection was grand. Apple, apricot, peach, and nectarine. "In the late summer, nothing is as sweet as this." Leroy, plucked a peach from the tree and sniffed it, handing it over to me to do the same. "Go ahead, take a bite." He smiled devilishly and laughed so hard his head rolled back when I took that first bite.

The flavor was like peach candy from a soda saloon. The nectar dripped down my chin, and it was so juicy. The skin was taut and perfectly ripe. My eyes widened as I eagerly took another bite. Leroy grabbed a handkerchief and handed it to me, pointing at my chin.

"That was the best thing I've ever tasted, thank you, Leroy." We picked a few more peaches for some tarts he was making tonight. If the fruit tasted that good, imagine what his baking would be like?

It was enchanting as the estate slowly revealed itself to me. The area was hilly; ponds with lily pads were frequent but naked to the eye from a distance. Our property line was far out and marked with a massive pointy oxidized fence, lined with Hollyhocks as tall as me, dancing in the breeze. The longer we were out, the more there was to discover.

Mysterious garden statues appeared randomly placed throughout the property. Some were cherubs extending their hands to birds, and others were angels with stars. "Was Victoria religious?" As soon as I asked, I regretted the question.

Leroy's smile fell as he gazed up at a tall angel statue. A blue jay landed on its shoulder. "Yes. But she never felt good enough to be," he spoke under his breath as if answering his own question.

There was great sadness in Leroy. A burden that wore down already sagging shoulders. After taking care of the house for so many years, it must have been tragic losing Victoria.

"Do you mean the angels?" he asked, turning to me. "Yes, well, those were bought by Frank, Josephine's late husband. He always said Josephine was like an angel, and it is said he picked each of these sculptures because they reminded him of her."

We chatted on about the sculptures, Leroy even pointing out one that had my likeness. We kept walking and talking, going in a half circle around the front of the house, paying no attention to the elephant in the room— the sheer cliff the mansion was planted on.

"Leroy, will you show me the rocks in the back? I promise I won't climb them!" I laughed, imagining Leroy thought I was a child last night when he prevented me from looking.

"As you wish, Madam. Right this way." Leroy took her hand and walked around the back.

The property backed up on a cliffside that wasn't seen from any angle of the house except back here. The drop, being around a thousand feet, was very interesting geologically. I wondered what possessed the original builder to have a home constructed so close to a trap like this?

"Well Madam, this is truly a sight, isn't it?" Leroy nodded as if rehearsed.

"Yes, it's quite scary, actually." Mumbling, I took a step back, afraid of heights.

There was no barrier to prevent a fall if one looked over the edge. I pictured myself or someone else falling in, shaking my head in fright as I took several more cautious steps of retreat. Leroy put his hand on my shoulder, proud to see I was human, after all, and escorted me back to the front of the house.

When we were far enough away, Leroy stopped. "Madam," he spoke, in a shaken, raspy voice, turning me and taking my hands. "You must not go to the cliffs alone under any circumstances. Don't even look at them. They are very dangerous."

"Okay..." He was so serious that it made me feel awkward. "Don't worry, I won't!" Why would I want to go hang out at the cliffs? If they were in my thoughts at all, it would be in my nightmares.

"I suppose you should know that Victoria and your grandmother Josephine both died in that water below."

A bitter gust of wind chilled my body. I closed my eyes. The lives of these women— of my family— of my entire family— what did it spell for my fate? I knew it was a morbid thought, but I couldn't stop myself from saying it aloud. Leroy, still holding my wrists, paused.

He let go of one of my wrists while he reached into his pocket, pulling out a small vial of pale blue liquid. He placed it firmly in my hand with a smile that didn't reach his eyes.

"This is a special fragrance I made for you, Madam. It is pure Parfum, made from the flowers in my garden. I hope you enjoy it. The countess Victoria did." He looked down.

"Oh, well, thank you, Leroy! How special. I'm sure I will love it." I held it to my chest, and he turned away, speaking but not looking at me. He really knew how to keep me on my toes.

"I will return to the house now, Madam. You can find me in the kitchen, baking some strawberry lemon tarts. They sure are good for the soul." He walked off.

I was left alone, surrounded by ruby calibrachoa and obsidian elephant ear plants. Leroy had told me about each item in his garden, and what special meaning they had to him. "This pansy may look dark and ominous, and its name is 'Black Devil', but it gives you glowing porcelain skin and has the most wonderful fresh mint flavor. And over here, the dahlias."

"What do the dahlias do?" I eagerly asked.

"Well," Leroy chuckled, "they made Victoria happy. They were her favorite flower." Leroy held a large bloom in his hands, looking deeply into it. The flowers were exceptional, all different colors in red, pink, and deep purple. Almost black.

"As you can see, most of these are flowers. I have an herb garden around the willow tree. Let me show you."

Now, as I walked the garden solo, it felt magical knowing these plants all had a secondary purpose. Just then, I stumbled upon a unique flower. It was dark aubergine, with weird vines and globes of blossoms like antennas dripping wet from the center like it was crying.

The longer I gazed into it, the more disturbed I felt when I noticed the center of the enigma had what resembled two small eyes. I was still a few feet away, careful not to trample the coleus surrounding it. I took a small step and leaned in as far as I could, reaching over to touch—

"Madam Sarafina!" Leroy called out firmly, appearing beside me out of thin air.

I screamed, falling backward. "Madam, let me help you." Extending his hand, he caught my eye.

"May I explain anything to you about the orchid?" Unsmiling, he looked worn from the day. I felt guilty for being such a pain in his neck.

"Oh, is that what it is? That's alright. I will let you get back to— um— I suddenly feel very tired." It was true. The day had taken a toll on me. We walked the property almost two times over and covered each plant. I was exhausted.

"Very well, Madam. I will have dinner served at 6:30 tonight if you are hungry." Turning on his heels, he marched away. I looked at my watch. It was 5:15, and I was feeling weak from the day.

After freshening up in the guesthouse, I took a stroll back to the kitchen. My legs were sore and unsteady as I made the trip back. The air grew crisp, and I was only in a light jacket, so I hastened my pace.

Upon entering the home, I wondered if Victoria had hand-picked the stones in her chandelier. I would have to ask Leroy about that, as the gemstones felt familiar to me. I remembered my mother had a smokey quartz ring when I was a child. I realized I hadn't seen or thought of it since her death.

I ventured upstairs to explore some more before dinner. This time, I took the left hallway. The farthest room back, with its glass doorknob shaped like a square, shocked me when I touched it. It was odd, considering I was standing on wood floors, wearing rubber-soled boots. My exhaustion made me feel jumpy, and I took a step back and touched it again, turning the knob.

If a gut feeling told me what to do, I would nail a board over the door of this room and never look back. It had an eerie feel to it. All of the bedrooms I'd been in the house were circular and in beautiful shape with stunning embroidered headboards, unique embellishments to the furniture, and slightly modern Victorian decor. Not this room, though. Someone had torn the flooring up, and by the looks of it, rather abruptly. There were scribbles over the floorboards, which had some jagged pieces of cherry wood left over.

Surprisingly, there was a large window in this room that I didn't see outside of the house. It had large purple drapes begging to be parted, and I obliged. I peered out, expecting to witness the horrifying heights of the cliffs. But that's not even close to what it was. In awe, I yanked the drapes open as wide as they would go to take it all in.

It was the grandest view I'd ever seen— with cliffs covered in clusters of amethyst, pieces more prominent than in any museum in the world. Even under the overcast sky, golden flowers sparkled sporadically throughout the mesmerizing rock. Fog encapsulated the peaks like haloes. It was a true wonder of the world.

I noticed a balcony outside the adjacent bedroom that offered a better overlook. That must be Victoria's room, but its location was puzzling. There were no doors past the one I was in now. Drawn to the view again, I observed gold vines growing out of the amethyst right before my eyes. I was in pure awe, yet an ominous feeling struck me. Turning away, I screamed to find that Leroy had been standing behind me the entire time.

Without a word, he shuffled out of the room. I sank onto the bed, still reeling from the view. I didn't know what had gotten into Leroy, but I decided to speak to him at dinner about it.

I lay back, head against the footboard, a better angle to look at the painting above. The walls beautifully framed it with crown molding, as all the rooms had. It was at least 48x72— enormous dimensions that so many of our customers would kill for. Oil was the medium, but what was the subject?

The longer I gazed at it, the more it evolved. At first glance, I saw a stormy sky. Or maybe, the wind blowing smoke from a fire. My breathing grew shallow. The bed was so comfortable. I felt like my breathing was merging with someone else's. My eyes grew heavy when it struck me, clear as day, what the painting was. "Must take note of this..." I muttered just as Leroy barged through the door.

"Madam! Dinner is in five minutes," he barked, urgently standing above me like a teacher just caught me cheating. I got up and pointed at the painting, mumbling nonsense about it as I sleep-walked my way across the room. Leroy shut the door behind me and, when he thought I was looking away, locked the door. "Nothing to catalog in there, Madam." He squared his gaze with me.

"Oh, I thought— ", I thought the whole place was mine.

Reading my expression, he sighed. "I suppose you should know anyway— " he trailed off. "Look, Sarafina. Josephine, your great-grandmother, was a very pained woman. She'd seen more tragedies in the first few decades of her life than many see in a generation. She used that room to try and communicate with her deceased family members." I gasped at the thought. Was she into… Witchcraft? A very dark feeling washed over me.

Leroy's eyelids fluttered as he shook his head. "Do as you wish, Madam. Just know, things are not what they seem. And don't fall asleep in that room." He stormed off, leaving me speechless once again.

Things are not what they seem. Where had I heard that before? My hands crawled over my clipboard of papers from Victoria's attorney and shaking, I shuffle through to find the letter she sent. Why did she say that and send me a holy cross necklace? My thoughts raced and my mind became very clear as the adrenaline pumped through my veins. Things were certainly not what they seemed to be. I triple-checked that the door was locked, and I stepped backward as if to trace my steps, so that the room could be wiped from my memory.

I couldn't shake the heaviness I felt when I entered the room and the shock of my actions. I had laid on a bed used for witchcraft. I broke the silence of my anxiety with a nervous laugh and went into the closest washroom to splash water across my face. Gazing into the mirror at my frizzy reflection, no evil witches were staring back at me— no horror movie scenes— no ghosts. I was okay, just shaken from my brush with the occult. Before I retreated downstairs, I felt a slight breeze brush my back.

Was there an open window somewhere? I could only think of one place that could be, as I'd been in the other rooms that would've had a breeze coming from that direction. Where was the room with the balcony? There were no doorways on the back wall of the house, just a tea table and bookshelf. I turned around to make sure I was alone. No one was there, and I heard some pots and pans rattling downstairs. I was alone for now, so I tested out all the usual mystery movie suspects. I twist a candlestick— pulled a book— and flipped a switch. Nothing, no doors magically appeared from the bookshelf.

The dark wallpaper has vertical matte stripes of a deep ocean teal color. It must be here— this hidden entryway. I took a step back, analyzing the tea table, tall and bronze. It didn't match the blue and silver chair. Wait a minute— this was planted here! I pulled it away, to discover a beautiful crystal beveled doorknob.

The tea table was very cumbersome and made a ka-plunk noise when I moved it. I tried sliding it to no avail. Each attempt grew louder. This would have to wait for tomorrow, as it was time to retreat for the day. After all, Leroy seemed rather sour. I better not be late for dinner.

Downstairs, the kitchen was off to the right, and as I made my way down the hallway, I heard yelling. At first, I thought Leroy had dropped something or burned himself, but then I thought I detected another voice.

As I got closer, I heard Leroy demanding something.

"You MUST GO! Now. You are not welcome in this house!" Leroy pleaded. Was there a struggle? I heard grunting. Maybe Leroy needed my help!

"She didn't want me here, but now that she's gone…" The other voice was very calm compared to Leroy's shrill cry.

"I DON'T CARE, GET OUT! AHHH!"

It sounded as if Leroy was being attacked, so I ran to save him.

I barged through the swinging door, and caught a glimpse of Leroy before he threw his hands out and knocked over a bowl of flour. A cloud of white was all I saw before I slipped on something wet and crashed to the floor. Covered in egg yolk and flour, I was ready to be fried. Leroy snapped his fingers.

"Your Holy Water does not work on me," a stranger's voice whispered.

A masculine hand appeared out of the mist, and I reached for it. Staring in confusion, I traced the man's arm to a collarless dress shirt. Continuing up to the neck, I find a perfectly chiseled chin and jawline, a strong nose, and soulful, bottomless green eyes.

"Milady," he barely moved his lips and deadlocked on my eyes. His voice was whiskey, the dialect unclear. I was startled by his appearance—otherworldly— godly looking— strange but familiar. He reached for my other hand, and suddenly we were in a tango pose. "Hello." The word flowed off his tongue and wrapped around me. He wasn't from here nor there or anywhere at all. Lifting the tension in the room, he kissed my cheek and released me. I was so mesmerized that I could almost ignore Leroy's scowl and crossed arms.

"Sarafina, may I have a word with you, dear?" Leroy asked, but it was more of a demand. Couldn't he see that I was clearly busy and preferred he left us alone?

Leroy huffed and gently pulled me by the arm while I stared deep into the stranger's eyes as I was hauled away. We stepped out into the hall, and Leroy spoke loud enough for the man in the kitchen to hear. "Now, you MUST listen to me. That man in there— you want to stay as far away from him as possible. Do you understand? He is not GOOD. He is not like you, sweet Sarafina. I do not know you well, but I know him, and you must take my word for it!" Leaving me, he stormed back into the kitchen.

I heard him loud and clear but I didn't feel like listening. He had verbally slapped me in the face, and now I sheepishly stood in the hallway, waiting, hoping to meet the stranger again. As a distraction, I decided now might be the time to do some cataloging in this gorgeous hall. I took refuge in a corner, sizing up a purple silk tufted chaise lounge, but couldn't touch anything when I remembered I was covered in egg and flour.

The kitchen door opened, but my back was to it. There were no footsteps, and I glanced curiously over my shoulder. Leather-shined shoes and fitted black dress pants fluidly approached. I felt myself turning to the stranger and straightening my hair with my fingers.

From this short span of maybe two yards, I drank him in. He was frightening and mysterious, dark and stormy. His combination of features was unusual, almost uncomfortable. The term 'devilishly handsome' was meant for him. He enchanted me.

"Hello, Miss Sarafina," his 's' stirred goosebumps on my arms, and I felt faint. I didn't know what Leroy spoke of— this man was of a different caliber.

"Killian Sparr," The introduction rolled off his tongue with smooth charisma. He reached for my hand and slowly pulled it towards him, kissing it. It felt like accidental electrocution when his lips touched my skin. "I bid you adieu," he said, gracefully bowing. My jaw dropped until Leroy appeared behind him, nodding.

"Oh, so soon?" When my voice finally worked, I sounded like a five-year-old asking for candy.

Killian still had his intense gaze on me and my right hand in his. We broke our gaze and looked over at Leroy, who was livid.

"I feel that is what's best to remedy the situation," Leroy huffed, "Madam, if I may…you have so much work to do. I don't think it's a good idea to get distracted right now." Leroy used this last effort to change my mind. He was looking down at the floor when he spoke.

I let go of Killian's hand and tried to play it cool. This could get awkward.

"I don't have a problem if you want to stay for dinner tonight, Killian. Leroy is making more than I can eat as it is." The words flowed confidently off my lips, and I felt better until I remembered I was covered in flour. "Excuse me while I go wash up. It was nice meeting you." With a nod, I turned and left. Killian was smiling at me and never said yes or no, but I wasn't about to go back in there to get an RSVP.

With a spring in my step, I had my second wind as I speedily raced to the guest house. I drew a bath in the clawfoot tub the moment I walked in and peeled my clothes off. I laughed at my reflection in the large floor mirror propped up against the wall. After some soap, suds and shampoo I looked half normal again, and rested a few moments in the tub.

A handsome stranger had just kissed my hand. My mind wasn't fighting off thoughts of Dean for the first time in years. I felt a little strange, never having considered I'd meet anyone else I was attracted to like Dean. I didn't know anything about Killian, except that he was the definition of attraction.

I gave my face one more wash to ensure it wasn't crusted in egg. A little too much soap got in my eyes so I scooped water over them and reached for my towel. I groped blindly but couldn't find it. I opened my eyes and felt the burn. Then I screamed at the top of my lungs. There was a woman sitting on the edge of the tub.

***

VICTORIA

Josephine wasn't prepared to be a mother or a grandmother and especially was not ready to take custody of her granddaughter. But just like all the other things that had happened to her, she had no say in the matter.

While trying to enrich this child's life, she pointed Victoria toward her personal library. She seemed to take to all things of wisdom and knowledge; she had a great thirst for words. Much of Victoria's life was spent searching for something that explained her existence. Her feelings of abandonment ran deep, although she always tried to put on a brave face in front of Josephine. Still, the void in her eyes was ever present and clear to anyone who looked upon her.

Once, in passing, Victoria said something slowly and quietly under her breath when Josephine mentioned a trait she shared with her late father. She had read something in a book of poetry that rang true to her, quoting, "We go on in more ways than here; though our minds remember, our souls cheer." It was something her young mind took to as a way to find comfort, but Josephine reacted poorly and out of character. "Your great-great-grandfather cursed this family to tragedy, misery and hell."

Victoria's eyes widened as she digested the statement. Josephine immediately wished to undo the words she spewed. It was the brutality of watching a young child suffer for the deeds of a man who lived so long ago, unfairly taken out now. Josephine promised herself she would never speak of it to Victoria, and if she decided to, she'd wait until the girl was older. And now, only a child of nine, she'd let it slip from loose lips.

Victoria retreated without questions after the exchange, diving deep into the library. Josephine would watch as she dedicated her young life to a more significant meaning— finding a purpose for her existence. Victoria as a child was raised without any religion. Her parents never told her a word about God, and she didn't know of anything regarding His existence until she was in the library at Josephine's house. Josephine had not been religious as she felt it was off limits to her as the darkness of her life consumed her being.

Victoria picked up a Bible out of curiosity, started reading it, and felt love and peace wash over her. She learned all she could and put her faith in God, ceaselessly praying for the answers to the unspoken questions that always lingered.

When Victoria was sixteen years old, she lived and breathed the gospel and felt spiritually prepared to know the details of the 'curse' as Josephine referred to it. Josephine never told her the details of what actually happened, but Victoria was ready. God was the most high, almighty, and powerful. There was nothing He couldn't reverse, fix or heal. She spent years preparing for this, studying Christian theology, history, and the word of Jesus. She was so immersed in the texts Josephine was stunned it had taken such root as it did in Victoria.

The day Victoria came to Josephine and asked the details of the curse, Josephine leaned back in her chair. "What took you so long to ask, Victoria? I disclosed that to you nearly seven years ago."

Victoria shrugged her shoulders, but she knew the answer. "I wasn't ready for a rebuttal."

Josephine looked at this girl, now a young woman, who was as beautiful as her mother had been, but had something more. There was a stillness to her, a deep understanding of what was to be, a silence of her soul. When Victoria first came to her as a child, she was lively, energetic, and bubbly. The events to follow swiftly blew out the candle in her heart, hardening her for the cruel realities of the world. Now, she came to Josephine wanting answers she didn't find in any of her studies or from the ancient texts of Egypt to the Spirit of the Lord.

Josephine, nodding, sat upward. "My dear, your great-great-grandfather bound us to evil and torment. You see, there is no hope for us. It started with him, and though you and I are still here, notice how everyone we love has died. He traded our souls to a devil on a promise for wealth."

"What does that mean for us, Josephine?" Victoria had never addressed her aunt by her first name before; the sound of it alone was slightly alarming, but it let Josephine know that Victoria was tapping into her inner strength. She was old enough to know the truth of her history, the blessings, and the curses.

"Well, my dear, if there really is a heaven and a hell— I just don't know. His entire bloodline was bound to a man; one made of evil and he torments our lives and minds," Josephine was hesitant about the last part. "I know you are a spiritual person. I admire that, actually. I wish I could live that life."

"But Josephine— you can!" Victoria cried out. There was emotion in her voice. "God can save us from anything!"

Josephine smiled, but the cracks were forming in her mind. She had spent years being consumed by grief to the point where she could not imagine a way out. The things that had been put upon her made her unable to live a normal life, find peace, and most importantly, unable to raise her only child.

"I'm sorry, dear. I just can't get there with you. But again, I admire everything you have become. It's been beautiful to watch." Josephine rose from her desk and left the room.

"Do not believe every spirit." Victoria, quoting from her Bible, slowly turned from her and retreated. She was determined to find a breakthrough to her grandmother, to untie her from the chains of doubt that the devil had consumed her in. But Victoria began to wonder if something even deeper lay within Josephine.

Every so often, she would catch Josephine in the act of something peculiar. Once, she walked into the library and found Josephine facing the wall and mumbling under her breath. Victoria had tried to call over to her, and desperately tugged on her arm, but nothing would break Josephine's trance. "They were poisoned," Josephine whispered.

"Who was poisoned, Josephine?" Victoria responded in a shaky voice, afraid of the outcome. An air filled the room that could only be described as ominous.

Josephine snapped out of her daze, her body looking sunken and hunched as if she'd been standing for hours. Maybe she had? Josephine quietly glanced around the room, a look of realization washing over her face. "Oh, my dear, what did I walk in here for again?" A nervous laugh broke out of her, but it sounded forced, as she appeared to be distressed.

Then one beautifully crisp evening, Victoria wanted to invite Josephine to make hand pies with her and Leroy, and they believed her to be in the loft. Victoria knocked on the door, imagining Josephine admiring her grand birdcage that hung from the ceiling. It begged to share its beauty with a winged creature that Josephine always promised to get, but Victoria was still waiting on. There was no answer, so Victoria quietly stepped into the room, only to find Josephine sitting in front of the parallel mirrors. Her eyes bore into one, in a trance-like state– while she held a candlestick before the other.

Victoria was alarmed, but she yearned to understand what was happening in her home, so she whispered to Josephine, "Grandmother? What's going on?"

Josephine remained frozen, but the candle suddenly blew out with such force that Victoria yelled in fear. She ran out of the room, down the marbled stairs, and into the kitchen, where she choked out what she had seen to Leroy.

Another time, Victoria found Josephine in her garden, clipping off the buds of the dahlias, her favorite flower. Leroy had been standing at a distance, not wanting to reprimand her as she employed him. But the look of pain on his face said it all. Victoria jogged over to Josephine to see what this madness had been about, but when she reached Josephine, her eyes were wild. They were wide like moons and glassy like marbles. A glance in her direction was enough, and Victoria again felt that same darkness around her.

But God didn't give Victoria the spirit of fear, and she recited a verse to herself. I will fear no evil, for You are with me. The familiar calm came over her heart. She called out to Josephine with her eyes closed, so she may not see the eeriness again.

Her grandmother, with her back to Victoria, froze at the sound of her name, dropping the pruning shears. Victoria called out again, "Grandmother Josephine, what are you doing to your precious garden?"

Josephine let out a small cry. "Oh no, no, no! What have you done?" She was speaking very softly, but not to Victoria. In fact, Victoria did not know who Josephine was talking to.

"Are you all right, Josephine?" Leroy called out from the porch, where he'd been painfully watching the butchering of the flowers that he put so much work into.

"Yes, I am without harm. I'm so very sorry for the damage, Leroy."
Josephine still had not turned to face either of us. Leroy nodded and shrugged
off, back into the house. Victoria soon followed, but Josephine remained in the
same place.

After that day, Victoria believed there was a larger problem with
Josephine, and she decided to question Leroy to see if he agreed. "I first noticed
something– " he searched for the word, "– off with Josephine, a little after she
gave birth to your mother." Leroy looked physically pained by the memory. "She
would appear to be having conversations with her late husband. But at that
point, no one knew he was dead, except for her."

"What do you mean she knew?" Victoria was puzzled by this.

"She told me he would come to her in her dreams and said he was dead at
the hands of her Aunt Cora."

The name sparked many questions in Victoria's mind, as it was the first
she'd heard of her.

"But that's not nearly the most disturbing part of that story. You see,"
Leroy paused, giving the young woman's face a once over as if gauging whether
she could handle it. But her ability to handle it was proven to Leroy when she
faced this manic episode of Josephine in the garden. "Her late husband, Frank.
He told her he was in hell."

A pit formed in Victoria's stomach.

"Then the news reports came out. A list of those dead on the Triton–
Frank was among them."

Victoria nodded; she had read Frank's obituary a few years back. It was in
a scrapbook of articles related to his career, his factories, and accomplishments
that Josephine kept in her library, which was a vast collection of books that she
had never read; but were books that Frank had owned that she now treasured.

Victoria had diligently studied a collection of writings and publications,
sourced from all different religious beliefs, on deliverance from demonic
possession. Her obsession didn't just lie with the salvation she so desperately

wanted for Josephine— eternally and otherwise— but a way to get through to Josephine; it was something she could freely have. One day in Josephine's library, she uncovered a box full of ancient texts. Within this box, along with the dust and mothballs, was an old Egyptian book; the cover a large Eye of Ra. She hesitantly opened the book, imagining bats and curses flying out, but remembered there was already a demonic curse at play. Smirking at the thought, she flipped through the papyrus papers. They were handwritten in Old English, with words that she'd become familiar with in the Hebrew Bible. A page about the demonic power of curses caused her to slam the book shut. It's heresy, she mumbled. The book stated allegiance to the god of the underworld, which brought up many questions in her mind. How did this curse come about, and why? Not knowing the full extent of the curse or its meaning, Victoria decided that she wanted to know the truth.

Victoria played out the conversation in her mind. Josephine would give it to her straight and further discourage conversation about it, saying nothing would ever break its spell, they are all damned. Victoria would plead with Josephine that they are not damned. Jesus is the Almighty and can save them. Josephine would dismiss her, though Victoria would not be discouraged, and knew she could be saved. She would then have the perfect response, that she has the way to break the curse once and for all, to free Josephine from this madness. Josephine would cry, begging her to untie her.

Victoria set off getting ready for bed, fired up in the Spirit. Anyone and everyone can become righteous, and she would prove it, starting tomorrow morning. Holding the Hebrew Bible, she noticed something she had not caught before. The inside cover had a name pressed into it: Franklin Bagley. Why, if that wasn't enough reason for Josephine to pay attention, Victoria didn't know what was! This was his bible. Maybe he was in heaven after all? Her eyelids were heavy; reading these texts so late at night made them cross and grow blurry. The beautiful baby blue hand-blown glass oil lamp glowed next to her. She lay in the center of her bed, where her arm just reached the handle to turn the oil off. She whispered a few prayers before drifting off.

"Our Father in Heaven,

Hallowed be your name."

"And lead us not into temptation,

But deliver us from the evil one."

Victoria awoke the next morning with a feeling that could only be described as dread. Something was off. No sunshine came from the windows, nor did the bird's chirp.

She donned her robe and her house slippers and trekked downstairs. Leroy wasn't making an early morning pot of energizing tea, nor were there any lemon and rose biscuits on the table. The flowers in the entry wilted, something Josephine always took pride in keeping up with— but then again, she'd just butchered her flowers, so maybe she had nothing to replace them with.

"Leroy? Josephine? Are you here?" Victoria's voice carried through the manor, and a frigid gust of air was all she got back in return. Looking around, there were no windows or doors open, however.

Detecting motion out of the corner of her eye, Victoria thought someone had walked by the window. She ran to it, the soles of her slippers sliding on the marble floor, nearly causing her to fall. She grabbed the windowsill, searching outside, but couldn't see anyone on this side of the house. They headed left toward the back of the mansion, which led to only one place: the cliffs.

Quickly changing clothes, Victoria opted for her rain boots as it was a little muddy out there this time of day before the sun dried out the grass. She peeked in Josephine's room, which she never did— her aunt liked her privacy. That said, she was always available to Victoria during the day— unless of course, she was having what Victoria had come to know as a demonic episode.

She wasn't in her room. The door was shut, and her bed was perfectly made. A small spray of yesterday's flowers had been lying on the bed; Victoria recognized the ribbon, as she had recalled cutting it and handing it to Leroy. She remembered him pruning the rose bushes, and they had been laughing about him wearing her pink garden gloves because he'd misplaced his and the thorns were exceptionally difficult this year. The roses were pale pink, almost colorless, like they had been drained. Her empty vase was sitting at her vanity, so Victoria boldly ventured into the room and placed them inside.

She always respected her grandmother enough not to snoop in her room, but she just couldn't walk away from those roses that looked desperate for a drink. There was fresh water in the vase, just as she'd hoped. Victoria pictured Josephine hearing a bird chirping out on her balcony or Leroy calling to her, distracting her while in the middle of this small task. Victoria quickly placed the flowers in a vase. She knew she needed to vacate the room before being seen, but something told her to walk out to the balcony. And that was her first regret.

Victoria opened the curtains to the balcony, revealing a stunning view of rocky cliffs that glistened with the moisture just below. Half the year, a powerful water system washed beneath, but this time of year, it was barely a trickling creek. When Victoria opened the doors to the outside, it sounded unusually loud for autumn. She tried to rationalize it; maybe the mountains had an early snowfall that melted off? Thankfully, meteorologists would handle that part of life. It was a beautiful morning, so much so that Victoria nearly forgot everyone was missing from home. After a few moments of drinking in the fresh air, she turned to go back to her mission. But just then, the clouds shifted, and the sun appeared, beckoning her to spend a few more minutes at this gorgeous altitude on the private balcony she'd never experienced before.

Along with the sun came the beautiful song of the birds. The cliffs almost turned purple in the sunlight, or maybe it was just the angle she was looking. What she thought was glistening from the water now appeared to be within the rocks itself. What the— ? Surely, they were not sitting at the base of an amethyst fortune? She laughed it off. Josephine had never told Victoria explicitly how much money she had, nor did Victoria ask, but she was aware it was great, the kind that never ends. Victoria rubbed her eyes. What am I seeing? The longer she stared at the cliffs, it appeared that they had something slowly growing from them. Small gold shoots began to form, their speed accelerating, now growing towards her. They got closer and closer, and she reached out, ready to meet a vine with her hand. It was about to touch her palm as she wondered at its beauty. The shimmering delicacy had formed into a dark golden rope, ready to lasso her hand.

"VICTORIA!" Leroy shouted, frightening Victoria to the point of a scream. She snapped out of the daze, turning to him, who looked like he was a kettle about to burst. His face was piping red. "What is it you are doing in here? Hmm?"

She had never seen him this worked up before. In fact, she'd only seen him joyful and disappointed. Never angry.

"Well, I– " She was pointing behind her, turning to explain the golden rope. But when she looked back, it was gone, along with any purple hue of the cliffs. "I was, well, I thought– "

"You know you shouldn't be in Josephine's room." Leroy held the door open, motioning for her to exit along with him.

"Yes, I know, but have you seen her? I was looking for her– and– and there was someone outside." She now felt frantic, trying to explain herself and her actions, which she knew were breaking all respect and unspoken rules of the household.

Leroy's expression softened, turning into a frown. "I haven't seen her either. I was hoping she was with you." He paused, narrowing his eyes. "Who did you see outside?" he demanded.

"Well, that I don't know. I thought it was a man, I saw, or thought I saw, very dark short hair out of the corner of my eye. But I was in my slippers, and then somehow, I ended up here."

Leroy, squinting his eyes and pursing his lips, turned and left the room. A visible change in his demeanor made her anxious and she followed him to find out what happened.

Victoria stayed on Leroy's heels as he took off from the house, stomping his way to his garden shed. He wasn't dressed for gardening; his wingtip Sunday shoes were usually only worn in the house. Now they, along with the bottom few inches of his slacks, were covered in mud. He reached into his shed and grabbed a short, rusted shovel. It was solid metal, and the weathering on it made her think it must've come from the original dig of the house, with how old it looked.

Leroy spun around, going to the back of the house, only acknowledging Victoria when he mumbled, "Excuse me," as she'd been standing very close and he was trying to get around her. He was in deep focus, but instead of possession like Josephine had been exhibiting, Leroy's intentions seemed purely defensive.

They slogged through the mud to the back of the house, where the land slipped off ten yards away into an utterly landslide-looking cliff. Victoria remembered when she was younger, asking Josephine if one day the rest of the land would fall; taking the house with it? Josephine laughed, saying, "I hope not!" But neither of them really found any comfort in that.

Around the back of the house were many small stone structures; old smokehouses that Leroy still liked to maintain. Leroy walked to the third one on his left, which was about seven feet tall, rounding the smokehouse to see behind it. He swung his shovel as hard as he could, making a cracking noise that brought a stranger to his knees— a man that she could only see the top of his head from her perspective. It was enough to confirm that it was the dark-haired person she'd seen. Victoria screamed, not knowing who this man was or the threat he posed. Leroy hit him again and again. Afraid but needing to see the stranger's face, Victoria ran behind Leroy to catch a glimpse of the certainly-unconscious man. But when she got closer, the man jumped up, sprinting away as fast as he could. Leroy shook his head in disgust, still not acknowledging Victoria being a witness to any of it, and walked off.

She watched Leroy march away, and a small glimmer of blood on the back of his shovel held more questions than answers. As she looked down at this matted plot on the ground, Victoria saw a beautiful pocket watch with a cracked glass face and an engraving with the letter, 'K.' She didn't dare touch it, feeling the familiar sinister feeling she seemed to carry around with her these days, as often as the stranger who kept arriving unannounced. She worried that if she turned her back on this pocket watch, the mysterious villain would reappear. Yet she couldn't resist the impulse to look over the edge.

Victoria had no fear when she stood on the balcony, but now, standing on tumultuous soil without the railing for protection, she'd offered a quick prayer to God that if she were to fall to her death, that Jesus would meet her immediately. Her tiptoeing turned into a muddled crawl; the slippery slopes taunting her with every step forward. She was on all fours and made it close enough to peer down to the water. It wasn't surging like it sounded, rather the water just roared as if something was in its path. She analyzed the creek bed for dams that could be causing the slapping, and then she saw her.

Josephine lay lifeless in the water, her flaming red hair dulled by the stream, but the bright yellow dress she wore billowed around her body like a blooming flower. Victoria, collapsing into the mud, screamed into the abyss. She screamed until her voice made no sound at all, well beyond when Leroy returned to her side.

CHAPTER EIGHT

WILLIAM

William stood, gathering himself and brushing off the sand he was covered in. The waves were crashing loudly and carrying the voices from the balconies of the hotel he was staying in. He looked up to see that many people had an eye on him, wondering if he was dead. He lifted his arm up and waved while realizing his body had been very bruised during the night.

He hobbled back into the hotel, kicking the remaining sand off of his shoes and swiping at his clothes. The front door of the building had a wooden sign hanging by chains. 'Siren by the Sea.' Sounds about right, William thought. He reached for the door handle and paused, looking in the window. The reflection of the man who stared back at him was off; he knew it to be himself, but he felt something had changed within him. There was a pulsating fire within his veins. He peered closer into the glass— it was as good as a mirror in this light. Something had changed outside of him, too.

A woman at the desk, one that he hadn't seen before, looked up at him with piercing blue eyes and smiled. She was a sight for sore eyes, but he needed to gather himself before he could make a proper introduction. She introduced herself to William as Geraldine Kippling. He nodded and found himself stumbling around with words and walked off.

William climbed the stairs to his room but he wasn't alone: darkness walked beside him. And for the rest of the days of his life, it would share his company.

He stepped into his room, peeling his damp clothing off and draping it over the seashell bed frame. The balcony door had remained open all night, the cool air sending chills down his body. William drew a hot bath, while he ran his fingers over his upper lip repeatedly.

William never let his facial deformity bring him sadness, despite people in his youth having an issue with it. But once, after he had been traded to the white men, the woman who housed him for those short weeks commented about it. "You are made by the hands of God himself so there ain't nothing wrong with you. There is something wrong with the rest of 'em."

Though he never knew what to think of God, he knew what happened last night wasn't God but rather something darker, and now his facial deformity was gone without a trace. And who was to thank for that? When the water went cold, he decided to shave the beard he'd grown in his old life. Whatever lay ahead of him now, didn't need the guise of Scarsbeard. He slicked his hair and put on his cleanest clothes, closing the door behind him as he made his way back downstairs.

"My name is William," he tried to speak eloquently to the back of the woman who had talked to him earlier. She paused, hearing the words before she turned to him, smiling.

"William– ?" It was customary always to include a last name, not that she could've done anything with it at that time. But there was just one problem: William was, after all, an orphan and had no surname. Sitting on her desk was a catalog, which he skimmed out of the corner of his eye.

"Sears." It slipped off his tongue with such beauty that he swore there was a sparkle in her eye.

"Nice to be of your acquaintance, William Sears."

The conversation turned into a courtship, and soon after they were married. They exchanged vows in the hotel courtyard, which coincidentally Geraldine's father owned. He was into property development and had many buildings and land, offering William a position in the dealings, which William accepted. Her father, Jameson Kippling, wanted to do right by his daughter by giving them a piece of land for their wedding. Anywhere they chose, he told them, and money was no object.

William knew precisely where he wanted to live– in the cabin that belonged to Lowell's father. After the honeymoon, he traveled by horse and carriage to the countryside. When he came upon the house, he stood outside for some time before walking up to the door.

The last time he was here, he was just a child. Now, a married man, surely on the brink of having a family of his own, his greatest desire was revenge. Revenge on Lowell. On his childhood. And his memories. His mind never wandered from the curse that the creature on the beach promised she'd lay upon them, and he wondered if it was true.

Knocking on the door, he was surprised that someone had answered nearly immediately. And it wasn't just someone: it was the woman he'd threatened to leave her care.

The look of fear washed over her, but she didn't waver. Time had not been good to her, and she looked gravely ill.

"If you've come to finish what you've started, just do it. I'll be returning to the Lord soon anyway, and I do not fear evil."

William looked at her in pity, shaking his head. "No, ma'am. I am inquiring if you'd like to sell me this homestead. You see, I'm in the market to buy it."

She stood in silence for a moment, then let out a cackling laugh, exposing several missing teeth. She agreed and waved him in, explaining her husband had died in the war he'd recruited William for, along with the remaining sons they had. They settled on a price and which day she would leave, as he needed several to collect his wife's belongings and set the home up before she arrived.

At her polite questioning about his life, William shared some of the positive details. She said she was genuinely happy with how things turned out for him. He shook her hand, standing up, and walked to the door prepared to leave. One more question bubbled up inside of him.

"Do you know the whereabouts of Lowell?"

She was still reeling in her joyous windfall on what she described as an "Indian-ridden" homestead and didn't think anything about the question.

"He came a few years back, after his father died, to see if he was around.

Boy, by the look in his eye— I can tell ya, had his papa not already been dead, I think he was going to kill him. I don't know where he is now, though. He became a painter." She pointed to a small frame that hung next to the door behind him.

A rugged beach scene lay before him as he delved into the painting. Small shadowy figures were in the water, the land above them harder to distinguish. He pulled his head back, eyes refocusing. This was an Indian camp. He could make out the teepees now. Eyes widening, he looked at the signature on the bottom corner. 'K.S.'

***

VICTORIA

"Father, please don't leave. Stay with me! Can't you just stay with me forever?" Victoria's heart was in her throat. She had never been without her family before and wasn't sure she was capable.

"My sweetie, be a good girl and I will be back in a few weeks' time, okay? I have to go to work, but I do wish I could stay here with you." He wiped the tear from her cheek and kissed her forehead. "Every night when you say your prayers, I will do the same. It will be just like we are together, alright?" Daniel reached in for a hug to console Victoria.

Rose, her mother, was already getting in the car, calling out after him. "Daniel, we better get going. Don't want to be driving through the night now, do we?"

He nodded back at her, though she was already inside. Lilith, in the backseat, waved at her little sister before slumping back into the shadows.

"Goodbye for now, Victoria," he whispered. Her eyes were wild with panic as he drew back.

A small gust of wind blew through the open windows of the manor, and a sweeping scent of lavender from the dormant bushes took over her senses as memories flooded her mind. Lavender was in bloom when she first came here all those years ago.

When her maternal grandmother, Josephine, lived on the estate, she invited Victoria's family to stay a weekend here. Victoria, upon first sight of the mansion, screamed in joy. She was only a child but fell madly in love. Josephine Bagley was so pleased, as her daughter, Rose, was less than interested in anything to do with the estate.

The weekend had its obligatory visiting and catching up, but Rose seemed frazzled, out of focus. Her other daughter, Lilith, was an uninterested teenager who had just met the love of her life, Robert, and unless the conversation was about him, she had little intrigue. Rose's husband, Daniel, was doting on her and being his charming, outgoing self, almost to the point that no one noticed how withdrawn Rose was. Except for Josephine. She knew her daughter wasn't interested in spending time with her or this house to which she credited her 'lonesome, desperate' childhood to. Sure, there were no other children out here and most of the world didn't even know she existed. But Josephine never wanted this life either, and her solo pregnancy was the most challenging time of her life. Though she had been inseparable from her mother, she felt inadequate for the role. If only her husband Frank had been here to help raise her, surely his tenderheartedness would have made Rose a better person.

Victoria had a beautiful weekend at the estate. Josephine had given her free reign inside and out. She toured the library while snapping up books that she planned to read. After long walks in the garden, she napped near a bed of flowers that she had picked for her mother. Then on the day they were to leave, she studied some beautiful birds while sipping iced tea with fresh mint sprigs on the sun porch. Her mother called her to the car, and she felt her world crashing.

"But we can't go yet. I was going to learn how to make lavender lemon tarts today. We already milled the flour! You can't make me leave!" The tantrum wasn't like Victoria, she had always been well mannered so Rose and Josephine were taken back by this sudden outburst. Daniel tried to reason with his wife, nudging her that they didn't have to leave for a few more hours.

Josephine smiled to herself. She was flattered. She hadn't seen Victoria since she was an infant and she craved more time with her, but she wouldn't ever tell Rose.

"It's fine if Victoria stays with me the rest of the summer." Josephine smiled demurely. Lilith looked very concerned for a split second, as she had been lying in the back seat of the car and got up during the commotion, but then proceeded to lay back down. Daniel was visibly conflicted, but Rose knew the truth. She had never confided in Daniel about these matters, nor did she plan on it. Rose nodded to Daniel and pulled out a long cigarette from her brass case.

Saying his goodbyes to Victoria, her father looked deep into her eyes, holding her hands in his. He kissed her on the forehead and made her promise to be gracious and respectful. Leaning on the side of their gold Chevy, Rose took a drag of her cigarette, her perfectly painted red nails shining in the light. She tossed it to the ground, rubbing it out with her high heel, got in the car, and didn't say another word.

As her parents drove away, Josephine kneeled down and explained to Victoria that it was clear Rose was not in a good place. It wasn't Victoria's fault, and while it did not make sense to her now, one day it would.

As her parents drove away, her father began to tear up when Rose scoffed at him. 'Pull yourself together, Daniel. She will be fine.' But it was Rose and Daniel that would not be fine. The closer they got to their home on the beach, the foggier it grew. Lilith asked to be dropped off at Robert's house, even though it was nearly 8 pm. Rose instantly said yes, which took Daniel by surprise, and after a pause, he agreed and said he would return to get her at 9 pm. Lilith was sixteen years old, and she was always such a sweet child. He had met Robert recently and approved of the relationship, though Robert was two years older than Lilith.

Getting out of the car, Lilith ran to Robert's front door, where he was standing with open arms. Daniel could see his parents in the living room drinking tea. He sighed and drove off.

The fog intensified as they turned onto the rural highway. They couldn't even see a foot in front of them, only the lines down the middle of the road. Rose sat wide-eyed, nodding when he suggested that they pull over.

But it wasn't in time. A truck pulled onto the road and hit them head-on, killing them instantly.

Josephine had been preparing some cardamom tea when the phone rang. Who could that be? It was nearly 9 pm.

"Hello? Hello, Josephine?" The caller shrieked in a high-pitched tone, but the voice was unmistakable.

"Yes? Lilith, is that you? What's wrong?"

"It's mom and dad." And just like that, Josephine felt her insides drop to the floor while she was still upright.

"They were in an accident," Lilith was bawling uncontrollably into the receiver. "They are gone."

"I– I will be there as soon as I can." Josephine didn't know what else to say. She was overcome with emotion.

"Rose," she whispered into the abyss with her eyes closed. Doubling over, she choked on her tears in silence. Rose must have seen her death. That explained it, just like Josephine's own mother had forseen hers. Our family was cursed in that way, Josephine thought, stricken by the knowledge.

"Are you still there?" Lilith whimpered into the phone, which Josephine had been holding this entire time. "Yes," she whispered.

"You don't need to come yet. I am staying with Robert's family and I just need to know that you will take care of Victoria."

"Of course, I will."

"Thank you. I'll keep you updated on what's happening here. I'll call you later." With that, she hung up and Josephine didn't know why, but she had a feeling she would never hear from Lilith again.

Then Josephine remembered Victoria was here with her. She was safe, unharmed, and this was her chance to honor her daughter, Rose, by taking care of Victoria. And just that she would do. She pulled herself together, straightened the tea on its tray, and picked it up. Backing out of the swinging butler's pantry door, she traced her steps neatly into the kitchen, hallway, up the stairs, and then Victoria's new bedroom.

Victoria had a look of awe and bliss when she saw Josephine walk in with a tray of goodies. There were small biscuits that smelled like sweet cream and lavender, an ornate tray with fresh honeycomb on a drizzle of dark chocolate, and the loveliest smelling tea that soothed her bones before she even took a sip. She dove right in the second Josephine set it down on the tea table, not waiting to finish chewing the biscuits before drizzling honey on them and taking another bite. Josephine felt warmed; it was comforting to take care of this child. She had yet to hear the worst news of her life.

"Grandmother?" Victoria whispered, bringing Josephine out of her deep thoughts. Victoria had crumbs on her chin that were stuck to the honey. "Yes, my dear?"

"This is the best day of my life!" Victoria leaned in, hugging her deeply. Josephine went rigid, enjoying the hug from this sweet child but deciding she would spare her of the devastation. At least for tonight. She would save the heartbreak for tomorrow.

Josephine lay in bed staring out at her balcony, restless. She recalled her own mother's death and the many that followed. It never got any easier, and she hated to admit her daughter's death paled compared to that of her mother's— or her late husband.

Before she knew it, the sun rose and she slipped out of her bed, into her slippers and robe. Tiptoeing through the halls, she wanted to get to the kitchen and make Victoria a beautiful spread. But when she got there, she could see the dining room light was on, so she nudged the door open and let out a gasp when she found Victoria sitting at the table.

"My dear, you startled me. What are you doing up so early?" Victoria looked up at her; at that moment, she knew Victoria knew.

Victoria, staring down at the table, spoke softly. "I wanted to call my father first thing, since he always gets up so early. I wanted to tell him about the tea and the honeycomb. We usually only get honeycombs at Christmas. But Robert's mom answered. She put my sister on the phone."

"Victoria, I am so sorry you had to find out this way. I was going to tell you today. I just wanted you to get a good night's sleep first."

Victoria nodded, understanding.

Josephine pulled out a chair and joined her granddaughter at the table, taking it in just how small she really was.

"Is there anything you want to ask or talk about?" Josephine wondered what conversations would come from this; would there be feelings of abandonment? Anger? Resentment?

"Lilith said she is marrying Robert. What will happen to me? Will I have to go up for adoption?"

Josephine took a breath, relieved that she would not be taking in Lilith, and smiled. "You will stay with me, of course, my sweet granddaughter."

Victoria closed her eyes and shed a tear. "I am so relieved to hear that," she whispered.

"Good, it's settled then. Now, how about I make us something special for breakfast and we can continue this conversation? There is nothing you can't ask me, okay?" Josephine had many regrets, one of the biggest was her relationship with her daughter, and this was her chance to make it up to Rose.

"Can I help you in the kitchen?"

Victoria had many ups and downs over the next few weeks. She said all of her thoughts out loud, and Josephine would help her analyze and work through her feelings. Victoria's mother had been cold and neglectful, but her father was kind. She never forgot that. But there was something she always held back from Josephine. For years, whenever the telephone rang, or she heard a car in the distance, she had hoped it was her father. Since there wasn't a funeral, and she never returned to the family's home, in one way, it was never real to her. But the only call that ever came was years later, well beyond when Josephine died, from her sister Lilith's attorney. Their lives ended abruptly, the same fate as her parents; the difference being that Victoria hadn't known about their young daughter, and the lawyer said the girl, Sarafina, didn't even know who Victoria was. Lilith had been explicit about that in her will, not to reveal that part of her family to Sarafina. "She didn't want her daughter to know about, well— you," the lawyer had no delicate way to put it but said it was in Lilith's precise instructions that he call her.

"Look," the lawyer was very blunt, with a nor'easter accent thicker than honey. "My work here is done. I don't know what happened between you, nor do I need to. But now you know her name, you know she exists. I'm sorry for your loss. Oh, and there is a letter from Lilith being mailed to you. Bye now." Click.

The finality of the phone call left Victoria grappling for answers. "Leroy? Are you here?" He was her rock all these years, the first one she told things too or rather— the only one. She had no friends, and now, no family. Except there was a small glimmer of hope for the latter. She had a niece.

***

LILITH

Dear Victoria,

After much thought, I've concluded that I do not wish to expose my life to whatever evil Josephine dabbled with.

You see, our mother shared it with me when I turned thirteen, as surely, she would've with you.

There is some sort of 'spell' that she believed tormented us all, and I do not choose to live that way.

I hope you don't either. But for now, know that though I keep my life from you, I will always love you and pray for you.

Lilith

***

VICTORIA

Josephine had a seashell-shaped jewelry box given to her by the love of her life. The most fascinating accessories were inside and it was such a treat whenever she would show Victoria. An emerald ring with a thumb-sized stone, two trillion cut diamonds on each side, in a deep gold setting. Also, a pear-cut 7-carat blush sapphire with a diamond baguette on each side, set in a lovely warm gold. But the showstopper was her cherished cross-cut gemstone necklace. It matched the wedding ring that she never took off, and was quite the peculiar color.

"May I try it on?" Victoria once asked as a child, nine or ten years old. Josephine was very sweet and patient, but firmly said no. Smiling, she put the jewelry one by one back into their exact positions, adding, "This stone is very precious. You see, it's the rarest stone in the world. It was given to me by my mother, who, well…" She looked away, recalling something, before staring me dead in the eye, and placing her hands on my shoulders. "When you are older, you can do more than try it on. It will be yours, Victoria."

Victoria's eyes widened. She couldn't wait to be older, to be beautiful like her grandmother Josephine, and wear her cross necklace. She had long red hair that never lost its richness. Even as she reached her older years, Josephine remained youthful. A few weeks before she left, when Victoria was milling around her room, she broke the news that a friend was coming to stay.

"He's an old friend of mine, and he's accepted a caretaking position here at our home to help with the landscaping, cooking, and cleaning. His name is Leroy, and he will be living out in the guesthouse."

The news was startling. Until now, the two women had managed pretty well. They gardened and grew beautiful vegetables and purchased food from a neighboring farmer once a week. The lawns were mowed by two young men, one whom Victoria had a bit of a crush on. "This means I will be canceling our landscaping service." She said with a wink, and although Victoria never acted on it, it was fun for her to admire a boy.

After Josephine left her room, Victoria realized the manner in which she had strategically changed the subject from hiring this strange man, Leroy, to firing the two lawn care men. Why suddenly hire help, especially to be in the home? They hadn't had many guests. The last one was an artist visiting for a few weeks to do some portraits, and before that, Victoria's family visited when she was a little girl. They left her there, and her parents left the earth the same day.

Sometimes, that thought pained her. She had felt a strong connection with her father when she was a child, but her mother never seemed to bond with her young daughter.

That day they left her, Victoria's father looked back before driving off. His face was pained, but he continued driving. Ever since then, Victoria made the decision not to feel sorry for herself; looking to Josephine for the lead on that outlook. Her grandmother's strength and grace were enamoring; she'd been dealt the worst hands you could imagine, but she'd never given up on her life or Victoria.

Once every few weeks, Josephine would take Victoria out to the markets. They were home dwellers, so seeing other people with their stares and biased whispers was always strange.

Neither of them liked the attention, and it became less and less that Victoria would want to go.

But when Victoria was older, Josephine would insist, "You need to be out, to meet a suitor. I want nothing more for you than to find a prince! Don't be an old maid like me." Josephine was always encouraging, but aside from Victoria thinking the lawn boy was cute, there was no spark with anyone. Her only desire was to go back and get away from these people.

Josephine would always cause quite the stir out in public because of her remarkable beauty. She barely aged in her sixty years of life. The gossip of the town would ensue along with a whirlwind of rumors. Josephine would always smile, and let them wonder. It wasn't a defense mechanism; she truly didn't care what people thought. And that was the most beautiful thing about her.

Back to reality, Victoria walked over to her bedroom balcony, pulling back the purple velvet curtains and peach sheers, staring out at her existence.

"The cliffs of amethyst and gold," she softly spoke, half expecting Josephine to respond, as Victoria had heard her mumble those words in a trance once. She'd been gone for decades, and Victoria accepted her death long ago, but Josephine was always heavily on her mind, along with the feelings of regret.

She would often pray that Josephine, wherever she was, had accepted Christ before she died, even though she knew Josephine had been adamant against the idea. While Victoria didn't believe in hauntings, she knew evil spirits walked the earth to do the devil's bidding— she often felt like these spirits were posing as Josephine, taking on her characteristics in order to confuse Victoria into thinking it was something else.

Still, when the voices came, and Victoria started blanking on more significant gaps of time, her rationale told her it was likely a mental illness, though that clarity faded as fast as it came. It was immediately outweighed by the darkness that she'd been attracting her entire life— a darkness she fought so hard against. Josephine had always encouraged her to study and learn as much as possible— the implication that it was pointless to try and be righteous, because they were doomed anyway. She had only verbalized it one time; and before Josephine's death, Victoria's faith was so strong she wouldn't allow her mind to entertain that idea for a moment.

Victoria's scriptures taught her about God's eternal love for us, and her life revolved around Him. But as the years went on, she felt something terrible was creeping in. When the wind blew, she'd smell a sweet lilac fragrance, only for it to turn sour. Or she'd return to her room and some belongings were gone, only to reappear a few days later in a different location.

The years following Josephine's death were taxing on Victoria. She would experience bouts of depression that would last for months at a time, losing all interest in her studies in the Word— only to be brought out of it suddenly and without notice. She would then be in a near-manic state of joy, working in her gardens, writing poetry and prose, and walking in the evenings with Leroy. Until the voices would start up again, sending her a dump load of doubt, darkness, and grieving, until she would slip back into the abyss of her wandering mind.

***

SARAFINA

Reaching for a grip in the tub, water splashed everywhere. My screams had not subsided and the woman was still locked in a dead stare. I hastened out of the basin and grabbed a towel. She had her back turned to me now, not posing an immediate threat, so I demanded to know who she was.

No answer. I yelled it again, nothing. Now I am angry.

I marched over to her in my dark purple towel. She looked up at me and all at once, I saw it so clearly. The striking resemblance to my mother took my breath away. I let out a cry as I stumbled backward, catching myself on the wall. Could it be? "Victoria?" My face twisted. I barely whispered the words in my confusion. After a short stare down, I reached out to touch her. She mouthed something to me, but I couldn't hear anything.

My fingers felt the slightest texture of her dark green dress before she vanished into thin air.

"Wait, wait!" Screaming into the empty void, I added, "I'm not afraid. I'm sorry, please come back!" Just then, my foot caught a slippery spot on the tile and I yelled out, grasping for the tub as I fell down. My head connected with the pearly white basin; all I saw was stars.

I woke up still in the tub. It must have been a night terror. Or was it? The water had gone cold, and my teeth were rattling. My head throbbed in pain, but not from one central location. I got out of the water and reached for a towel. How strange, there was a towel before I got in the tub, and now there's not.

I looked around the room. A damp towel is dropped to the floor about where I was standing in my dream. I grab the towel and wrap myself up in it. My chills are taking over me now, and my hands are shaking. The bathroom light is bright compared to the dim glow of the living area outside, and I tiptoe, straining to find my way. Suddenly I sense I am not alone.

My mind takes me back to the Sunday church teachings of my childhood. One week, I overheard a woman begging the pastor to cast a demon out of her. She had sworn she had one that was giving her paralyzing nightmares; but the pastor said something about it being the wrong kind of church for that.

Feeling a new awareness of the possibility of evil around me, I immediately began praying out loud. "Dear Jesus— it's me, Sarafina." My teeth chattered uncontrollably, and my mouth felt dry, my tongue a foreign object behind my lips.

"I know it's been a while. And I'm so sorry." Sobs take over, my tears flowing into a river. What was supposed to be a prayer for protection shot me into long-winded repentance.

"I'm afraid there is evil here, Lord. Please protect me from it."

A strange noise began, almost like music, but muffled. It grew louder and more distinct. It was a woman humming a song with a few words here and there.

Now I started crying louder as the chandelier began to sway. The breeze outside couldn't account for that. This was something else. A bloody edge of the tub made me instinctively reach for my head. My hand came back red.

It was a fast-paced song, sounding like something from the early 20th century. The only words I could clearly make out were 'maniac'. The sound was coming from above. A faint, choppy sound that only a phonograph could produce started up. An upbeat piano and a man singing— it was the song that was being hummed, and it was growing louder and louder.

I backed out of the room and closed the door. My body tingled uncontrollably as I made my way to the loft and dressed. My mind calmed as the Lord did his work on my heart, but I still wanted to get away from this cottage as soon as possible. I combed through the closet with shaking hands. Strangely, some of these were not my clothes. Megan must have forgotten them and taken mine by mistake, and I couldn't find my corduroy jacket I'd been wearing yesterday.

I found a long sleeve chartreuse blouse and jeans with boots. I blotted the wound on my head, covering it with my hair as I pulled it down from its clip. What just happened? And why did I feel like something darker was at play?

A tree tapped on the window, making me scream again. I couldn't get out of the guest house fast enough. My mind shifted to my gorgeous house guest. I felt a little safer knowing he was on the premises. I went downstairs from the loft and flipped on four lights throughout the place. The bathroom door was now shut, with the light on inside. Staring at the crack under the door, I decided I would never go back in there under any circumstances.

"Looks like I don't have a bathroom anymore." My voice was raspy, and I reached for some water in the kitchen sink. Twisting the faucet, nothing came out. I get a creeped-out feeling I have company again as I reached the door, finding my jacket hanging on the rack that wasn't there before.

The wind had picked up outside, and it was unseasonably cold for this time of year. It was a long walk to the mansion that I took in a half-jog. A little perspiration dotted my hairline when I made it to the front door.

"My dear, you look like you've seen a ghost!" Leroy was taken aback by the look in my eyes. He took a step towards me and whispered, "Who was it?"

"I– I don't know what or who it was. I think it was a night terror." He nodded with a look of understanding. He whispered again, asking where the necklace was that Victoria had given to me. I reached around my neck, knowing it had fallen off days before, but I was hoping it would turn up still.

Leroy crossed his arms, his smile fading. "My dear, there is something you need to know about Josephine." His voice dropped into a whisper. "She was deeply into the occult practices. You must protect yourself from that evil because it's still here today." He reached into his pocket, pulling out a necklace with the most unusual gemstones, different from the one Leroy wore. There were three charms; a thin cross and two small stars. "This belonged to Josephine when she was a girl. You can wear it. But know, it is just a symbol that's completely empty of meaning if you don't have the faith in God to protect you." His eyes implored me to put the necklace on, and I did.

"I do believe." My eyes grew moist again. When the river of peace washes over your spirit, it must flow directly from the eyes because I couldn't stop crying.

Leroy was relieved to hear it. "And madam, about our house guest. You see, Josephine– ", A wine glass being tapped with a knife summoned us into the dining hall. Leroy was once again angered by Killian's presence as he huffed and stormed off into the kitchen.

CHAPTER NINE

VICTORIA

Victoria watched as Leroy dug a grave in the garden. She had been particular about where she wanted it. Although the property had a cemetery, she wanted her dear grandmother to rest amongst the flowers. For her marker, he had someone from town come out, and together they drug over one of the angel statues. Victoria didn't have a preference as to which. She thought they were all beautiful and had a likeness of Josephine, which she assumed was why Frank had chosen them for this estate. But after they brought the closest one over and turned it to the top of her grave, Victoria immediately regretted not choosing one.

It was the saddest angel she'd ever seen— or maybe it was just in this context? The angel's arm was outstretched, and when the men turned to walk away, a bluebird landed on its hand. This brought tears to Victoria all over again. She had cried more in the last few days than she ever did for her parents. But her parents, though her father was dear to her, left her here. Josephine was the one to raise her, and Victoria felt very pained that she was unable to change her grandmother's mind about God and heaven before she died. She would continue to feel unbearably guilty for the rest of her life.

The following weeks threw her off her orbit so entirely that even Leroy couldn't keep things together. He'd known Josephine since she was pregnant with Rose, and he'd been with her through it all, now helping her in death. He would stay on at the Bagley Manor, picking up the pieces of her mysterious death, and help her kin— Victoria.

The two would often sit together at the dining room table neither speaking nor eating, both minds rambling off what-ifs, how's, and whys in unison. They never talked to another about their feelings as things this strongly felt went without saying. Loss this great, which neither of them were unaccustomed to, had to make its way through the body and through their lives, tearing it up completely piece by piece. By sitting together, they gave each other permission to feel, to question, and to wonder without judgment— or a timeline.

But after a while, their seatings became shorter and shorter, then began to be filled with chatter. Idle talk at first, Did you see the ivy is turning colors? I need to paint the shed this week. Wow, this tea is phenomenal. This went on for a short time until they both felt they had the unspoken permission from the other to come out of mourning. One day, out of habit, Victoria went to the dining table shortly after waking, like they had done for months. But Leroy wasn't there— instead, he was out in the gardens. This pleased Victoria, and she enjoyed watching him pruning the flowers. She, too, felt that she could continue doing what she enjoyed before the tragedy. The only problem was that her entire life focus, other than God, had been showing a way for Josephine to escape from her demons.

There were so many questions she'd never asked Josephine, and now she was afraid they'd remain unanswered.

"Leroy," she called from the porch, walking towards him in the gardens.

"Yes madam?" He was smiling. He always used to say how much joy the garden brought him.

"I— I hope I'm not interrupting." Not one to impose, Victoria knew she needed to gain independence from him, but he had just been with her constantly lately, and now she felt reliant on him.

"I have a few questions for you." Where would she even start? The cliffs? The man she watched as Leroy beat him with a shovel, before he disappeared?

Leroy's smile turned to a frown, and she immediately regretted following him outside. She anxiously changed her mind, "You know— never mind."

Leroy's eyes softened. He had to tell her eventually. He took off his gardening gloves, putting the clippers into his wheelbarrow.

As Victoria turned away, Leroy sputtered out the words that he could barely admit to himself.

"His name is Lowell Killian Sparr. He's related to me— in a way— distantly. From a long, long time ago. And unfortunately, I believe he is also the one that possessed Josephine."

Victoria's jaw dropped, but she had been so drained from the shocking moments in her life that she found it easy to understand. She knew demons to be real, and possession, evil— this world was full of it. That morning she had read in her new copy of the Holy Bible, which she received as a gift from Leroy after Josephine had died. "A way to find hope again," he said. The Bible had its way of revealing things when you most needed to hear that message, and this morning it had been about life not being without troubles, but God was always a constant. We must stay on guard for the things of this world.

After Leroy spoke for some time about his relative, who Victoria learned had been born in the late 1800s and had some otherworldly abilities, this became very clear: he was obsessed with Josephine; an infatuation that had a twisted core; since it wasn't for love, but rather, for control.

And it was very plausible he had been responsible for her death.

"I was the firstborn to my unwed mother, Adelaide." Leroy's voice was pained, sounding like a tidal wave of emotion was nearing the breaking point. "She was a young girl still, and my father, Nicolai, was from the poorest family in town. But, they were deeply in love." He shrugged his shoulders, feeling the wisdom of the situation. "Adelaide came from one of the wealthiest families, and her parents were less than pleased with the situation. They forbade the relationship, rejecting me before I was even born." He looked away, withholding something. "She left me in a basket on Nicolai's family's doorstep when I was an infant." Victoria took a deep breath, feeling the anguish in the air.

"My mother's parents had already committed to her marrying another young man in town; uniting the two families would create a monopoly in business for them, and that's all it was. But the marriage didn't last long because they never loved each other."

"Nicolai never hid anything from me. He was a wonderful father. I was always content with my upbringing; it was full of love. Something that I know my mother never had. And my father instilled a work ethic in me at a very early age. But oh, did I love to work with him." Leroy shined in delight at the memory. "We worked in a bakery together. And that was when I saw my mother for the first time."

"She rolled up the cobblestone streets one morning in a carriage. She had a long-brimmed hat, and when she looked up after stepping out of the cab, she saw my face and knew I was her son. And I recognized her from the photographs.

"She had two other children by then. She kept walking, but later came back alone to tell me that she was going to marry again. A man named Killian Sparr."

If Victoria's jaw could've dropped any lower, it would have fallen off.

"He took my mother for a ride, to say the least." There was a bitter tone to Leroy's voice, and the sounds of regret. "He came into the marriage with many gambling debts, but she paid them all off. They were only married for a year before she tragically died, the cause never determined. But he inherited all of her wealth. And now he can't keep himself from tormenting your family."

Surprisingly, this did bring some strange comfort to Victoria, of foul play, meaning Josephine hadn't just grown tired of her life with Victoria and decided to check out. Then it dawned on Victoria that Leroy had questions about Josephine's death and didn't mention it? When the policeman came from town, roughly an hour's drive on unpaved roads during a very wet spring, Leroy had every chance under the sun to say something, say anything. They all assumed it had been self-inflicted. But in Leroy's defense, how exactly would, "My distant relative born in the 1800s is still walking the earth and possessed Josephine to do this" sound?

"What about the cliffs? I saw— things, that morning." Leroy's nodding turned into a head shake. He knew it all too well.

"That's one of his tricks, making you see things, experience fragrances and think things that aren't possible– real, or Godly in any right."

Victoria awoke from her daydream. She didn't often allow herself to travel down memory lane, but in honor of today, she was permitting herself to feel it all. Today was the anniversary of when she last saw her father. She had been staring out her window for so long that her eyes hurt from dryness. She rubbed them with her frail hands, the tears she didn't feel before, now soothing her. A sparkle from across the room caught her eye. It was the chandelier lighting up her jewelry in the reflection of her vanity mirror.

Staring at her reflection, she wondered if she still had her father's eyes after all these years.

A voice interrupted her thoughts, saying, "Your father never loved you." She immediately dismissed it. It was just a part of the torment she'd been battling for the last twenty years or more. She wondered if it was the same demonic force that fought with Josephine that, in some debatable way, caused her death– whether it was self-inflicted, looking for relief, or convincing her to do so.

"Leroy?" Victoria called out. Her head tilted sideways, resting against her headboard as she returned her empty gaze to the window.

Leroy appeared at her bedside immediately. "Yes, madam?" He smiled, but it didn't reach his eyes.

She looked at him, the only person who'd ever stayed in her life, but now he was an old man. "I feel terrible." Her face turned away and she spryly got out of bed.

He looked very concerned at first, but then laughed. "Victoria, you appear to be in perfect health, maybe lacking some comfort is all. Why don't I go get us a cup of that tea you like, with extra cardamom and ginger?"

She hadn't been listening but obliged. "I'd like that. Thank you, Leroy." She reached out and held his arm before he turned away. "Leroy– " she hesitated,

"– you are my family." She stared into his face as if searching for something, a reason, or meaning. The voice in her head returned, "He's only here because you pay him."

Leroy, tearing up, suddenly knew what this was all about. This time of year was always hard on her, with unresolved feelings of abandonment from her family. "Madam Victoria, I simply think of you as my world, and it has been my honor, as it will continue to be. Now, let me go fetch that tea." He broke the gaze, acknowledging her holding his arm by gently squeezing hers, and swiftly turned on his heels to go out the door.

What Leroy didn't know was that she was slipping again. For reasons he may never understand, she couldn't live like this anymore. Pretending there wasn't a problem in her world, like it was a good place, studying, praying. Pretending she wasn't going absolutely mad. She would pray ceaselessly, and in fact, that was the only time she ever found peace from the darkness, the voices, the spirit that wanted her to doubt. She knew the devil wanted her to doubt, and would have that clarity while in prayer. But the moment she would wake from her deep meditation and hear the voices, and see the evils that surrounded her– the remembrances of things that happened– she had the unbearable urge to end it once and for all. She wondered if there was a medical intervention that may help her. When Leroy came back, she would ask him to set her an appointment.

Victoria took a look around the mausoleum of the room, full of ups and downs of life and emptiness. Everything had once been Josephine's, and that weight was always present. Victoria went to the vanity, which was carved exquisitely to look like two hands holding a mirror. Sitting on the tufted bench, she held the jade comb her father had given her for her seventh birthday. It was an extravagant gift for a child, as her mother objected, making her love it all the more. A small etching in it read "V". Pulling back a front section of her hair, she slid the comb in and took a look at herself. Despite her five decades of existence, she was uniquely pretty, with long auburn hair that hadn't grayed yet.

She had evergreen eyes and smooth skin; the soft freckling of her tan cheeks encapsulated a tender youthfulness. She took herself back to the biggest compliment anyone had given her; when her late grandmother Josephine said, 'You look just like your father when you smile.' But as her life raged on, there was less and less to smile about. Her real life would start in heaven.

She often wondered if her father had been a Christian man. They never went to church as children, but she knew better than that. Church never made anyone anything. It went so much deeper than that. She wished that Leroy had met her father. She often told him how much he would've liked him because everyone did.

With a feeling of finality, she got up from the vanity and went to her tea table near the window. Gold vines had been placed there, which startled her, though she didn't remember doing that herself. Twisting back to the mirror, she was no longer wearing her comb either. A bird chirped on the railing of her porch. She thought it to be late afternoon, but it was still morning by the light. Take a deep breath. It's just your mind playing tricks on you. Things were not always what they appeared, she reminded herself. Sitting on the edge of her bed, she prayed.

Victoria picked up her favorite book from the tea table, admiring the red leather-bound Holy Bible with black embroidery of her name on the cover, the gift from Leroy all those years before. She wrapped one of the long, gold vines around it and set it down in a pile of dahlias that had also just appeared. Leroy always picked them for her. They grew to become her favorite flower, or did she just love them because of Josephine? She added the comb that was now back in her hands, and there was a small collection of rare gemstones and a carved cross. These were her most prized possessions in a home full of Edwardian antiquities, and now they lay on a cocktail table in the corner of a room. She heard a voice, 'Wherever you are going, you won't be needing these.'

What an odd thing to say, she thought to herself. Could this be death? Movement out the window brought her back to her muddled reality. Thinking there had never been a more beautiful day, she walked out on the sprawling balcony, which she usually didn't trust herself to do. The cliffs were shining magically, and taking a deep breath, she let herself enjoy it. Gold sprouts were popping out before her eyes, and more appeared with every breath she took. A bird sang in the distance. At the sound of its beautiful song, she closed her eyes, and a tear rolled down her cheek. The air felt so good. She found herself leaning on the railing and then swinging a leg over. Her laced boots barely had any traction, and her grip was even less reliable.

When the gold flowers started blooming, she swung her other leg over the railing. Her green, muslin dress was very thin. The cold air shocked her skin. Drinking in the fine air mist with all of her senses, she felt alive in her madness for the first time. A presence loomed over her, but she outstretched her arm into the sun, and it was gone. Laughing to herself, she mumbled, "This must be heaven." But she never forgave herself of the guilt for not getting through to Josephine before she died and couldn't believe she deserved forgiveness from the Lord. She cried out to him, "Lord, am I forgiven? Please forgive me." The whisper of her words felt clear in her mind but sounded jumbled as she spoke.

With a gust of wind, a small blue bird fell from the sky and landed on the balcony. Victoria gasped and reached out to him, suspending all of her weight on one leg. The bird appeared to be stunned, but then another bird landed on the railing next to her. Strangely, its pulse matched hers.

The amethyst cliffs were sparkling, as they often would. She knew it wasn't good or right or normal to be seeing this, and in years past, she would do everything in her power to keep her focus away. Because with the cliffs, the demons, the devil— the voices would come.

Just like Josephine felt before her death, Victoria knew it wasn't true, but she, too, felt damned. Damned by this presence. Damned by this illness. This fog, these cliffs, this house, and everything in between. Victoria started to recite the Lord's Prayer, still awkwardly sitting on the railing.

"…and deliver us from the evil one."

Snapping her head towards the cliffs, the vines and flowers were gone. Just then, God spoke in her heart, and she had the overwhelming knowledge that she was Saved by grace, and it was not time to go yet. The awareness of her position on the railing also flooded her. She cried in her newfound joy while she doubled down on her grip, trying to lean backward to the balcony floor.

She had finally received the answer for her soul that she needed at the right time. But she became slightly twisted on the balcony, and as she tried to shift her weight, her front shoe lost its footing. She needed to lean forward and balance her foot on the outside in order to kick off to go backward. A sweat broke out over her body as she dangled. Coming up the hallway, Leroy had the tea on its cart that he kept atop the stairs. He was hollering out that he had something extra special just out of the oven when he discovered her on the railing. His sudden yell jolted her and ultimately pitched her body forward, neither her wrists or feet strong enough to keep her upright. She screamed out as her body relinquished itself to the rocky waters of the river hundreds of feet below.

"Victoriaaaaa!" Leroy cried out, crashing the teacups and cart to the floor.

He rushed to the railing as if he could grab her and hold her back. He was distraught at his delay, frantically searching for her body at the bottom of the ravine. What had she been wearing? It was definitely dark in color. All he could see were stones. There was a stinging mist on his face and he could taste the tears pouring from his eyes. Devastation took over as he gasped for breath, crashing to the floor of the balcony. "Lord, I can't do this again!" he cried out.

***

SARAFINA

"Well, speak of the devil!" I shouted as I saw Killian in the corner of my eye, a little too excited for my good, immediately regretting the tone of my words. I waited a moment, catching my breath. Wait. What just happened? Now my great-grandmother is coming to see me? I hear Killian call out my name and am brought back to earth.

My heart led me into the dining room, with its tall, vaulted ceilings and emerald and copper accents. Large picture windows facing the aspen woods give it an eerie ambiance, but staring at him, I felt safe for the first time in my life.

Killian stood as I entered, taking my hand in his. With a long pause, he kissed it. Never breaking eye contact, he pulled out the chair next to him and motioned for me to sit. When I did, he took my face in his hand and brushed my cheek, running his fingers through my hair. Those deep-sea eyes drank me in as he leaned in with his lips to my forehead. I couldn't get close enough to him. A yearning in my body made me feel crazy and whole. His breath was on my hair as he held me, still sitting in separate chairs, waiting for Leroy to enter and break the ice. Waiting, waiting— hoping he never did.

It felt like minutes had passed when Leroy rang a small bell, announcing his presence before he entered. My body sprang backward, the fear of getting caught between these two horrifying me. Killian boldly grabbed my hand with his, holding it atop the mahogany table, challenging Leroy with his eyes. Leroy wouldn't return Killian's look as he silently served the food. I felt bad for Leroy, and my guilt took over as I released Killian's hand.

Leroy had served a delightfully fragrant salad first. There were diced oranges, a rainbow of kale and a flavorful pomegranate dressing. An edible flower lay on top making this meal even more memorable.

Killian had the same arrangement, but his flower was different. He looked at it for a moment, before taking a napkin and pulling it off to the side, leaving it on the tablecloth. "It's edible," I mentioned to Killian, and he shook his head in return. "Not this one," he spoke softly and his voice made me tremble. I didn't really hear his words. If I had, things would have quickly gotten out of control. All I heard was a soft song coming from the ballroom across the hall.

Our second course was a prime cut filet with a purple mashed potato. Leroy had left the skins on, which made a gorgeous presentation. My steak was cooked to perfection and tender. I glanced over at Killian, whose meat was seared rare. Blood covered his plate, but he never spoke a word about it.

Rosemary and thyme bread rolls made from scratch were placed at the center of our table, lying on a bed of fragrant lavender. Leroy also lit the candelabra for us beforehand, setting the atmosphere as the music grew louder outside the door.

"Do you hear that song?" I asked, smiling at Killian, thinking Leroy had put it on for some dancing after dinner. He wasn't as mad as he seemed to be.

Killian's chin tilted, and he paused his movements, listening. He shook his head. "It's coming from the ballroom. After dinner, I'll give you the tour." He smiled, taking my face with his hand and pressing his forehead into mine. Things were moving a little quickly, and my heart raced with panic. I felt a fire in my soul when I looked at him, as anyone would with his stunning appearance, but I have yet to learn anything about him. Except, of course, that Leroy hates him.

To make matters more confusing, he didn't say much at dinner. I had expected a long conversation, ending the evening with us both having told our life stories, and if we weren't together, dreaming of it. Dinner ended with Leroy announcing it was time for dessert. Killian again reached for my hand, but this time not to defy Leroy. He leaned over to me and kissed my forehead.

The dessert was black tiramisu with a deep red strawberry on the top. Killian took his strawberry and fed it to me. I giggled, leaning in for a bite, and experienced a flavor I didn't recognize. It was a deep, dark flavor, almost bitter. My tongue felt thick as I chewed. I searched anxiously for a napkin as I spit it back out. "What was THAT?"

Leroy scuffled out of the kitchen. "Is everything to your liking, madam?" His eyes widened as he saw the only thing eaten was Killian's berry.

"This strawberry tastes…off."

"Oh, does it? My apologies. I just picked that this morning. Here, let me get you a different one." Leroy took the half-bitten berry and looked at it, smelling it. Finally, he tested it himself. "Oh, my goodness, madam, you are right! That berry is perturbing. So sorry to have served it to you." He flew into the kitchen and returned with several strawberries on a copper platter, some even dipped in chocolate. I started on my black tiramisu, which was to die for. Killian began toying with my hair which made me too nervous to chew in front of him.

"Don't be shy in front of me."

The words reminded me that I must be acting dorky. I tried to take another bite but ended up pushing it around my plate with my spoon. Thinking about feeding him a taste, I became alert when I heard Leroy coughing in the kitchen. We both turned our heads and waited for him to stop.

"Is he choking?" In a panic, I slid back the chair and peeled myself out of Killian's grasp. He followed.

"Leroy!" I ran to him when I saw the scene. He had vomited across the kitchen floor before we entered. He was beet red, sweating, lying on his side on the black and white checkered floor. He moaned as I told Killian to get me a wet cloth.

"Of course, my love." My insides melted when he spoke those words, but I had to wait to revel in that.

"What happened?" Blotting Leroy's forehead with the cloth, I needed to piece the details together.

"Poison berry," he squeaked out.

What is this, Snow White? "Who would poison you!?" Looking around the room as if an unknown menace was going to appear. "Kill— -ill" Leroy was gasping for air and couldn't get the word out.

"Don't worry, I don't think this will kill you," I assured. "If it was going to, I think it would have already! What do I do? Should I call poison control?"

Killian came up behind me with a small vial of blue liquid. He opened it up and Leroy tried to roll and crawl away. Killian stood over him, and then knelt down, pouring the liquid right into his mouth.

"An antidote, of sorts. Leroy made it himself. Not sure if it will help."

Killian put the cap back on and set it on the counter. He shrugged and returned to the dining room without a second glance. Still in shock, I watched Leroy's breathing normalize until he felt well enough to have a glass of water.

After things calmed down with Leroy, he was back to puttering around the kitchen. He offered to open a bottle of wine and I agreed, grabbing three glasses for us from the bar in the dining room. He was surprised he was invited to join us when he saw the third glass, but sat down, clearly uncomfortable by Killian's presence. Leroy barely uttered a word, but Killian came alive for the first time that night, wildly recalling a story about an African safari he took with university professors.

"The mother giraffe came over to me in our topless jeep and licked my head! Her tongue was bigger than my leg!"

My wine-stained lips hurt from laughing so hard. He was funny, charismatic and charming. Leroy even cracked a smile.

When the wine was gone, Killian stood and held his hand out for mine. "Ready for that dance, Sara?" I awkwardly rose, suddenly feeling the alcohol hit me, but couldn't say no to this fairytale prince, who was already on nickname status, apparently.

The music coming from the ballroom had since stopped, but upon entering, a record player was set up on a table. A wooden bookcase with beautifully carved stars displayed a host of records to choose from. I had only been in the ballroom once on my first hasty walk-through, at which now I felt tremendously lame for not appreciating this home for its unique treasure. At that moment— being full of hope, happiness, and wine— was when I decided I would keep it.

Killian put on a record that was a soft sway, slow-dance type. He took my hand in his, and the other moved around my waist while he led. A marvelous dancer, he must have been professionally trained. He certainly had the body for it. I moved effortlessly, following his lead.

At first, I was looking around the room, but when the song changed, we broke our grasp momentarily and made eye contact. It was deep and intense.

Gazing into his eyes made my body feel like it was on fire with desire. It appeared like the room was full of people in my peripheral vision, but I didn't want to break away from his beautiful gaze. Smiling at me, he closed his eyes and kissed my forehead while we quickened our pace at the beat of the next tune.

As we spun faster, my vision was blurred, which I accounted to the wine, but the ballroom was suddenly full of people watching us dance. They were cheering, clapping, and lighting cigars. The dining room bar was in here, with a dapper bartender pouring scotch to men with thin mustaches. They were all dressed in black-tie attire; however not from this century. I looked down at my body and I was wearing a light blue gown and very distinct jewelry. I stumbled to a halt as Killian took my face in his hand and whispered, "Don't fret, my darling. Just enjoy it for the moment." And he too was in a tuxedo.

Nervously laughing, I nod. The song slows, and he dips me and dramatically kisses me. To say I saw stars would be an understatement. I saw planets and moons, and my whole life flashed before my eyes and my future, from my mother brushing my hair as a child to seeing the mansion for the first time and meeting Killian. Picking wildflowers with Killian in the fields, long summer days of him reading poetry aloud, and then being alone in the mansion, awaiting his return. The familiar feeling of devastation and abandonment choked me up inside.

When he broke away from my lips, ending our passionate kiss and pulling me upwards from the dip, the room was empty and we were in our normal clothes again. Killian was staring into my eyes lovingly while I felt fear. Why was I alone in my future? Where did he go, I wondered. Does Killian die? I pulled him closer and decided to kiss him again to have questions answered.

Pulling him into my embrace, I couldn't help but smile. He was remarkable, as was his soft kiss on my lips. I closed my eyes as tight as I could, waiting for… something. His kiss grew deeper and more passionate while I started pulling away.

"Is something wrong?" His eyes bore into mine with concern.

"No…it's just, well… did you see anything when we kissed?"

He laughed, winking at me. "I saw fireworks."

I decided to drop it. I didn't normally drink alcohol. I was weak to the effects.

We slow-danced to one more song, and he asked if he could walk me back to my guest cottage. I happily obliged, walking outside, but then I remembered the unwanted presence waiting for me there.

"Where are you staying tonight?" I had assumed he'd stay with Leroy, but after tonight I realized they were on hostile terms.

"I hadn't planned on staying at all," he said, taking my hand, "until I met you." Leaving a kiss on my forehead, he leaned in to kiss me again when a flock of bats flew overhead and startled us, so much that I let out a little scream and ducked. We both broke into laughter. He grabbed my hands and looked into my eyes, his silhouette defined by the moonlight.

"Why did you come?" I asked. "It doesn't seem like you are– close– with Leroy." Regardless of the answer, I was so grateful he did show up.

"I just heard the news about Victoria."

I felt ashamed for asking the question. As I scrambled to find the proper words, he looked down at his feet.

"I– I'm so sorry, Killian." I reached to hug him. "I didn't realize you were close."

He took me in his warm embrace and whispered, "Thank you. She was a very special woman. I would have loved for you to have met her."

Head down, I decided now was the best time to clear the air. "What happened between you and Leroy?"

Killian nodded, ready to answer. He put his hands in his pockets and looked up at the full moon.

"Tale as old as time itself– a misunderstanding now swept into the darkness forever, it seems. I just can't seem to make it up to him."

Darkness. I understood that. Searching this man's face under moonlight that never seemed to wane, I wondered if things were really what they seemed with him. My mind argued that he was enigmatic. But my energy was drained, so I hugged him, offering him to bed down in one of the rooms of the guest cottage. I would be sleeping in the house from now on.

***

WILD HORSE

Days after Ehawee passed in childbirth, the tribe felt the evil was spreading rapidly. Spirit Shadow became unwell and spoke of darkness around him; he could no longer feel Lakeena with him. There was only one thing they could do, and that was rid their lives of the spirits which haunt them now.

The women bundled up the babies in a soft hide with a layer of fur as the snowstorm raged on. The sky was overcast, and the air stung their eyes as Wild Horse and Spirit Shadow loaded up the infants and got on their horses. Their tribe watched them leave, while the women solemnly stared at the babies, they also mourned the loss of Ehawee, as her body lay wrapped in a blanket with scattered offerings surrounding her. Enahee, her brother, was inconsolable for days and never felt the desire to even look at the babies she brought into the world before they were taken away. He would later imagine what they would look like, if they grew with her likeness and round face and bright smile; would he recognize them if he saw them in a clearing or made trade with their people?

Spirit Shadow stalked the edge of the woods, placing the babies in a frozen meadow. Wild Horse knew the children wouldn't be found there by Spirit Shadow's design; the loss they brought to his family was immeasurable. Once he left them, he cried out to the spirit of Lakeena again, to ask if she was there.

The clouds then cleared, bringing out the sun for the first time in days, to which Spirit Shadow took as an omen that she was.

But Wild Horse couldn't help but notice the sun was shining on the babies, warming them from the frozen tundra on which their small bodies lay. Wild Horse told his brother to go back to camp to Ehawee and prepare her burial. The ground was too frozen, but they would make a way for her to be honored in death.

Wild Horse stayed behind, looking upon the babies as they stirred and cried, wanting to move them to a clearing where they would be found, but also wanting to honor his brother by letting them be. Wild Horse stayed, watching the children, until he heard horses pass by just beyond the trees.

He thought he ought to call out to the people but knew it would risk more evil coming to his tribe. But Wild Horse could not let these children die, because Ehawee wouldn't have wanted that. Though she didn't choose this fate, she wanted to raise the babies amongst her people and teach them what was right and true and beautiful. Wild Horse, being the leader of the tribe, had consoled Ehawee before the birth, when she told him that. Now, he was torn between being the leader of his people, where he was obligated to make the right and moral and wise decisions for his tribe- and the brother to Spirit Shadow, whom he would die for.

Before Wild Horse could decide, the babies let out a loud cry; loud enough to alert the people who were near, and he heard them talking before the footsteps became closer.

"There's a child out there!" A woman sang. "Take your gun with you, Billy, and go get that child."

The man's footsteps crunched in the deep snow. Wild Horse was long hidden in the trees, his horse he directed back towards camp while he remained with the babies. Wild Horse watched as the man who looked filthy but kind, who was a White Man like the father of the infants, scooped them up and told them they would be alright.

And they would be alright; Wild Horse repeated the phrase in his head. And he knew it was true, that they would, and he softly ran back through the trees to catch his horse, never to be seen by the White Man again.

CHAPTER TEN

WILLIAM

Years passed, and William and Geraldine welcomed two daughters that lived past infancy, Cora and Sophie. As they grew, he would listen to their mother teach them about Heaven, Hell, and the God that rules.

But William wanted a boy, and not just any boy. He wanted to adopt a child from the very orphanage he grew up in, to save a mind from the prison that it represented. Just like the Indians had saved him.

Geraldine was hesitant about the idea at first, but after thinking about it for a day, she suddenly became thrilled at the thought. It was settled; and they would make the short journey to the orphanage a fortnight later.

As they approached the doors, William suddenly felt very small. Here he was, with his bride and two small daughters in tow; but he wondered if he was good enough for a son. To teach someone how to be a man. When he caught his reflection in the glass window, he remembered just the kind of man he truly was. He was about to turn around when Mrs. May answered the door.

The reunion was everything they both had hoped it would be; she met his beautiful wife and family. He explained where he was living, to which her wide-eyed gape flashed her memories of just who else lives in those woods, and she wanted so desperately for him to bring up just what had happened that night, in this place, all those years ago. The event that left everyone in her care traumatized, plus the death of Denny, and he was nowhere to be found.

But he didn't say a word, and Mrs. May knew better than to bring it up to him in front of his new family; the writing was on the wall, he didn't want her to know about it, and who would?

One holler from Mrs. May and ten boys came rambling out of the main room. William and Geraldine smiled at the children, and a few were quite charming and talkative to her. William wondered if he remembered his childhood differently, seeing these sweet, adorable children that were bubbling over some old train set. But he didn't. The children that he lived with were cruel.

Geraldine turned to William. "Well, should we just take them all?" Her jovial spirit was contagious to Mrs. May, who was now sharing all the children's favorite foods, colors and chores.

"And Jack loves to garden, just like you did Wiliam!" William liked the sound of that; Geraldine cooed at the words.

"Which one of you is Jack?" Geraldine smiled at the children.

"Boys, where is he?" Mrs. May swiftly took down the hall, opening the back door and calling out to him. "Jack, come in for a moment, there are people here to meet you." She was beaming with pride when she walked back a boy, who'd been holding a small hand shovel and had dirt on his hands, arms and face. But even with the dirt shrouding his appearance, there was no mistaking that this boy was Indian.

The feelings overflowed from Williams' heart when he saw him, and there wasn't a doubt in his mind that this child, who was the likeness of the people he'd longed to return to, would be his son. "Hi Jack. My name is William. This is my wife Geraldine and our daughters, Cora, and Sophie." William pointed to their heads as he spoke their names. "I think you are very special, and I am wondering if you would like to come and live with my family and be my son."

Geraldine was surprised he chose the boy so quickly, but she felt it too, from the moment he came into the orphanage, Jack was her son just as much as Cora and Sophie were her daughters. Geraldine also knew there was much she didn't understand about her husband and never would; he had a connection to a world she would never know. She had seen in William's pocket once, shortly after they met, he had a small piece of beaded leather he carried around. But as much as she wanted to ask, he never volunteered the story behind it, so she chose early on to respect his past and not meddle.

Mrs. May walked them out to their carriage. She nodded in approval at the beautiful black horse who huffed in waiting. As Geraldine loaded up her three children and carefully put Jack's little suitcase in the front, Mrs. May turned to William to thank him.

She told him they had about one adoption per month now, with all the homesteaders moving out this way, and she explained the children now coming to her were younger and younger. But she was so pleased to see Jack get a nice family, since he'd been here since he was just a few days old, as she recalled the snow falling on his bundled-up body, marveling at the fact he was strong enough to survive being left in the woods. And as always, she would wonder about the parents.

The next years went by in a heartbeat for William and Geraldine. William loved his son as much, if not more, than his own blood, for the boy represented the life he had wanted for himself all along. Jack reminded William of his dear friends in the Indian tribe; he had Ehawee's smile and Spirit Shadow's eyes, and for that, he somehow knew this was her son.

For William had learned that night, on the beach, that Ehawee had tragically died in childbirth. It was serendipitous he could now do right by her, the girl he loved all those years before, and raise her child in a way that would honor her.

Jack was the only one to learn of William's secret life among the Indians; it was the men's secret, as they would say, and Jack never repeated any of it to his mothers or his sisters. William would teach him what he had learned among his time, such as minor flint knapping, though he wasn't as good as he remembered, Jack was incredibly gifted at everything he did.

William would always attend the weekly church service with his family, and he was pleased that his offspring were maturing into Godly young people. He never knew anything about his own salvation. Instead, he just assumed in trade of the things he'd done, he could never have it. When he was younger, he envisioned a 'great awakening' something he would experience that would bring him closure, acceptance and most of all, forgiveness from God for the lives lost directly and indirectly at his hand, the fate he didn't protect Ehawee from and whatever happened on that beach, all those years ago. And he couldn't release the threat of Lowell, searching for him, lurking to kill him, from his mind.

Believing this, he worried about what would come of his family. These children had never known struggle; even Jack would fondly speak of the woman who raised him and William both; sharing stories about the antics of the children, the songs they would sing whilst Mrs. May played the piano. In fact, William often wondered if Jack wished to return to the orphanage.

He even assumed Geraldine married him on the belief he was related to the catalog home giants of their time, as he couldn't believe anyone, his children included would ever love him for him, if they knew who he was. A killer, a thief, a very bad man. And then his mind, as it always did, traveled back to the days spent among the Indians, when things were beautiful.

Seated on the porch of the farmhouse where he chose to live, William stared blankly out into the evening. Geraldine had asked several times over the years why they lived so far from the hustle and bustle. She had enjoyed the city life of shopping, wining, and dining. William had given her some excuses as to protect their daughters from it, and Geraldine always accepted that. But the truth was, William wanted to be right here, where the Indians once were, and he would wait. Wait for them to return, to finish him off, or to take him back. He still, to this day, in all his personal successes, wanted to be the man he felt the potential to be when he lived among the Indians.

William turned to Geraldine and asked if she was happy with their life. She was beaming, constantly verbalizing she was so proud of her husband for their love, children, and comfort. She, of course, said, "Yes," to which he responded, "Good... Because there is a man made of evil waiting for his chance to murder us all." He was mumbling, unaware of his words as he sipped a glass of whiskey. The shock wiped her expression from her face, as she instinctively gripped her cross necklace. "Why, William, what do you mean?" Her face cocked sideways, frantically searching his expression for a hint of a smile, a sign this was just a joke. Nothing, and it wasn't. She turned away, her mouth still agape.

William took a breath. "As long as our family lives, there will be a man alive that is looking to kill us all. And that's not even the beginning of it." The weight of that time again pressed on his mind as he reclined in his rocking chair, closing his eyes, waiting for death.

Sophie and Cora, in their teens, had been just on the other side of the wall listening to their parents' conversation.

For Sophie, hearing these words incited fear in her mind and heart; she swiftly went to her Bible and into long moments of prayer. She had often wondered about her abilities that others didn't share, like her visions of things to come. Sophie had early on declared them to be a sign of the devil and she squashed them from her mind whenever they appeared. She didn't want to be this way. No, she wanted to be Godly. She did not want to be damned like her father believed he was.

Cora extracted a different feeling from her father's words; she was energized. While her sister Sophie often confided with her about her clairvoyance, Cora decided she wouldn't indulge about her own level of ability. She felt she was gaining more power by the day; as she now couldn't just see the future, or see the past, but she could step into it.

Cora, hearing her father speak, silently thanked him. Because of his choices, whatever it was that did it— she would always be wealthy. As for the man, she also had the power to see him coming a mile away. And she would use both for her advantage, indefinitely.

***

SARAFINA

The days flew by, and less work was completed each hour than the previous. I was basking in the beauty of our surroundings while enjoying the companionship of our house guest. Leroy kept trying to have a word with me, but Killian kept me distracted and engaged in many activities in what could only be described as a courtship.

One morning, Killian surprised me with an amethyst pendant necklace. It wasn't nearly as beautiful as the necklace that I already wore, nor as pretty as the one I'd lost from Victoria. But I was gracious for the present from this man I dared to love, and swiftly put it around my neck, mindlessly wearing it atop the cross necklace.

"Aren't you going to remove the one you are wearing, milady?" Killian smiled, but it didn't reach his eyes. My mouth nearly dropped into a frown. I didn't want to remove the necklace, which was evident to Killian at this point, but I hesitantly obliged. I thought of God, my newly re-found faith in which I didn't need a symbol to be proven, but I couldn't help but feel like I'd be struck by lightning the moment I took it off.

"It looks beautiful on you, Sara." Killian kissed my forehead and led me over to the pomegranate tree. "There are people who believe the fruit Eve bit into was a pomegranate," he sheepishly spoke with his eyes squinted. A feeling washed over me like I was Eve, but this man was a snake, which surprised me, considering I was already planning my wedding with him in my mind.

"I have to leave for a short time, but I promise to return very soon." His words went through me like a dagger as he looked over me when he spoke. Turning, I saw Leroy watching us from the steps. I felt juice dripping down my chin when I realized I had taken a bite of the pomegranate I didn't remember picking. I don't even like pomegranates. A dark feeling washed over me as I started to feel like I was losing control of my body– and my mind.

***

WILLIAM

After the children married and moved away, Geraldine desired a grander lifestyle, away from the humble homestead. She had requested William to look at the land her father had gifted them all those years before. Her father had never approved of the homestead and hoped that throughout the years of paying his daughter's husband very well, he would have the urge to move out and into something more luxurious.

The land was several hours away by carriage, and no structures of any kind on it, so they would have to bring provisions for sleeping. This excited Geraldine even more, as she sang words about it being a 'blank canvas'. Her father had even found an architect to tag along on the trip.

William was hesitant to leave his home because as he got older, he grew more paranoid about the Indians returning. He felt they would burn his house down, something he used to crave more than anything— even if just to put an end to his beliefs of a cursed existence.

They were to embark for the land this Sunday after they attended church services. William had gotten up earlier than usual to prepare for the trip, he told Geraldine, but he was really going down to the church to have a word with his pastor.

When he got to the humble chapel, the pastor was inside at his makeshift pulpit, turning a few pages in his bible, nodding to himself when he opened it to the right page. He glanced up when he heard the door shut behind William.

"Good morning, William. How are you today?" The pastor smiled, expectedly, for it was never unusual for people to come in outside of church hours with a nagging conscience, a personal crisis, or spiritual battles. He came to wait for it, arriving a few hours before and staying hours after every service, checking in during the week and often finding someone poking around, waiting for him to show up to council them.

"Good morning, Paul. I was hoping I could speak with you in private."

Paul glanced around the room and waved his arms to show William that they were alone. He stepped out of the pulpit and took a seat in the front pew, motioning William to join him.

William sat in the pew, looking straight at the wooden cross on the wall. "Do you think God will forgive me?" His voice was intentional but soft.

Paul, also looking up to the cross, firmly replied. "Yes."

"But you don't know what I've done." William's gaze was steadfast.

"And my answer will not change." Paul reached into his breast pocket for a small book of the New Testament. He read a few verses, but William was trailing off in his mind.

"The things I've done can't be undone."

Paul paused. This was nothing he hadn't heard before. He knew many murderers and thieves in his life, and while he never felt any differently about them, he suddenly felt whatever William was wrapped into was somehow worse. Darker, maybe. He pondered to himself, not wanting to confront or ask directly what it was, as he felt it best not to know.

"That's why you need to be born again."

***

SARAFINA

I heard a knocking on Victoria's bedroom door and turned my head to see Leroy standing in the doorway. He had a cup of tea in his hands and the sight of it instantly made me thirsty, so I reached out for it. With Leroy's skills in the baking world, I was used to intoxicating scents at every turn, but this tea had no fragrant aroma whatsoever. I peeked up at him before I took a sip, him nodding back at me. At first touch to my tongue, it was sour, almost bitter, but I instantly felt a spark in my senses. A tingle ran down my arms and legs, a fog clearing in my mind.

"Wow, what's this all about?" I laughed, holding the teacup up.

"That, my dear, is a very special blend I made just for you. You said that you were leaving soon for a little break?"

"Oh, I was? I mean, yes. I definitely need to check back into work, check on my apartment, pay my rent, water my plants– " A quick panic of urgency washed over me. "I need to leave by Monday." Nodding, I reassured myself that everything would be fine since that had been my plan all along. I came out here for eight days and would return to work and life on time.

"Monday is tomorrow, milady." Leroy quipped back, cocking an eyebrow at me, as if to say, 'now what?'

"Ok, good then. It's settled. I leave first thing in the morning." Another sip of tea and another shockwave to my senses. How was tomorrow Monday already? I glanced around at Victoria's diaries which surrounded me. Suddenly it felt a little morbid to be in this room.

"I think I will return to the cottage tonight." Running my hand through my hair, I felt stressed at the mess I had made in here.

"I think that would be good to get a nice night's rest before your drive. I'll take it from here." Gesturing to the mess, he waved me out of the room.

"Thank you, Leroy. You're an absolute lifesaver." I felt a very strange sensation to get out of the house as quickly as possible. Stepping outside, I was alarmed at how cold the air felt. My teeth were chattering before I left the porch, prompting me to return back into the house to grab a shawl. Leroy still stood in the entryway, alarming me.

"Oh!" I let out a small shout, nearly falling over. "I thought you were upstairs."

He had a fake smile as he said, "I wanted to make sure you made it out of here, is all."

How peculiar, I thought.

"I just thought I'd grab a shawl, it's quite cold out, but on second thought, I'll just make a run for it." I felt very anxious and perspiration broke out on my forehead.

"Very good then." Leroy spoke matter-of-factly, turning on his heels and continuing back up the stairs.

The following day I was to return to the city, to work and life as I knew it before this ever happened, and I found myself lingering, dragging through the routine of waking, stalling for time as if afraid I would leave something important behind. It seemed like if I left, all of this would disappear. My worst fear of it all being a dream would come true. In truth, this was the biggest thing to ever happen to me, and I didn't want it to leave my sight. My stalling turned into confusion when I couldn't locate my purse, or any personal belongings that I had brought with me. Not even my mobile phone. I asked Leroy to call it, but then I couldn't remember my phone number.

He nervously laughed it off but then grew concerned. "Would you like me to do a once-over in the cottage, madam?"

I nodded, waving him off. But instinctively, I felt nothing that belonged to me before would be found.

The frigid air slapped me once again. Why is it so cold? Before Leroy left earshot, I quickly hollered out to him. "Leroy— what day is it?"

He stopped in his tracks, taking a deep breath before responding. "Miss Rayne, it is November fifteenth." The shock hit me like a gust of the outside air, making the hair on my neck stand up.

"How could that be? That would mean— " I trailed off, trying to calculate the very days, weeks and months…I had been here for months.

Leroy continued up the stairs, whispering back to me. "Look at what you're wearing, madam."

I looked down and saw I wasn't wearing anything recognizable. My wardrobe usually consisted of jewel-tone clothing, but this was a gray lace dress that looked decades old. I didn't even own any dresses back home. Where did this come from? My nails were bitten, a habit I never had. And my feet screamed, laced in a heeled shoe that must have been two sizes too small.

I ran to the hallway powder room, knowing a full-length mirror was on the wall next to the tub. But when I got to it, the door was locked. I reached into my phantom pockets for the keys, but, of course, they were not there. I had no keys or pockets. Kicking off the boots, I raced through the grounds barefoot to the cottage. The turf was frozen; small patches of slippery ice threatened to take me down. I managed to make it to the door without injury and burst inside. The interior was nearly as cold as the exterior, which I immediately found odd, as if Killian hadn't been staying here at all.

After an exhaustive search, I couldn't find any of my belongings in the cottage. But I did find a bag belonging to Megan. When did she leave? Had she been trying to contact me? The reality I've been here for nearly a year hit me again. My apartment, my job, my friends— what must they think happened to me? Why hadn't Megan sent a search party?

I opened her bag and found a parcel of photographs inside. Photos of people I recognized, but with Megan. A beach trip with an older couple. Dinner parties and birthdays. This is her family. I have no family. My vision grows foggy. I'm fading away. Wait, I'm not ready to go. The pictures of the people— I loved them. I don't know them. I am Josephine. I am Sarafina. I am no one.

I'm slowly slipping away for good.

***

JOSEPHINE/SARAFINA

The blood left my cold cheeks as it returned to me before vanishing again. I'm fading in and out. Tears are falling. I laughed in my madness and felt the darkness leaching my bones. I sensed Killian was nearby.

I dropped the bag, and its contents scattered across the floor. The wind is blowing hard outside as dusk is near. As I walk towards the door, I grabbed a cloak hanging on the coat rack and made my way, with frozen feet, to the manor.

Leroy took one look at me, and he knew. He shook his head in disbelief, crying out, "Madam, you didn't have to do this! Why can't you just move on like the rest of the dead! She is a very young woman with her whole life ahead of her!"

I made it to my old bedroom. The gold vines started to shimmer in the moonrise.

"Killian will keep bringing me back as long as there is a body in my bloodline for him to do so. I will end them all if that's what it takes. This isn't right— he won't let me go."

"But Josephine— " Leroy appeared, "— she's barely lived at all! Won't you give her the chance?"

That pleading note struck a chord with Josephine's spirit. She swiftly turned to him, intimidating him into backing off a few steps. "I bet you can figure out that I didn't go to heaven. You were right all along. Now it's too late for me."

"It's not for Sarafina." He retreated another step, wanting to escape the wrath of her eyes. "Sarafina believes in God."

Josephine's expression turned sour when she heard this. Her voice became contorted, like talking into a microphone too close to the speaker. She quickly went to the balcony, Leroy running after her, screaming for her to stop.

The balcony railing was warm to the touch. She swung one leg over, overwhelmed with an intense sense of déjà vu. Leroy pulled her body back over immediately. She laughed at the fiery sunset, her parting goodbye in this mortal form. The amethyst cliffs glittered in the warm glow, the golden flowers accelerating with every move she made. She heard the dark voices calling her home. Frank's voice was among them. He told her to jump so they could finally be together, though she knew it meant eternal torment once she was released from earth.

But Sarafina's body couldn't muster the strength to break free of Leroy's hold on her arms. It reached and pried— this body exhausted, and by the taste on her tongue, appeared to have just consumed a sleeping tea. But there was another taste Josephine's soul couldn't quite make out.

"Sarafina, I know you're in there. You must pray with me, even if you can't make the words with your lips, okay? Put on your full armor of God and try to repeat after me." Leroy began to recite the Lord's prayer, in tandem putting his knees on Sarafina's arms.

"'Our Father in heaven,
hallowed be your name,
your kingdom come,
your will be done,
on earth as it is in heaven.

Give us today our daily bread.
And forgive us our debts,
as we also have forgiven our debtors.
And lead us not into temptation…" Pulling out a small cross on a silver chain from his shirt, carefully setting the cross against my forehead. "…but deliver us from the evil one." (Matthew 6:9-13)

CHAPTER ELEVEN

SARAFINA

The soul inhibiting my body left with such a force that my nose started gushing out blood. Tears of relief fell from Leroy's eyes, mixing with the sweat dripping from his brow. He helped me up but first pulled me from the balcony, propping my body in a half-up position next to the bed, immediately locking the balcony doors behind me. I felt wobbly on my feet as Leroy assisted me to the bathroom while holding a handkerchief to my nose and tilting my head back. With arms outstretched, I trusted him to lead me down the staircase as we found ourselves outside the house.

"Let's go to the guesthouse and get you cleaned up. This house is riddled with him, madam. It is not safe for you to be here."

"With who?" I mumbled; nose plugged.

"Killian. He is responsible for all of this, madam. I tried to warn you, but he has a very charming effect on everyone. You see, he's cursed to walk the earth as long as your family is alive. Aside from flirting you into attempting suicide, he now has a pattern of using Josephine to speed things up. He's ready to die, and in many ways, Josephine is blindly ready for him to die, too."

I bore into Leroy's eyes, searching for the truth in his words. Taking a deep breath and digesting the information, I knew it to be true.

"I'm sorry I didn't listen to you." I was full-on ugly crying now, my words breaking up with every syllable.

"It's the past, madam, and it doesn't matter. What matters is that you're safe."

I begged for more details about Josephine and Killian, but he played it off at first, only to bring it up moments later as we reached the guest house door.

"He was— is infatuated with Josephine. Killian walks evil, as you can see now. He's been the puppeteer behind much of the pain— if not all— that's happened in this land. To Josephine, driving her into the world of the occult. He wanted Josephine to himself the moment that he met her. I saw it in his eyes when I first came to the estate. I couldn't believe it for years, but what everyone thought was cholera, was actually a poisoning."

My heart sank hearing Leroy speak. To think I'd loved a man that was capable of the worst evil I'd ever heard was disturbing to my core. Entering the cabin, Leroy pulled out my things from under the bed and inside the closets, stuffing them into a trunk. He knew I would be leaving immediately.

"It's disturbing, but true. The saddest part was a note the family had placed on a bedroom door, in which they tried to protect the children there. Killian tore it in half when he found them, and I found the rest of it under a rug."

He pulled out the note, in two pieces, to my disbelief.

"Have mercy on" – "the children, please, sir, I beg of you."

"You've carried this around for all these years?" It was so long ago; I couldn't wrap my mind around it.

"It was my constant reminder that the ways of this world are evil, and I must keep my eyes on God. I just wish Josephine could have found that peace."

***

WILLIAM

William waltzed out of the church that morning with a feeling of peace. He strolled home, conversing with the Lord the entire time, catching him up on everything he'd done in his life since that fateful day.

When he arrived home, he told his wife they would leave straight for the land to explore the new beginnings of their future. She was thrilled.

After several long and bumpy hours, the stagecoach arrived at their new property. The driver started unpacking while William sat inside, staring blankly out the window in disbelief.

"It is so beautiful, William. It reminds me of our painting. Let's go walk around!" Geraldine was beaming, not noticing William's expression or stiff stature. As she reached for the door lever on the stagecoach, William grabbed her arm.

"We will not be doing that, Geraldine. This is not the land for us." As she begged and questioned him, he tuned her voice out. He couldn't explain to her this land was cursed— that this land had been touched by evil. Geraldine was spot on; this land was the landscape that Lowell Killian Sparr had painted; the portrait that hung in the ship William sailed all those years ago. It was clear as day, and he wouldn't be stepping a foot on it.

"Wait. I thought you said there were no structures already built?" Geraldine searched quizzingly out her window. William peered over her shoulder to see what she was looking at, and a small A-frame building stared back at him. In disbelief, he told her to remain in the cab under all circumstances. She didn't look at William like she took him seriously, but as he stepped outside, he told the driver to ensure she stayed put. He nodded.

The land grew wider and bigger with every step he took towards the building. It was crudely constructed; the materials reminded him of Sarafina's Revenge for their color, just like the planks. And the sogginess of the exterior; they looked like they were about to rot away into the water that he could hear somewhere nearby, or in his soul.

In his blurred vision, the home reminded him of something, but he couldn't quite place it. When he reached the door, knocking on it with force, his legs were anxious to keep marching on. He took a deep breath, waiting for someone to answer, but it didn't happen. Looking around to assess the land, behind him, he could see his wife's big eyes staring out of the coach, the driver leaning against her door. Trees lined the west, and the water sounded like it was north of him but much further away. While inspecting the nearby woods, he saw someone move behind one of the old oak trees.

It had been decades and more, but he could've placed that lanky body anywhere. He knew exactly who it was. William had felt Lowell's presence the moment he recognized the property from the painting. He took a few steps back to the a-frame, pulling the small lighter from his pocket that Geraldine's father had given him before he died, and he lit the place on fire.

Watching it as it burned before him, knowing undoubtedly that Lowell was looking on, now William realized what it reminded him of. With the smoke coming from the top it looked like one of the teepees from the Indian camp. William fell into a trance, watching the flames as they roared until all that was left was the structure's frame.

William decided that immediately upon his return home, he would keep the deed in his safe, never to be handed out to anyone. As far as he was concerned, as long as Lowell-Killian— whatever name he went by— inhabited the land, it was cursed.

William returned to the stagecoach, and seeing the wide eyes of Geraldine and the driver made him turn around again. The only thing now standing from the A-frame was a perfect cross. The flames dying off rapidly.

William wondered what it meant.

***

He lived to see another sunrise, for which he was half surprised. The day before had been as unsettling as a man could experience— that coming from someone who had seen it all. He prayed through his morning, overlooking the rich forests surrounding his homestead. The planks creaked when he rocked his chair back on the porch. He watched the woods, but for the first time, not anticipating the return of the Indians as he had since the day he was traded. He remembered what the pastor said yesterday about being born again and accepting salvation. Though William sat shrouded in darkness, he felt the light on his face as he slowly closed his eyes for the last time.

Geraldine found William holding a small piece of beaded leather. She tossed it aside, trying to revive her beloved husband, but he was gone. There was a smile on his face. At first, she didn't recognize it, for the man she looked at had a facial deformity.

A long and lonely year went by, and Geraldine often felt like the forest had eyes on her. She realized she didn't fear death, however close it approached with each passing day. Geraldine decided that she would never leave her and William's homestead. She was going through documents in the safe and found the deed to the land she so dearly desired but decided to lock it away, hidden in time, under the floorboards.

Often, Cora would time travel and check on her mother, though she never made her presence known. She didn't want to scare her mother, whom she loved dearly. But the day she saw her mother placing a deed under the wooden plank floor, the wheels of her mind started turning, and she wondered how she could use this to her advantage.

***

KILLIAN

If the man on the bench looked as exasperated as he felt, it surely must be visible to others. If darkness had a physical form, it was Killian.

"I must be leaving now. Thank you for your storytelling today. It was a pleasure listening to you." The man shot up from the seat but had an overwhelming pain in his leg, nearly sending him back downward. Suddenly, he doubled over with nausea.

"I'm afraid I can't let you do that, chap," Killian said. "You see, it took me years and years to find you. The adoption records were sealed. And honestly, I'm surprised you survived after your great uncle left you in the forest to die."

The man didn't know what Killian meant, but the words stung, and he felt tears form in his eyes, a pain that only those who have been given up experienced.

"Did you know you have a twin? He was adopted years after you by the very family I spoke of today." Eli felt a tear fall down his cheek.

Killian laughed. "Yes, it's true. And yes, I did a very bad thing, all those years ago to your mother. But you are my son."

The man felt pins and needles all over his body as Killian spoke, calming himself with the memories of his very loving and doting parents. God rest their souls.

"Now's where I need the favor, son." Killian's devilish smile turned darker and his teeth were gnashing out the words that barked from his lips. "I was cursed to live as long as the descendants of William's family exist. I've failed to kill them all, and now I need you to break the curse. I've given it much thought, and it's simple. I'm cursed because of you, so if I kill you, it's over." Killian's words were becoming more contorted with every syllable, and the man grew more confused.

"So, you need…me…to…die so that you can die?" The man asked Killian, who he considered the closest taste he would ever have of the devil himself.

"I know, the logic is choppy, but I'm willing to try." Killian's voice was animated and bouncy, and he stood up, the two men now facing each other. "Eli, right?" Killian spoke to the man, using his first name. Eli gasped and nodded in return. "Eli, it doesn't have to be painful. It will be quick, I promise. There are many arts I've mastered, one of them being poison." Killian held up a small vial. Eli looked away, feeling utterly helpless and overwhelmed. He asked Killian if he could have a few minutes of reflection first, to which Killian grudgingly agreed.

The pain in Eli's leg subsided. He walked over to the pier only a hundred yards away, knowing full well that he couldn't escape the darkness that was his birth father. He reflected on his life, searching for any truth in this stranger. Eli had been lovingly raised by his adoptive parents. They always said he was Native American and encouraged him to explore his heritage. He moved to an area rich in the history and culture of many tribes, and as he sat in the rickety chair on the porch that came with his house, he swore he could hear their music that had long passed, in the wind that blew by.

Of course, the tribes were gone now, as no one had seen them in decades. Eli felt alone in the last few years after his parents left the earth, believing that whoever his birth parents were, they were likely gone as well. Now, as Eli faced this stranger, who gave him the answers he had long sought, the fear washed over him.

But then Eli remembered something else; that he had another father who loved him eternally. He put his head down to pray.

After a short while, Eli returned to Killian, having found peace in the matter. Killian sat back on the bench and looked at him matter-of-factly. "Well, what'll it be, chap?" As he repeated the same line to Eli, he saw now that this man had hunted him, and while there was no way out now, he had one last thing to say.

"I forgive you." The words calmly poured from Eli's mouth.

Killian's face contorted into a laugh.

"I forgive you, Killian," Eli repeated.

Killian became piping hot with anger, balling his hands into fists. "That's not what I asked for!" Killian screamed at Eli, pushing him backward, who took the shoving without a fight.

"And I believe God would too."

Killian, releasing the vial from his hands, dropped to the ground and wept.

***

SARAFINA

Leroy placed the trunk on the outside porch, reaching into his pocket for his stopwatch.

"The cab service will be arriving in twenty minutes, Sarafina. I've so enjoyed our time together, as in my years, I feel like I, too, will be leaving the earth soon. But I anticipate waking again at the pearly gates of Christ."

I hugged Leroy and thanked him for everything he'd done for me. "Your unwavering faith in God and…Humanity is inspiring." Tears mingled with my smile.

"Leroy, I can't thank you enough. I– I'm not sure what I will do with the estate." I grinned sheepishly, expecting commentary from him, but he just nodded instead. "I have loose ends I need to tie up in the city, and after an exorcism here, I'd like to return to see you." I laughed lightheartedly, and Leroy looked off into the distance. We sat outside the guest house on the porch swing, waiting for the car. I remained silent, waiting for Leroy to state whatever was on his mind.

"It's true," he began. "Killian had demonic power over Josephine. Darkness– no doubt about it. After he tormented her mind for years, she finally gave in– only to be toyed with again and again, for his bidding. When she was alive, Victoria tried every way she could to convince Josephine she wasn't bound eternally to his evil. You know, that was the real curse of Josephine's life. It wasn't the death of everyone she'd ever loved, or that something inherently evil controlled her– but that she refused to believe God could ever change it."

About the Author

Cassandra discovered her passion for writing at the age of seven when she purchased a diary at the Scholastic Book Fair. What began with journal entries about her school and home life later evolved into a collection of poems, short stories, and novels. Her hobbies include skiing, traveling around the Rocky Mountains, and reading. Much of her writing inspiration stems from her Onondaga heritage. Cassandra's favorite genres of books are Christian Thrillers, Native American literature, and anything British.

She is a full-time writer and resides in Wyoming with her husband, Chad.